A WITCH'S REVENGE

A WITCH'S REVENGE

CHRONICLES OF AN URBAN DRUID™ BOOK 4

AUBURN TEMPEST

MICHAEL ANDERLE

DISRUPTIVE IMAGINATION

Copyright © 2020 LMBPN Publishing
Cover by Fantasy Book Design
Cover copyright © LMBPN Publishing
A Michael Anderle Production

LMBPN Publishing
PMB 196, 2540 South Maryland Pkwy
Las Vegas, NV 89109

First US edition, December 2020
eBook ISBN: 978-1-64971-390-2
Print ISBN: 978-1-64971-391-9

THE A WITCH'S REVENGE TEAM

Thanks to our JIT Team:
Dorothy Lloyd
James Caplan
Diane L. Smith
Jeff Goode
John Ashmore
Daniel Weigert
Deb Mader
Rachel Beckford
Kelly O'Donnell
Dave Hicks
Micky Cocker
Debi Sateren
Paul Westman
Larry Omans

Editor
SkyHunter Editing Team

CHAPTER ONE

"She shoots! She scores!" I choke up on my stick and raise it over my head as Kevin, Dillan, and Nikon bring it in for a round of victory high-fives.

"And there you have it, ladies and germs," Dillan says in his best Ron McLean impression. "The Lucky Pucks win the round-robin series four games to three leaving the Hat-trick Heroes broken and buying the booze for the night. *Looosers.*"

Aiden, Calum, Sloan, and Emmet bow to the terms. Emmet points at Dillan and frowns. "We prefer to be called the graceful non-winners rather than losers, thank you."

I giggle, take a final bow, and jog over to where poor Sloan looks defeated in the net. "Sack up, Mackenzie. You grew up as an only child in a castle. No one expects you to be Patrick Roy out of the gate."

"Good, because I don't know who that is."

Emmet screeches in horror and throws Sloan a look of disdain. "How about Martin Brodeur? Johnny Bower? Felix Potvin?"

Sloan's blank gaze has all of my brothers giving him the stink-eye.

"Seriously?" Aiden says. "Is he fucking with us?"

I shake my head. "Nope. I don't think so."

"Okay, Irish." Dillan holds up his hands. "This is serious. Forget about the best goalies of all time. For all the green Skittles, this is your Final Jeopardy question. Can you, Sloan Abercrombie Fancy-pants Mackenzie, name one notable hockey player?"

He looks at me for a hint, and I lift my hand, blow, and make like I'm drinking a coffee. We talked about this just this morning. Come on, dude....

"Tim Horton's?"

Dillan snorts. "Tim Horton is the hockey player. Tim Horton's is the coffee shop he opened when he retired."

"*Ding, ding, ding*...close enough," Nikon says, coming to his rescue. The blond immortal looks good windblown and pats Sloan on the shoulder. "As the other non-Cumhaill add-in and hockey flunky in attendance, I vote Sloan gets the point."

Dillan then turns his attention on Nikon. "Okay, Greek. As an immortal god, sticking your neck out for Sloan puts you in no peril, so let's up the stakes. Can *you* give us one notable hockey player?"

Nikon rolls his eyes. "I'm a Greek immortal, full stop. Not a god."

"You're stalling. Full stop. What's your answer?"

He flashes a cocky smile. "Wayne Gretzky."

My brothers nod and the tension eases.

Dillan holds up his finger. "You get a bonus point for picking a local boy. Greek, you pass the test. Sloan... you're on probation. We're watching you, Irish."

I laugh at the alarm in Sloan's gaze and pull him out of the net. "Relax. They're razzing you. You upgraded from my annoying but talented druid friend to potential love interest. The boys will bust your balls for a bit."

"First off, *potential* love interest? I thought we'd jumped that hurdle and second, I thought they already like me."

"Oh, they do. That has nothing to do with it. They've tormented every boyfriend I've ever had. It's a rite of passage. Don't worry. You'll do fine."

"Showers and Shenanigans?" Kevin tosses his gloves on the top of the net.

I shake my gloves off so I can check the time on my Fitbit and nod. "Yeah. It's five-thirty now. Let's say burgers and beer at seven?"

"Done deal." Dillan raises his stick. "Bring it in Clan Cumhaill. Our blood, our sweat, your tears."

The five of us *clack* sticks and that signals the end of the Cumhaill side lane four-on-four tournament.

"Don't worry, Hat-trick Heroes." Calum jogs off to catch up with Kevin to get cleaned up for the pub. "We'll get 'em next weekend."

Sloan frowns at me. "You do this *every* weekend?"

He's too funny. "It's an October and November thing. It's too hot in the summer and too cold by December to schedule anything but a shinny game now and then. Look at it this way. You can only get better."

Dillan snorts. "Yep. As far as hockey skills go, you're nothing but raw potential."

Sloan's scowl is classic. "I could've done better if you'd let me cast a spell."

"Cheater, cheater, pumpkin eater." Emmet stacks the nets and lifts the crossbars with his shoulder to carry them back into our yard. "Oh, and fair warning. In this family, if you're caught cheating or lying, we actually do make you eat raw pumpkin."

"And it's gross." I grimace, and the back of my throat heaves a little. "Those goopy stringy bits in the center are nothing but slime worms in your mouth. They slither down the back of your throat and make you gag."

Emmet snorts. "It's a cruel and effective punishment. Usually lying is a one and done offense in this family."

Sloan looks at me and arches a brow. "What did you cheat at that got you condemned to a squash sentencing?"

It's embarrassing, but hey, if you do the crime you do the time in this family. "I sold Brenny's scooter to a kid at school and took the money to buy makeup and a training bra."

My cheeks flush hot.

Sloan chuckles and brushes a finger over my traitorous cheek. No doubt, with my pasty complexion, they're now flaming, blotchy pink. "I take it when ye got caught, ye lied about it?"

"She sure did." Dillan opens the back gate to usher us all into the yard. "She put the blame squarely on Emmet, and we all believed her. After all, our baby girl wouldn't lie."

I bat my eyes and throw Emmet an apologetic smile. "In my defense, I was eleven and Emmet was bragging about all the new Yu-Gi-Oh! men he bought with the twenty bucks he found on the forest path to our fort. He made an easy patsy."

Emmet scratches his eyebrow with his middle finger, and I giggle. "He's not just flipping me the bird. He's also showing you the scar he has to remember the occasion."

Sloan's head cranks around like he's part owl. "Ye framed him fer yer crime and beat on him?"

I snort. "No. Brendan punched him."

Sloan checks out the line of skin that cuts through Emmet's ebony eyebrow. "Yer twelve and yer older brother hits ye hard enough in the face to give ye stitches? I'm all for a good donnybrook, but that seems harsh."

Dillan laughs. "No. Brendan punched him in the sack and Emmet piked and cracked his face off the fireplace hearth. What do you think we are… barbarians?"

Sloan's horror makes me bust out laughing. "Oh, surly. You missed out by not having brothers. Don't worry. I'll share. My brothers are your brothers now. You're welcome."

Dillan and Emmet laugh. "Yeah. You're welcome."

Shenanigans on a Saturday night is always a good time. The music is upbeat, the bartender happens to be one of my favorite people in the world, and for some inexplicable reason, the Redbreast Whiskey tastes best served here.

"So, you and the uptight GQ model, eh? How's that going for you?"

I swivel my stool at the bar and glance back at the tables we've commandeered in the back. Once I've made sure our convo is our own, I check back with Liam and try to gauge whether he's upset or razzing me for the fun. "You know I love you forever and always."

He chuckles. "That's a two-way street, Fi-bee."

I snort. "You haven't called me that in a million years."

"Right about when you stopped buzzing around Aiden, Brendan, and I and getting us into trouble."

"Mostly so you'd stop calling me Fi-bee." The two of us chuckle, and I tip back my tumbler and let the liquid goodness warm its way down to my belly to join the growing pool of intoxication. "Seriously. You're okay with Sloan and me? I didn't mean to get us tangled up."

"It wasn't you who tangled things up, Fi. That was me." Liam shoves a lime slice into the neck of a Corona, sets it on a tray, adds two Guinness, and knocks his knuckles against the bar to signal the order complete.

Kady shuffles over from the soda fountain with two Cokes and sets them on the tray as well. "Thanks." Her gaze falls on his face, then flits around the back wall of the bar.

He winks at her, and I put my fingers over my mouth to stifle my laugh. "Oh, and here I was twisting myself up about letting you down. That's how it is, is it?"

Liam scowls and stalks up the bar to close the distance. "Drop it Fi. You don't know what you're talking about."

I peg him with a look and waggle my brows. "You'd like to think so, but you know I've got you pegged. What happened to the no fraternizing with staff? Did she catch you at a weak moment by the grease trap? I know, it was one of those nights when you dropped her home. She invited you up…one thing led to another…."

He rolls his eyes and leans closer. "It was the dry storage room after close and stop. No one knows. You're not supposed to know."

"The storage room? How cliché. Every bar movie ever has people getting busy between the racks of dried goods."

"You're full of shit. Name one."

"*Roadhouse*."

He rolls his eyes. "You're such a freak. What's with you and that movie?"

"Um…hello, it's a classic. Patrick Swayze and Sam Elliott on the same screen busting heads in bar fights. It's adrenaline perfection."

He snorts. "If you say so, crazy lady."

I realize I've squirreled off on a tangent and get back to the point. "So, back to you and Kady."

He checks that our convo is still private and leans closer. "A little louder. I don't think you alerted the entire bar."

"Oh, please. I won't embarrass either of you by exposing the sordid details of the two of you tossing rules to the side. Although, I *am* concerned about the hygiene of the dried goods. Where are we on that front?"

"The dried goods survived unscathed."

"That's a relief." I swirl the whiskey in my tumbler and sip. "Next question. Was it one perfect moment that shall never be repeated or are we talking shadowed corners and stolen moments?"

He looks at me and bites the inside of his mouth.

I burst out laughing. "Well, this *is* getting interesting."

"You totally suck."

"Hells yes, I do. Now, come clean."

"Okay fine, it's *maybe* turning out to be more than a moment of horny restocking."

His fluster is so adorable I want to squeal and stomp my feet. I don't. I meant what I said. I'd never jam him up. "Good for you two. Seriously. Kady is lovely, and she's been sad since she and Dillan broke up."

An order pops up on the register's screen, and he sets to work mixing a blender drink. "Do you think Dillan will be pissed? I'm in total violation of the Bro Code here."

I consider that and dismiss his concern. "Dillan called it quits because our druid lives are dangerous and Kady doesn't do well with violence. She didn't like him being a cop. She would never have been happy knowing what other things go bump in the night."

He pulls a draught and sets it on the tray to grab a second glass. "Sitting on the sidelines is a tough burden to bear. Especially when you're the odd man out with no powers."

"Don't sell yourself short. You took on vampires and hobgoblins and lived to tell the tale. You have powers, just not fae magical ones."

Liam pours the fruity frozen cocktail into a mason jar and measures out gin to add to the shaker. "Part of me envies your brothers and Sloan because they get to join you on this massive journey of danger and adventure."

"But the other part?"

He grips the stainless steel cocktail shaker with both hands and starts shaking. "The other part remembers how much it hurt to be shot and how scary it was to be kidnapped and threatened by psychotic members of an empowered world no one knows about."

"I never wanted that for you." I tip back my tumbler, empty it, and smack it on the bar for a refill. "I hate that it happened and will forever feel responsible for your suffering."

He sends that order off and grabs the bottle of Redbreast before coming over to me. "I know that, and I don't hold any resentment at all. The thing is, you took it as another bad day dealing with bad people. There's something about you and your family. You're built to take things like that in stride. I think it's why you make great cops, and I know it's why you'll make great druids."

He tops my glass and leans his elbows on the bar across from me. "You know I love you and the family, but I'm wired differently. I want to work in my bar, binge *Schitt's Creek* on Netflix, and snuggle my girlfriend on the couch without ever worrying that vampires or werewolves will *poof* in and rip our throats out."

"That's disturbingly graphic." I make a face and watch the spent bullet hanging around his neck sway against his chest. "I get it. I've never been half as scared for myself as I was for you the day you were hurt. The idea of losing someone I love—especially so soon after Brenny—is too much. I want you to be happy. I want you to be safe. This is good. Kady is a good choice."

The relief that flashes in those mesmerizing mint green eyes of his tells me how much this has bothered him. I stretch out my arm, and we clasp hands. "Do you want me to field the question with Dillan and run block?"

"No. I'll do it. I'm just really freaking relieved to have your blessing."

I pick up my refilled tumbler in my free hand and raise my glass. "I've always got your back. That's a basic tenet of being a bestie."

He squeezes my hand and then straightens. "And man, I couldn't ask for a better."

With my tumbler in one hand and the Redbreast bottle in the other, I make my way back to the two tables we pushed together to fit our group. Aiden went home after his burger to read the kids their stories before bed, so that leaves Nikon, Dillan, Calum, Kevin, Emmet, Sloan, and me.

"Fi!" Emmet waves me in and points at my seat. "Just in time. We've been telling Sloan embarrassing stories about you. Dillan was starting the one about the well-hung guy who took notice of you in your life drawing class."

My eyes bug wide and my ire rushes to the fore. "Why would you ever tell that story? Are you drunk or stupid? When have I ever set out to tarnish you in front of one of your girlfriends? If that's the way you want to play it, you boys are going down."

Emmet laughs and points. "See, there it is."

Sloan shakes his head and gestures for me to take my seat. "Relax, Cumhaill, they're fuckin' with ye. They never told me a single thing other than to warn me about how to tell when yer right pissed. Supposedly, when I see the vein throbbing at the side of yer neck like that, I should shut my mouth or clear the area before ye detonate."

I glare at my brothers, and they all burst out laughing.

"I hate you all. You so suck."

Dillan pats the table, and I take my seat.

I offer the bottle, but don't let go. Making locked eye contact with each one of them, I make damned sure they're all paying attention. "To be clear, if you guys open the door on our most embarrassing moments, I have enough firepower to bury all of you ten times over."

Calum leans over from the chair beside me and kisses the side of my head. "Oh, Fi, we don't doubt that for a second."

We enjoy ourselves as the back of the bar rowdies until closing time, then arrive in Emmet's room under the *poofing* power of our wayfarer.

Emmet is polluted.

Calum and Kevin are each tucked under a shoulder to hold him up, and I'm on video duty. You never know when something might happen that could come in handy later.

Poofing right next to his bed was a strategic decision, rather than arriving in the back hall and trying to get him up the stairs while Da is sleeping.

"I love you guys." Emmet grins. "I seriously love you. Big love. Huge. Manly love."

"That's our Emmet," Calum says as he and Kev ease him down onto his bed. "He's all about the drunken love."

I untie his shoes and set them aside.

"Here, Emmet." Sloan holds up a glass of water and a couple of Advil. "Take these now and drink this. You'll thank me in the morning."

Emmet looks at the water in the glass and scrunches up his face. "Got anything stronger?"

"No. It's simple hydration this round, I'm afraid."

Emmet leans around Sloan and frowns at me. "Where'd you find this guy? Water? I thought you said he's Irish."

Calum chuckles. "Don't diss our DD. This bar-to-bed service was amazing. I'll tip you in the morning, Irish."

Dillan finishes in the bathroom and comes in stripping off his shirt. "Yeah, thanks for being our Designated Druid. Now, everyone get gone. I'm wrecked, and I'm about to go full monty. This is your final warning."

Sloan flashes out and returns a moment later with Emmet's glass of water refilled. "I'll put this here for later. Try to drink it."

I chuckle. "Did you and Calum drink water on your night of Canadian Shield bonding? As I recall, you were unconscious and hugging his shoe when I found you both."

Sloan rolls his eyes. "Your family should come with a warning label. Seriously."

"Damn straight." Kevin pulls Calum toward the door. "Night all."

"Shut yer feckin' gobs and get to bed!" Da shouts from his room. "I've got a gun!"

I make a face and wave goodnight to all. After a quick trip to the bathroom to wash off my makeup and pee, I head into my room. "Oh, hey," I say, finding Sloan on my bed. "You lost? I think your bed is one room that way."

"Not tonight. I thought I'd say goodnight before I head downstairs."

"Downstairs? You're not... Oh, Kev and Calum kicked you out?"

He chuckles. "Actually, the three choices were to join, watch, or vacate."

"What? They tried to poach you?"

He laughs and waves that away. "They're both gone with drink. In any case, I opted to grab my things and head for the pullout."

I frown. "I don't have it set up, and I'm too tired to get the linens now. Can we play PG roomies and you sleep here?"

The look he flashes me is far from PG, but it's gone as soon as he catches himself. "I'll be fine. There's that big, fuzzy blanket on the end of the couch. No linens necessary."

"That's better than my comfy bed how?" I grab my jams, step behind the open door of my closet and spin my finger in the air for him to give me his back.

He does as he's told and moves behind the screen of the door. "Not better, just wiser. We've both had a fair bit to drink, and sober Fiona made her intentions very clear. I don't want tipsy Fiona to blur any lines ye've drawn. I do, however, want to see yer leg before we go to sleep."

"In one sentence he vows to behave, and in the next, he plots to get my pants down. Mixed messages, Mackenzie."

He chuckles, but there's definite tension in his tone. "I said I'll not rush things, Fi, and I won't."

"I was teasing. I know you won't." I finish getting ready for bed and free my hair from the collar of my shirt. When I come out from behind the door, I can see by the way he's chewing his bottom lip that he's still stewing. "Okay, out with it. Say what's on your mind."

He shrugs. "It's nothin'...I'm simply a touch off-balance bein' held at arms' reach by a girl I'm datin' I mean."

"Why? You've never dated a girl who's not simply in it to strip down and jump you?"

"If I say no, will ye think less of me?"

I laugh and head across the room to my little vanity. Sitting in front of the mirror, I take the clips out of my hair and brush things out. "I'm a big girl. I've had partners, and you've had partners. No big."

"But it *is* for you...with me, I mean. Is that because of somethin' I've done or said? Are ye wary of trustin' me or somethin'? I want ye to be frank with me if ye are."

"All right, the whole truth is I want to be careful. You mean a lot to my grandparents, and they mean a lot to you. You're also my friend and someone I depend on for druid stuff. I need you as a sounding board and support. Our lives and our paths are intertwined. My life-axis altered less than six months ago. I don't want to rush into hooking up only to realize I was off-kilter and ruined something great."

He considers that for a little and nods. "Agreed."

"So, slow and steady to win this race."

He intercepts me when I stand and points at my leg.

I pull my pants down my thighs, sit on the end of my bed, and lean back onto my elbows. When he places his hands over the damaged tissue poisoned by me internalizing Morgan le Fey's grimoire, the warmth of his healing magic tingles across my skin.

"I'm not arguin' the logic about takin' it slow." A deep scowl forms between his brows. "I'm simply unaccustomed to spendin' this much time with a woman and not takin' those next steps. Yer not like any girl I've known before and *I'm* off-kilter."

I chuckle. "How am I that different? Other than the jumping your bod part."

"Och, let me count the ways." His focus shifts to the gross, gray flesh, and his lips move as he casts a spell. Hovering his hand over the wound, he closes his fingers and pulls his fist back from my leg as if he's tugging the poison out by an invisible cable.

I hiss and grip my duvet. "Fuck a duck, Mackenzie? What did you do?"

"That hurt?"

"Um, yeah, more than a little."

His scowl deepens. "I was testin' the grip of the dark magic woven into the tissue and muscle of your leg. If that hurt, it's wound deeper and tighter than I realized."

"There's no *if* about it. Dayam."

He shakes his head and looks up at me with worry plain in his dark gaze. "We need to convince yer father that takin' ye home to my father is the best thing. He dug his heels in and has Garnet lookin' for someone who might help, but it's difficult when we can't tell people what poisoned you."

"Da went to Garnet Grant for help about my leg?"

"He did."

Wow. That takes a moment to sink in. My father ranks Garnet only minutely above Vito Corleone in the hierarchy of hoodlums. If he's asking him for help, he must be seriously worried. "How bad is this? On a scale of one to ten—one being it's not good when your skin is dead and dying and ten being we need to amputate before you become a dark magic evil minion who mindlessly eats people."

Sloan frowns. "Seven-point-five... maybe eight."

I blink. "Oh. That's not good."

"Ye wanted me to be honest, didn't ye? That wasn't one of those women questions where I'm supposed to ice yer cake instead of bein' honest?"

"Yeah no. Always honest." Although him icing my cake sounds rude and slightly interesting. He straightens and steps back while I cover up and climb into bed. "So, that insight should make for a lot of interesting nightmares."

"Shit, Fi. I'm sorry. I shouldn't have said anything."

"No, it's not your fault." I pull my covers up to my chin and shake my head. "And yeah, it's probably best you sleep downstairs. I'd feel awful if I turn into a hideous possessed beast in the night and eat your face."

"Och, thanks. I appreciate that."

CHAPTER TWO

I wake to the gray light of an October morning in Toronto and breathe in the decadence of Sunday breakfast cooking downstairs. "Oh, thank you, baby carrots."

The deep chuckle beside me brings my attention to Sloan stretched out on his side, his brow arched. Man, how anyone can look so pretty first thing in the morning is beyond me.

It's annoying, really.

"Why are you giving worship to dwarfed vegetables?"

I swipe at the dampness on my cheek and pretend I don't drool when I sleep. "How long have you been lying here?"

He shrugs. "Not long."

"You could've woken me up."

"When ye sleep, yer quiet and still. Once yer blue eyes start shinin', yer a bit of a whirlin' dervish."

"And you're a weirdo."

He makes an Irish *harrumph* sound in his throat. "So, why the ode to root vegetables?"

"Don't you smell that?"

"The boys makin' breakfast? I do."

"Well, it's a long-standing rule in this house that whoever is up and at it first on Sunday morning—who isn't rushing out the door for a shift—is on duty for family breakfast. I love it when that's not me."

"Then couldn't you simply lay here until someone else gets up and gets things started?"

I frown. "Do you understand how the honor system works, Mackenzie, or is it a foreign concept?"

"I think I grasp it. But, if that's the case, then I think it should've been me who is cooking. I was awake well before Calum and Kevin headed down to the kitchen."

I roll to sit up and rest for a second with my feet on the floor. A wave of nausea rushes over me, and I focus on the floor while the tides slosh and churn. Yikes.

I swallow a bit of acidy barf and remind myself to take it slower. My stomach is still sloshy from a night out drinking.

Hey, Red. Bruin stretches a massive brown paw across my bedroom floor and yawns wide. My bear takes up most of the space between my bed and the door, but I love waking up and seeing my grizzly mound close by. *I take it ye had a night of savage craic out with the gang?*

"I did. And you? Did the Don Valley delights sate your hunger as usual?

They did. Ye know, for an urban area, yer river system has quite an abundance of wildlife.

"It's nice, isn't it?"

I think so.

Now that I'm sitting up, it quickly becomes apparent how full my bladder is. I really have to hit the bathroom. "Wow, okay. That explains the pee dreams."

"I'm sorry, what?" Sloan says.

"Pee dreams. Don't you get those?"

By his expression, I'm thinking no.

"You know…when you have to pee in real life, so in your dream, you go to the bathroom, then you walk out of the bathroom, and you still have to pee. Now you're in the library, but there's no bathroom, so you pee in the stacks, then you walk outside to the park, and you still have to pee, so you squat behind a tree, and on and on. A pee dream."

He looks at me like I've suddenly gone Hydra and popped out a couple of extra heads. "Yer ridiculous."

I hold up my finger and shake my head. "Not this time, Mackenzie. Pee dreams are real. It's a thing."

I stand to ease the discomfort, but before I head across the hall, my cell rings. The throaty, African chant of the *Circle of Life* intro tells me it's the Lion King calling. I giggle and swipe green to accept. "Good morning, Mr. Grant. How fare thee this fine Sunday morn?"

"Good morning, Lady Druid. Have I caught you at an odd moment? Did you just flash back from Elizabethan times? Had another adventure with your ghostly ancestor in the past, have you?"

I laugh. "No. Can't a girl add a little flair to life for no reason other than to add a little color? All right, I'll play it straight. Hey, Garnet. What's up?"

He chuckles. "Well, now I prefer the first greeting."

I shift my weight and make a face at Sloan. Man, I gots ta pee. "Did you call for a reason you want to share or is it a mystery I have to figure out?"

"There was an incident last night with the vampires."

"Not it! Wasn't me. Out drinking with the fam all night. My alibi is solid."

"You're not being blamed."

"Oh, that's different. I'm used to being rounded up as one of the usual suspects. I am not Keyser Söze."

He chuckles. "I'm calling because there's a Guild Governor meeting and you now hold the seat for the druids. Your attendance is required."

"Oh, cool. My first official duty. When and where?"

"Anyx will escort you. He can be at your back door in one hour. Will that work?"

"Sure. An hour works. And Garnet…"

"Yes, Lady Druid?"

"Thanks for calling to let me know. The fake summons to meet you where people try to kill me have gotten old."

"I'm sure they have. I'll see you soon."

"Dress code?"

"As you are, will be fine."

The call ends, and I look down at my Pikachu pajamas. He likely doesn't mean that literally.

"Fi. Yer dancin' around like yer gonna wet yer pants."

"Yes! Thank you." I turn and rush to the hall as his laughter echoes behind me.

"Yer ridiculous!"

I'm showered, dressed, and manage to down a plate of pancakes and bacon and a cup of tea before Anyx knocks. I open the back door and hold up my hand.

The man is a brawny blond with a bodyguard's stature and the leonine features that hint at his dual nature.

He looks at my proffered hand, chuckles, and makes spidery fingers on my palm. Then we meet palm-to-palm, and he folds his middle finger over mine. "So, we're going with this as the secret handshake, are we?"

"Yep. Fool me once it's on my head. Fool me twice I'm as good as dead."

Emmet comes out of the kitchen and snorts. "You realize that's not at all how that goes, right?"

"I made it more relevant to my situation."

"And everything is about you?"

"I never said *everything* is about me…but when it comes to empowered ambushes and unjustified attacks, it usually is."

"She's not wrong," Dillan calls from the kitchen.

"Fine. I'll give you that." Emmet leans in and holds out his palm. "I've seen you around, but we haven't officially met. Hey, there. I'm Emmet. Can I say, the whole turning into a lion thing —very cool. Congrats on that."

Dillan and Calum come out, and another round of intros and shaking ensues. When it's over, Anyx looks at me expectantly.

"I take it we should go?"

"He hopes for you not to be late to your first meeting."

"Set the expectations high, and there's nowhere to go but down," Dillan comments.

I laugh and grab my jacket. "Oh, I'm sure they'll learn soon enough to drop their expectations. Be good, boys. No picking on Sloan. He's new. I don't want you to break him."

"Och, what's this, Irish?" Calum lays on the brogue. "The wee lass fights yer battles for ye now? Ye haven't the stones to face us yerself?"

"My stones are fine, thanks." Sloan juts his chin out and casts me a look. "If they're dishin' it, I can take it."

I wince. "Oh, no, surly. You did not just say—"

"Challenge accepted." Dillan slaps high-fives with Emmet and Calum. "Oh, you're toast, dude."

I look at Anyx and back at them. "Okay, I'd say play nice, but that won't happen. Please, don't make him cry. I hate it when you make my boyfriends cry. Remember, I like this one. I want to keep him."

"No promises." Emmet waves over his head as he swaggers back into the kitchen.

I grab a cinnamon bear claw off Dillan's plate and dip it into his pond of syrup. Taking a bite, I hold out my free hand to Anyx. "We might as well go. The wheels of torture have been set in motion. There's no stopping that train now."

Anyx, as usual, shows no opinion on anything. He accepts my palm, and I smile up at him.

"Beam us up, Scottie."

I'm portaled into a room I've been in one other time. It's a sleek office behind the frosted glass wall of a lit clock face. The first time I was here, Garnet's men tried to put me in my place by roughing me up. That ended with one man portaled to the lair of the Wyrm Dragon Queen as a snack and a wolf shifter vivisected by my spirit bear.

Good times.

I glance down at the spot on the floor where the body fell and try to feel bad about it. Garnet was upset. I'm good with it. I quickly learned that when it's kill or be killed in the empowered world, I'd rather be the former than the latter.

You good, Red?

I brush a hand over my chest and send Bruin a warm and fuzzy across our bond. *Yeah. I was thinking about our first time here and how awesome you were protecting me from that attacking wolf. Killer Clawbearer to the rescue.*

My pleasure. A kill is even more satisfying when it's made to protect someone you love.

Awe, that's poetic. They should put it on a t-shirt.

"Lady Druid, is everything all right?"

I follow the deep, graveled voice to the host of the event, Garnet Grant. If life were *The Lion King* live-action edition, Anyx would be a muscled, golden lion Mufasa, and Garnet would be the strong, wiry, and slightly unscrupulous Scar.

Tall and darker in features, Garnet is bigger than me by a foot in height and a solid buck twenty-five in the weight category. I'm sure he was intimidating before he became the Alpha of the

Toronto Moon Called and Grand Governor of the Guild of Empowered Ones, but he has it down to an art form.

I finish eating Dillan's baking treat and lick the cinnamon off my fingers. "Yep. All good. How about you? Life good? Anything or anyone making you purr these days?"

His ebony brow arches and he gives me a look. Others fear him as a big, bad man, but I know the man behind the growl. He's a pussycat—literally and figuratively—who also happens to lurve my boss.

And I *may* have given them a magical nudge to get their love life back on track.

"Life is good, yes." The little quirk of a smile that almost escapes his lips makes my inner matchmaker smile. "Now, can we get to the business at hand?"

I glance around the room and frown. It's just Anyx and us. "Um...I thought there'd be more of us."

He rolls his eyes and grabs a black robe, which he shrugs over his shoulders. After he frees his ebony hair, he grabs a second robe from where it's draped over the surface of his desk. He holds it in front of himself. "Guild Governor."

I shrug into mine, which thankfully, is not one size fits all. My cloak is fitted to me. It hangs to the floor, and neither drags nor rises high enough to show my shoes—which is a shame because I wore the new druidy boots I got from Yes We Vibe. So cute.

My cloak has two gold bands embroidered over my right shoulder where he has five and the Guild emblem. I point at his. "Is this a hierarchy thing? Should I be earning points to level up?"

"How about you make it through the first meeting before you worry about leveling up?"

"Have I mentioned I'm a little competitive? Being the youngest of six kids, I tend to get my elbows out early."

Garnet chuckles and places a hand at the small of my back. "That's not a bad thing. I'm sure it serves you well."

When we arrive at the meeting room down the hall, the buzz of conversation masks our entrance. Which, if I'm honest, is fine with me. The place is swank and sleek. A long black table shimmers with a high-gloss finish in the center of the rectangular room. Silky silver fabric covers the walls, and the lighting from the coffered ceiling makes the sheen dance. I tilt my gaze up and scan the bazillion pin-dot white lights that look like stars in a distant sky.

Noice. That's what I'm talking about.

"Wow, the meeting on the *Jubilee* boat cruise was slumming it for you guys. No wonder people were pissed at me."

Garnet arches a brow. Now that we're in front of the masses, he has on his scary, autocratic face. "Don't kid yourself. It was much more than the boat."

I bark a laugh and the conversations come to a screeching halt. I wiggle my fingers in a little wave. "Hey."

"Fiona. Yay! You're here." Suede rushes over while flicking her hand at all the scowly faces sending us snide looks. Her silver hair is braided down her back, showing off the pointed tips of her ears. "Hey girlfriend, welcome."

I'm easing back from hugging her when Nikon sidles up, grabs me around the shoulders, and dips me back into a kiss. When he whips me back to my feet, he steadies me and smiles. "Hey, Cumhaill. Welcome."

Okay, that causes a stir.

"What the hell, dude?" I sputter, wiping my mouth. "Since when do you think my lips are public access?"

He chuckles. "We're giving them something to wonder about. Your brothers thought if you're hot and heavy with number one —that's me, by the way—maybe they'll lay off you and yours for a change."

"My brothers? Don't plot with them. They're goofballs."

Nikon chuckles. "Sloan thought it was a good idea too."

"Seriously? I highly doubt he approved you sticking your tongue in my mouth."

He winks, unrepentant. "I may have gone off-script. I'm a method actor. I pride myself on committing to the part. And yum, you taste like cinnamon bliss."

Another male chuckle brings me around to Zxata joining us. He looks dashing in his robe, his long blue hair and silver skin highlighted against the dark fabric. "Another entertaining entrance for you, Fiona."

I cast Nikon a glare as my cheeks flare hot. "That's me. Always making an impression."

Zxata squeezes my hand and tilts his head toward the table. "The sooner we start, the sooner we're done."

"Right you are," Garnet says. He turns to the room and gestures to the table. "Everyone, make your way to your seats. Let's begin."

It doesn't take long for the group to settle around the table. We take our seats, and I'm relieved we don't have to sit in the hierarchy ranking order of our powers as we did at the river cruise luncheon.

"That's because this is an action assessment meeting, not a general monthly meeting," Suede says when we settle into our seats. "There are fewer people, and we're dealing with a specific issue. These are usually quick and painless—unlike the luncheons."

She's right. At that luncheon, there were forty or more people. Today, there is half that.

"Where is everyone?"

"Well, other than those who couldn't come on such short

notice, you killed the head of the mages, the hobgoblins, and unseated Droghun as the head of the druids."

"No. I killed Salem to save the city from opening up a rift to hell, there is an unsubstantiated theory that my bear killed Kartak without my knowledge, and yes, I unseated Droghun as head of the Toronto druids, but I also had him reinstated as the head of the Toronto necromancers. See, when a door closes, a window opens."

She grins. "I'll be sure to point that out to him the next time I see him."

I press my hands against the table and take an assessing look around the room. Awesomesauce. Unlike the table at the harbor cruise meeting, this table bows wider in the middle, so I can see everyone when they're speaking.

No more anonymous hecklers taking potshots at me.

"All right," Garnet says from the center of the long side of the table. "Here's where we are. Last night, Xavier and his seethe entertained a few old country guests, and they threw a traditional celebration."

Suede leans close and whispers, "A.k.a, there was a vampire feed-and-fuck frenzy."

"Early this morning, his lieutenants did a headcount and noticed several of their flock had wandered off."

"Flock? As in sheep?"

"Figuratively," Garnet says. "That's what vampires call the in-house humans they feed on."

Suede pours me a glass of water and pushes it toward me. "We find it cuts down the incidents of vampires going too long between feedings, then binging on vagrants and late-night clubbers in the downtown core if each nest has a dozen or more humans who live with them full-time to satisfy their feeding requirements."

My mouth drops open. I'm not sure what I expected of the vampires, but that seems barbaric. "We allow that?"

Garnet nods. "We insist on it. There are strict regulations for vampire seethes to keep sheep and even stricter regulations to ensure that the humans who choose to serve them are fully aware of the pros and cons. They aren't prisoners, nor are they coerced. Believe it or not, seethes turn away volunteers who beg them for consideration."

I swallow and try to let that sink in. "That's cray-cray. So, normal people are all like, 'Yes. Please, puncture my neck and make me into a juice box. Oh, how I long to have my blood sucked?'"

"Something like that."

Rein in the horror, Fi, Nikon says into my mind. *Different species have different requirements to survive. There are others here who also feed on blood. Now is not the time to judge.*

Right, sorry. "Okay, so, the sheep make up the flock, and the High King vampire reported that during or after the blood orgy of the ancients, some of them got free from the pen and wandered off. Is that the gist?"

Garnet nods. "In a nutshell, yes."

The high priestess of the Toronto witches grunts. The woman is pleasant-looking with upswept hair and a frilly pink collar opened over her robe's lapel. That's how she looks with the naked eye, anyway. I've seen beneath her glamor. Her true face is gruesome and drippy and no doubt the result of a spell gone bad. "It's a wonder Xavier even reported it."

Garnet makes a note and lines the pen up at the top of the pad. "He had no choice. Three blood-drained humans wandered into the street and got picked up by the police. They may have been taken to the hospital. There might be people documenting a dozen fang marks. No matter what's happened, we have the potential for exposure in every direction here."

"Thirteenth Division covers Casa Loma," I say. "Have you got anyone inside the force who can fill in the blanks?"

Garnet shakes his head. "Our experience with the police was rather one-sided until your family descended upon us."

I chuckle. Yeah, we tend to swarm. "Do you want me to try to find out? Aiden's in the Thirteenth."

Garnet holds open his palms. "It can't hurt. Do your best and let's see where we are."

When they all stop and look at me, I take the hint. Oh, right now. Reaching under my robe, I find my phone and call my oldest brother.

"Yo, sista. What's up, baby girl?"

"Hey, there. I'm with Garnet and the Guild Gang and we have a sitch. Are you at work?"

"I'm in the parking lot. I have an hour before my shift, but I thought I'd tackle some paperwork. Why, what's the problem?"

I explain to Aiden about the vampires and how they misplaced three sheep from their feeding flock and that it would be bad if someone examined them too closely because they'll be down a few pints after hosting a feeding frenzy for the out of town crowd.

"Hang on. I'll check the logs and see what I can find out. Call you back in two."

I hang up and set my phone on the table. "He'll call us right back. He's checking to see what happened."

Garnet nods. "Next question. Ashod, when was the last time we audited the seethe and checked the accommodations and care of their sheep are up to standard?"

A man across the table and down a ways frowns and pages up on his tablet. "Nine years ago."

"That's too long. Let's send someone out right away. Maybe this is an isolated event, or maybe things have slipped over the past decade and we need to have a closer look."

My phone rings and yep, it's Aiden. "Hey, there. What do we know?"

"Okay, three women without ID picked up at Davenport and

Spadina. No charges. No reason to hold them. They were assumed to be on something because the officer who picked them up wrote them up as impaired but responsive. They're in holding sleeping it off."

"Cool. So, can I send someone over and have them signed out in our care?"

"If you're quick. There's a note here that someone called the woman's shelter. No one has shown up yet, but they don't usually take more than a couple of hours."

I look at Garnet, and he points at my phone.

"Hold on. I'm putting you on speaker with the group. Garnet looks like he has something to say." I switch it to speaker, set it on the table, and angle it toward Garnet.

"Aiden, thank you for your help. What's the address of your station house? I'll send Anyx over with one of the females from my pride. Can you meet them and help move things along quietly?"

"Yeah, and if they get here in the next fifteen minutes, it would be even better. The officers that picked them up are off shift. I can grab the file and get it sorted before anyone from SVU comes on duty and comes down to take a look."

Garnet nods. "Anyx, you and Zuzanna get them out of there and take them to Dimitri's. Get them something to eat, and I'll meet you there. I want to ask a few questions about what went on and how this happened."

Anyx dips his chin and is gone a split-second later.

"Thank you, Aiden. Anyx is on his way to you now."

"I'll be waiting."

Garnet looks a little more relaxed as the call ends. "Assuming the lost sheep issue is taken care of, who's up for the site visit to evaluate the conditions for their flock?"

"Let the druid go," Malachi says. He's a weasely man with mossy green skin and a beer paunch. "She has all the answers and opinions."

A flood of hands flies into the air and Garnet frowns. "Miss Cumhaill has no grasp on what our procedures are. How do you expect her to assess Xavier and his seethe?"

"The same way she does everything," he says with a fake smile pasted on his face. "With no tact and a horseshoe up her perky little ass."

There's a rumble of amused agreement.

"No tact? You're just pissy because I wouldn't let you play with my spirit bear warrior. I told you. That was for your protection. If you thought I was rude, I could rectify that right now. If he guts you, that's on you."

Malachi raises a hand. "I saw him at the druid challenge at the standing stones. No need to bother him."

"The vote's been cast," a heavily jowled woman with gold skin says from the far corner of the table. "Are we done? It seems the crisis is averted."

Garnet scowls. "No. That vote doesn't count. Fiona shouldn't be the one, and you all know why."

I blink and swing my attention his way. "I don't. Why?"

"Because Xavier hates you," High Priestess Witch Bitch says. "He makes no secret of it."

"Why does he hate me?"

"Because you've ended what now? Two or three vampires in the past few months?"

I think about that. How bad is it that I have to think about how many vampires I've ended? You'd think that would be something at the top of your head.

"In truth, I've only killed one. and that was in self-defense. Bruin killed the one in the Barghest warehouse, and Garnet killed the one kidnapping me for the mages. I killed the one who sold me to the hobgoblin king, and only because he shot my friend twice in the chest. If he doesn't want his men ended, they should stop trying to kill me."

Zxata leans forward and sends me a warm smile. "His

problem isn't so much that the kills were unjust. Xavier and his men think of themselves as the invincible force in the city. You ending his people on numerous occasions reminds everyone that they can be taken down. It's a point of arrogance."

"Well, I'm not going to apologize for defending myself or my friends. Maybe Xavier should be more careful about whose money he takes when he loans out his army of kidnappers. You lay with the Black Dogs you get fleas."

"You piss off Xavier, you end up dead," Malachi says with unveiled pleasure.

"Whatevs. Fine. If I've drawn the short straw, I'll do this assessment thing. I'm not afraid to meet the man on his turf, and I took the oath. Tell me what I need to do."

"I'll go with her," Nikon says. "We'll make it a date and hit the steakhouse first."

"I'll go too," Suede says. "I've wanted to try out the restaurant, and since I was part of the original committee that put together the rights and requirements of the human blood donors, I'm aware of what they should be getting."

Garnet checks something on his phone and addresses the group. "Very well. Our people have the sheep and had no problem at the police station. Our thanks to you and your brother for that, Lady Druid. Since we have the assessment planning sorted, I suppose this issue is closed unless anyone has other business? No? Then you are dismissed."

A couple of people flash out, but most of them get up and leave. Sloan said the whole wayfarer gift is unique, so maybe me expecting magical people to be able to portal in and out all the time is skewed.

The Moon Called can. Nikon can. I don't know enough about the other races and species of empowered ones to know who else has that ability.

"You look deep in contemplation, Red." Nikon slides into the seat next to me. "So, about our date tonight. I'll make the reservations, and of course, I'll pick up the tab."

I chuckle. "It's not a date."

"Oh, it's a date."

"Nope. In fact, make the reservation for four because I'm bringing my date."

Nikon snorts and waggles his brow at Suede. "I guess that makes you the lucky one, beautiful. I've already broached the idea of a throuple with Fiona and Sloan, and she nixed it."

Suede primps her glistening silver hair. "Elves don't have hangups about multiples. Feel free to broach any subject you like with me."

CHAPTER THREE

"Zxata says they voted you straight into oncoming traffic."

I pull the two Wiccan celebration books Myra asked for and add them to my growing pile. "Yeah, but honestly, I'd rather jump in with both feet than let Xavier and the vampires sneak up behind me thinking I'm afraid to face them."

"But aren't you? You should be."

Slow Descent. I cast the spell and lean over the rail of the third-floor mezzanine, dropping the stack of books to where my boss, Myra, stands waiting with the shelving cart. The texts and tomes fall at a measured rate, and Myra plucks them out of the air and stacks them on her cart.

"Da says we should always be cautious about danger, but never afraid. Fear breeds rash choices and often makes things seem worse than they are in reality."

Myra makes a face at me. "In the case of Xavier and the vampires, things are usually *much* worse than you fear."

While I climb down the metal ladder to the lounge and read area of the store, she finishes sorting the books.

Before we return to the front of the store, I press a hand

against the trunk of Myra's home tree. "Looking good today, Mr. Tree. Glad to see you lush and strong again."

Myra's vertically slit eyes glitter with pride as she takes in the restored health of her beloved ash tree. As a meliae, an ash nymph, her health and well-being is inextricably linked with that of her home tree.

Leniya, or Mr. Tree as I prefer to call him, was poisoned and almost perished when the Toronto mages attacked and Myra fell into a coma.

"It's good to see you looking so happy and healthy too." I sling my arm across her back and squeeze her shoulder as she pushes her little cart up toward the register. "Things are good, I take it? All's well in the land of impassioned lion lovers?"

Her giddy grin makes me giggle.

"Very good, I take it."

She raises her hand and twirls, her electric blue hair swinging into the air. "At the risk of scarring you for life, I gotta say Garnet Grant has skills that go far beyond very good. He's an absolute predator behind closed doors."

"I don't doubt that for a second. I saw how much he loves you when you were sick. I'm glad you two reconnected."

She groans and shakes her head. "I feel like I'm a crazy kid again."

"You *are* a crazy kid. Haven't you heard? One hundy ninety-five is the new thirty."

"Perfect, then I get to be your slightly older sister. No wonder we get along so well."

We're still chuckling and chatting when the brass bell over the door chimes. The influx of customers means we sober and put our professional faces on. The roar of cars and outdoor city sounds invade our sanctum but are quickly cut off as the door closes.

The storefront of Myra's Mystical Emporium faces out onto Queen Street. It would offer us a steady stream of foot-traffic if the business wasn't enchanted to admit only fae, empowered folks, or those who specifically need what we offer.

Most of the time that means there aren't more than two or three walk-in customers a day.

Most of Myra's business revolves around her locating and ordering rare books for repeat clients. Considering the store has been open for forty-five years, she has many of them.

However, this is the last week of October—and that means Samhain, the most significant of the quarterly fire festivals. It takes place during the midpoint between the fall equinox and the winter solstice and is revered as one of the Greater Sabbats, and honors the coming of winter and hibernation.

From the evening of October 31 to the evening of November 1, pagans welcome the completion of the harvest season and usher in the dark half of the year.

Hallowe'en. The Day of the Dead. All Souls Day.

BDL—Before Druid Life began, I dressed up for Hallowe'en, gave out Kool-Aid Jammers to the kids, then went to Shenanigans to get up to a lot of shenanigans.

ADL—After Druid Life began, I look at all the holidays through a different lens. Most, if not all the Christian holidays were adapted from or designed to absorb Celtic or Pagan Sabbats as far back as Constantine in ancient Rome.

Now that we're embracing our druid heritage, I'm reevaluating how we should celebrate the Wheel of the Year. Samhain is believed to be a time when the barriers between the physical world and the spirit world break down, allowing interaction between humans and the denizens of the Otherworld.

I admit, even knowing that magic is real, I'm not sure I believe that. Cray-cray, I know, since my long-dead ancestor Fionn mac Cumhaill visits me from time to time.

I used to pronounce it phonetically. Embarrassing really, now that I know one common Irish pronunciation is *Sa-win.*

"Merry meet, ladies." Myra greets the three women who breeze in. "Let me know if I can help you find anything."

I'm working on learning how to identify the different sects of magically empowered people in Toronto. Considering these women look one hundy percent human and are wearing pendulum crystals as pendants, I'm guessing witches.

It's a pretty safe guess.

One of the customers comes forward, unzips her jacket, and untucks her scarf. "We're getting ready for our annual Dumb Supper and need a few things. We were told you have authentic incense?"

Myra nods. "My crafter makes them in her greenhouse under the full moon and according to the moon cycles. All her products are made with natural and traditional ingredients and infused with an invocation at their time of crafting. You'll find them through the doorway there to your right."

"Perfect. Do you have Tarot or Angel Cards?"

"A small selection next to the incense. You'll find most of the Wiccan offerings in that area of the store."

Ha! Wiccan. Nailed it. Witches bitches!

The three of them hustle off, and I continue with the Samhain display I'm organizing. "So, this will be our first Samhain celebration, and I'm not sure how to bring it up with Da."

"Bring what up, duck?"

"Well, traditionally, druids celebrate the night with a ceremony to remember their dead. Some even believe the dead come through the veil to be with them."

"Yes. Thus the reason for the Dumb Supper feast."

"Right. I'm worried about Da. We're all still broken up and missing Brendan, but the idea that he might come through to us in a visitation is upsetting. I don't know that Da's ready for that."

"Uh-huh." She opens the bin she brought from the storage room and starts unpacking sugar skull decorations. "So, you're solely worried about your father and his pain around the loss of your brother?"

"Yeah, why?"

She straightens the wire legs of a giant, black, fuzzy spider and shrugs. "Just wondering, have you called the lady from the Widows and Orphans Fund to pick up the check waiting for you?"

"Not yet."

"What about the officer in the Death Benefits department? Have you called him to settle Brendan's claim?"

"No. Not yet."

"But it's your father who you think is having trouble accepting the loss?"

I pull in a long, unsteady breath. "All right, I admit it's not *only* my father who's struggling."

Myra rounds the old display counter we use as a desk and squeezes my hand. "No. Of course it's not, and that's perfectly natural. At least you visit him in your meditation sacred spot."

"Yeah, but that's his heritage spark mixed with my memories of him. As much as it comforts me to have him there, it's not *really* him."

"But if he comes through during a druid celebration, it would be really him, and you'd have to accept that he's gone."

I blink against the sting of tears and swallow. "My head knows he's gone. I'm not sure my heart has gotten there yet. So, yeah, maybe the idea of him coming through scares me. What if he's not him? Or worse, what if he is?"

Myra leans in and hugs me. "One thing I know about these things is this. Intent is everything. If Brendan is anything like the rest of you, he'll know what you can handle and what you can't. He may have changed his plane of existence, but he's still your brother."

"You think so?"

"I know so."

"Have you ever reached out to your son?"

Myra's smile tightens, but she doesn't balk at the question. "No, but maybe this year I will. Maybe enough time has passed, and I'm in a solid place with Garnet again, so I could survive it. I honestly never thought I'd get there, but I did—and you and your family will too."

I nod. "Okay, so not this year...but maybe another year."

The BlueBlood Steakhouse at Casa Loma is an upscale, fine dining restaurant with tons of ambiance. From the rich red of the wood paneling, beams, and fireplace mantels, to the large round booths with tufted leather seats and cowhide backs, the gold-mirror chandeliers with antlers on them—which could verge on being too much, but are pretty cool.

"Would you look at this place?" Suede's eyes are wide. "Is this how the other half lives? If so, I vote we do this more often."

I giggle at her enthusiasm but am in total agreement. "If the guys are willing to dress to impress like this, I'm game."

"Like what you see, do you Red?" Nikon waggles his brow and holds his hands so we get a full view. "Well, my offer stands. If you ever want to unwrap this package, you have permission."

Sloan scowls. "Are ye always on the pull or is it Fiona in particular who ye need to proposition?"

Nikon flashes a cocky smile, undeterred. "Both. Look how her cheeks flush beneath her freckles. Adorbs."

I roll my eyes, thankful the banter is friendly.

"You all look amazing." Suede flashes them two enthusiastic thumbs up. "Definitely drool-worthy."

Nikon leads the pack to the maître d' stand and leans in. "Party of eight for Tsambikos."

The maître d' gives Nikon a strange look, but hey, he barely looks twenty-one let alone the twenty-one hundred he is in reality. It's not the restaurant guy's fault for wondering why the blond kid is running the show. "Right this way. A table by the fireplace as you requested."

"And the wine?"

"Breathing to your specifications."

"Very good. Thank you."

We follow the maître d', and I chuckle at our party of eight. Somehow between inviting Sloan as my date and mentioning I'm being sent to assess the feeding habits of the vampires—who hate me—my brothers decided this should be a family affair.

So, it's me and Suede escorted by Sloan, Nikon, Emmet, Dillan, Calum, and Kevin. Calum didn't want Kevin involved, but he insisted. He knows what happened to Liam but says he won't be shut out of any part of Calum's life. To ready himself for what's ahead, he started Krav Maga and asked about joining us in combat training and our daily workouts.

So, it's eight for dinner.

Thankfully, Da is on the early shift and opted for bed. Aiden took a pass too. Kinu got a call from their landlord this afternoon, and they're meeting with him after the kiddos go to bed. So, eight could be worse.

It could be a party of ten. Cozy.

The well-dressed man in black tie leads the way to one of the large, round booths in the center of the room. Suede and I slide in from opposite sides and shimmy our butts around until we meet again at the back. Sloan comes in beside me, Nikon beside her, and my brotherly bouncers fill in two spots on each end.

The guys are still unbuttoning their suit jackets and settling in when Nikon takes the stage. "I told Fi this morning that I'm picking up the tab, so order what you like and spare no expense."

I snort. "You said that when you volunteered to accompany

Suede and me. Since then, three became eight. You don't have to pay."

"Unless you want to." Emmet holds up his hands when I glare at him. "The Greek is our host for the evening. We don't want to offend."

I shake out my napkin and lay it across the skirt of my dress. "Nikon, you've spent enough time with us now to understand the dynamic of my brothers. If you want to assert yourself, feel free."

Nikon waves that away and reaches for the decanter of wine. "Nothing to assert. I insist. After the hot chocolate drink fest and the road hockey bruises and the entertainment of watching you horrify the Guild Governors, I owe you all more than a dinner."

"Awe, he likes us." Emmet pushes out his lips and blows him a kiss across the table.

"Of course he does. We're f—" Dillan seems to remember the atmosphere and changes course mid-curse "—awesome. He's got great taste."

"You are f—awesome, and speaking of great taste," Nikon gives himself a full pour of wine, sets his glass down, and holds out his hand. "Who wants wine?"

"Have at it, Greek." Dillan hands his glass to Emmet and down the line, it comes. While that's happening, a girl in a tight black dress drops off a basket of warm rolls at our table.

She gives Dillan an appraising once-over I've seen a million times. Both Dillan and Emmet have a certain sexy something that the ladies always pick up on. Tonight it's even more evident because they're dressed snazzy in slacks and suit jackets.

After Nikon passes everyone their wine and we've all made our selections from the breadbasket, Dillan leans in. "So, is this restaurant owned and run by the...what can we say in public? We need a code word."

"Transylvanians?" I suggest.

Nikon chuckles. "That's not even close to accurate."

"Doesn't have to be." Dillan goes in for a second roll. "It's solely a point of reference for us, and it's a good one. So, is this restaurant run by Transylvanians?"

"No." Nikon sips his wine and eyes the people at the nearby tables. "It simply happens to be a high-end restaurant close to the Transylvanians' residence. Their king appreciates the finer things and frequents the establishment."

That seems to make Calum and Emmet feel better.

Honestly, me too. It's nice to know we're not surrounded by vampires waiting to pounce on us. If this is a human restaurant, there's a level of protection offered by the crowd.

"Where exactly is the nearby home of the Transylvanians?" Kevin asks.

"Emmet has a theory about that," I say.

He nods. "I found an article that said during World War II they made extensive renovations to the stables outside. The gist is that the renos were a front and a secret military research facility was built underground. It's widely believed that Station M is where they manufactured covert sonar devices used for U-Boat detection."

"If it's widely believed, it was a shit secret," Dillan says.

Emmet laughs. "That's exactly what Fi said."

"True story."

"Do you know what you want to order?" Sloan taps the menu in my hands.

"I haven't looked." I've barely glanced at the offerings, so I give it my full attention and have a look. Leaning sideways, I whisper close to Sloan's ear. "Why aren't there any prices on the menu?"

"Nikon likely asked for guest menus so we wouldn't worry about the cost of things."

"That worries me even more."

Sloan chuckles and kisses my cheek. "Yer sweet to worry, but ye don't need to. The Tsambikos family has amassed a fortune over centuries. A sixty dollar steak is loose change in the bottom of his couch."

"You see? The fact that there's even a steak priced at sixty dollars is terrifying."

"There are steaks priced at two hundred dollars when dining in nice restaurants, Fi. Sixty is nothing to worry about."

"Times eight," I whisper. "My brothers invited themselves."

Red. Stop worrying about the menu, Nikon says straight into my mind. *Just order. It's sweet of you to worry, but I've got this. Really.*

I roll my eyes and straighten. *Eavesdropping is rude.*

Not when the whispered conversation is for my benefit. Seriously, I'll enjoy it much more if you enjoy yourself and stop worrying.

Okay. Thank you.

It is genuinely my pleasure. Now smile and unclench your grip on the menu.

I exhale my anxiety and flash him a genuine smile.

"A toast," Nikon says aloud while raising his glass. "To new friends and new adventures."

Between dinner and dessert, Suede and I excuse ourselves to freshen up and the two of us stretch our legs and check out the ladies' room.

"That was so good, but I ate too much. I can't believe I let Sloan talk me into dessert."

Suede exits her stall and joins me at the sink where I'm washing my hands. "Your Sloan is a very pretty man."

I chuckle. "You noticed that, did you?"

She makes eyes at me in the mirror and we both chuckle. "And, at the risk of being brash and sassy, your brothers are hot toddies too. Is anyone single? Am I allowed to ask or are there boundaries to our status as girlfriends?"

"You're allowed to ask. Calum and Kevin are together, obvi, but both Dillan and Emmet are single at the moment."

"That's good news. Which one do you think would be a good match for me?"

I finish with my lip gloss and drop it back into my purse. "That depends. Do you like your man to be a little broody and snarky or a sweet goofball who takes everything with a laugh?"

"Oh, tough call."

When she finishes at the sink, we head to the door. "Honestly, you can't go wrong. I'm biased, I get that, but they're both great guys."

"Good to know."

"Good evening, ladies," a man says behind us from the shadow at the end of the bathroom hallway.

Funny, I don't recall the hallway being dark and shadowed when we went into the ladies' room. Now, it is.

"You both look lovely tonight."

"Xavier." Suede's easy manner evaporates, and she straightens while glancing up the hall toward the restaurant. "Sneaking up on ladies isn't nice. You could've come to our table and said hello. Or, you can step out of the shadows now and address us properly."

"Your table is too crowded for my liking, and I find I learn a great deal about a person from observing from the shadows."

"There's a word for that," I say. "My father and brothers would call you a stalker."

Suede's brow tightens, but I don't care if I offend the scary vampire king. He already hates me. How much worse could it get? Besides, I've faced off with vampires before, and he isn't about to attack me in his favorite restaurant and risk me releasing Bruin to defend myself.

"I heard through the grapevine that Garnet wants a review of practices."

Suede nods and adjusts her footing to ease closer to me. "After this morning's incident with your sheep getting loose, it seems reasonable."

"Fair enough. So, I understand you being here, but why the druid and the Greek?"

I smile and do my best to show him I'm unaffected by his naturally menacing air. "Because apparently you hate me, and the majority of the Guild Governors threw me under the bus and voted me here hoping you'll end me. Not my doing."

"I see."

I'm still wondering if the tone of his reply is a good or bad thing when he steps out of the shadows and—despite my determination not to react—a shiver runs down my spine.

Xavier is a stern-looking Korean man with a medium build and a trim beard and mustache. Nothing screams 'vampire' to look at him, but he does have oddly caramel-colored eyes. The warm, golden hue of his gaze makes me wonder if they're contacts or a weird side effect of his transition into a predator of the night.

It's strange enough that something feels off when you look at him, but not so obvious that you'd go screaming down the street if you met up with him in a dark alley.

I suppose that's how they survive living in the city among humans without being detected. If they were pasty white with fangs and blood-red eyes, it would be hard to keep their true natures under wraps.

I brush my hands up and down my bare arms to ward off the chill. "We retrieved your three missing humans from the police station. It appears that no one looked too closely into why they were dazed and confused."

Suede reaches out and takes hold of my arm. The gesture seems innocent enough, but by the grip she's using, I know she's getting ready to cut and run if necessary. "It was fortunate that Fiona and her family have ties within the police force and could step in."

Xavier nods. "I shall always give credit where it's due. That was helpful in an unfortunate moment."

My stomach squirrels and I press a hand against the wall to steady myself.

"Fi? Are you all right?"

"Yeah, sorry. Meat sweats. I ate too much."

"There you are." Nikon saunters down the hall to join us. "Sloan and I came to check on where our dates disappeared to. We didn't realize there was a parley in the facilities hallway we were missing out on."

Sloan looks at me and frowns. "What's wrong?"

"I'm fine. Just queasy all of a sudden."

Nikon frowns. "Sloan, you and the boys take Fi home. Suede and I will take care of the assessment and check in when we're done."

I open my mouth to argue but close it as quickly, afraid I might throw up. As much as I want to finish my first task assigned to me by the Guild and prove myself, I cave and take the out. "Thanks, guys. And thank you for the wonderful dinner." I squeeze Suede's hand and kiss Nikon on the cheek. "It was a great time, but yeah, I need some air."

Sloan returns to the table and comes back a moment later with my coat, my purse, and my brothers. The six of us take advantage of the shadowed hallway and *poof* out of the restaurant straight into my back yard. The crisp, October air hits my face. I try to breathe it in and tamp down nausea.

What's wrong, Red? Bruin's alarm surges within me, and I can't take the turmoil.

It sets my stomach roiling.

I blink as the yard spins, and I stagger a couple of feet. Twisting to break free of Sloan's hold, I drop to my knees. I'm barely doubled over before my stomach unloads my Cornish hen into my patch of black-eyed Susans.

From that moment, all manner of calm ends. Someone grabs my hair as voices echo and swirl in my head. "What's happening?" "Did they poison her?" "What do we do?"

I turn to tell them I'm fine when the night sky somersaults above.

"Fiona!"

CHAPTER FOUR

M y eyes pop wide, and I'm lying on my bed. Sloan is brushing my hair back from my face and assessing me with his gaze. "Fi, I need to examine ye. Can I lift yer dress?"

The thundering stampede of footsteps coming up the stairs signals the arrival of my family.

"In her room," Dillan shouts.

"Fi, yer dress. May I?"

I swallow against the acidic burn of vomit and the sensation of my throat closing. Oh, gawd, I need a bucket.

"Just do it," Da snaps while rushing in. "We'll not hold it against ye if yer tryin' to save her life. Calum, help the man."

I'm jostled and rolled. Cold air hits my heated flesh, and I'm shivering so hard I can hear my teeth chatter.

"Fucking hell," Dillan mutters.

"So, not food poisoning, then," Emmet says.

Sloan twists and points at my vanity. "Emmet, hand me one of the vials Dora sent over."

There's a shuffle and a lot of cursing, then Dillan scoops up my head and dumps liquid manure down my throat. Our friend Pan Dora—Merlin in a former life—was one of the greatest druids of all time and has been working to keep me from becoming possessed by a dark bond I made with Morgan le Fey's grimoire.

I gag and sputter as the rancid liquid hits the back of my tongue. Despite my body's instinct to reject the potion, I somehow manage to get most of it down my throat.

"Niall, it's time," Sloan snaps. "Enough is enough. I need to take her now. I checked her leg last night. For it to get this bad this quickly, it's way too much for us to be guessin' at what's happenin'. We *need* my father."

There's a great muttering of frustrated male voices, and I black out.

I rise from the depths of the cold dread and try to gain a sense of time and place. We're still in my bedroom, but the shouting has stopped. My red suitcase is packed and beside the bed. Sloan, Emmet, and Calum are with me as Da picks me up.

"Everyone ready?"

The next time I open my eyes, I'm lying on the stainless steel table in Wallace's clinic while people mumble and fuss. I've been stripped down to my panties on the bottom half of my body, and Sloan's got a cloth pressed against my forehead. He's saying something, but I don't understand…

Why can't I understand him?

Tears heat my cheeks, then Calum and Emmet are there, and they clutch my hands. Calum sings my favorite song from when we were kids, and the tune vibrates from a distance. It's like hearing carnival music from a couple of streets over.

Dillan pushes in. He brushes my tears and drops his face to

my neck. "Fight, Fi. It's bad, so you need to really dig deep and fight to stay with us."

I don't feel like fighting. I want to be wrapped in a warm blanket and cocoon for a long sleep. I'm so tired.

"Here we are again, Fiona." Wallace looks at me from down the table. "Ye've had a rough go it seems. Don't worry. We're takin' good care of ye now."

I recognize the people with Wallace. They were the ones who saved Liam when I was here last time.

That's good. Maybe they have another big win in them.

My eyes are heavy but every time I close them, Calum or Sloan or someone else shakes me.

Rude much?

"Fiona, look at me, *mo chroi*." Da's voice holds the stern censure he only pulls out in the direst of moments. "Ye need to stay awake. Fight the urge to sleep until the serum starts workin'. Do ye hear me, luv? We need ye to stay awake."

I'm so tired…

And I feel…

My stomach writhes, and Sloan rolls me to the side. There's a dish there to catch what I spew up. I grimace at the sight of what I expelled. It's a deep, dark green.

My heart lurches.

That can't be good.

"Well, that can't be good," Dillan snaps.

Right?

"It's the book's poison." Sloan hands Emmet the basin to rinse while he refreshes his cloth.

"Then it's *good* she's puking it up, right?" Calum says.

Sloan frowns and his current scowl is even direr than his everyday version. "We don't know. None of us has ever dealt with anything like this before."

Another wave of chills racks me. "C-c-c-cold."

"I'm sorry, baby girl." Calum rubs my arms. "They need your

fever to break. Then, I swear, we'll snuggle you up in fleece and blankets and settle you in front of a fire."

"Sack up, Cumhaill." Da pushes in beside me. "Grit yer teeth and bear it, luv. The worst of it is over now. Wallace and his people have things well in hand."

For all the skills my father excels at, lying isn't one of them. Maybe this isn't going to end well for me after all.

Damn it, and life was just getting interesting.

Death is a cruel asshole—a trickster even. Good men get shot in the streets and die protecting the innocent. Mothers get sick and leave their families behind. Yappy dogs fly across the front lawn and get snapped up by hungry coyotes. More often than not, life and death have nothing to do with growing old and our bodies passing into the next iteration of existence.

It's more random than that.

One minute you're sucked back into medieval times and watching the jugglers practice in the courtyard of an ancient castle. The next you're internalizing an evil grimoire and poisoning yourself for the sake of humanity.

Who would've guessed that was a bad idea?

Except tricksters also possess a twisted sense of humor.

Lying there, all comfy and warm, I'm not sure what happened or what to expect next. I open my eyes a crack. No glorious white light surrounds me. No puffy white clouds with cherubim angels strumming their harps within sight.

Nope. Plaid flannel sheets twist around me as I lay crowded and slightly crushed in a massive wooden four-poster bed.

I study the nature scene carved into the paneled ceiling of the antique bed and smile in recognition. King Henry. Not many men could pull off an antique of this size and style.

Sloan can.

Lifting my head, I realize why it's so dark. The heavy burgundy drapes are untied and drawn for privacy.

I also realize why I'm so squished.

Manx is curled up tight against my belly, his gray fur rising and falling in slow respiration. Against his paws, Sloan is fast asleep on the edge of the bed. Calum and Kevin spoon behind me, Calum's arm reaching over Kevin's hip to rest on mine. Down at the bottom, across the foot of the bed, both Dillan and Emmet are scrunched between my feet and the footboard.

Warm, soft fingers brush my cheek, and I tear my gaze away from my crazy brothers. Da is peeking in the curtains, his eyes glittering with relief. "They haven't left yer side since last night. Everyone's been out of their heads with worry."

"Am I fixed?" I croak, my voice raw and graveled.

His smile is tight. "So far so good. Wallace has never dealt with this, so he can't say, but he thinks he's got a handle on the poisoning from the book. I'm sorry I didn't listen to Sloan sooner. Ye suffered because I was stubborn and afraid. Maybe if he'd brought ye here earlier..."

"Not your fault. All we can do is our best, right?" I smile at the crazy cockerel comb of ebony hair sticking up off Sloan's head in odd angles.

There have only been two times that I've ever seen him when he hasn't looked GQ runway-ready. The first was the morning I flashed back from the dragon lair after my captivity, and the second is now.

Emmet lets out a breathy snore, and I check out the rest of my slumber party group.

"I am one lucky girl."

"Without a doubt."

I think Da is talking about me surviving. I'm talking about my family, but I leave it at that.

The deep grumble of my bear having a dream has me propping myself up on my elbow. "Bruin's okay? The poison didn't harm him while he was inside me?"

Da shakes his head. "It didn't. Still, Wallace asked that he stay in his physical form until yer well enough to take him in. The two had words about it, but yer bear won't jeopardize yer recovery, so he gave in. He'll be anxious to merge with ye though. He worried somethin' fierce. We all did."

I draw a deep, steadying breath and soak it all in. "I feel good now, though. Thanks for standing vigil."

He looks at the ensemble cast hunkered down around me and chuckles. "It's a good thing yer man has a bed the size of a football field."

"A very good thing." I wriggle to the top of the bed to get out from beneath the warmth of the sheets. I free my feet and look down at the wide strip of gauze wrapping my thigh.

"I'm afraid to see what's underneath."

"Then leave it a day or two before ye look. Yer body's been through an ordeal. It deserves a chance to heal before ye scrutinize it."

I run my fingers over the bandage and frown. At least if there's a scar, it's high enough on my leg nobody will see it unless I invite them to.

Da's right. That's something to worry about another day.

Right now, I'm thankful to be alive and well.

"Can you help me up?"

I raise my hand, ready for my dad to extricate me from the love-in. Manx growls as I ruffle his fur and Sloan's eyes pop wide.

"It's okay, surly," I whisper. "Go back to sleep. I'm awake and need to stretch my legs."

Sloan sits up, and our gazes lock. He looks alarmed at first but then settles once he realizes what's going on. "Hey. Nice to see yer not dead."

"It's nice not to be dead. Big points in the win column for you on that one."

Sloan sits up and rubs his hands over his face. "Yeah, well, I had a bit of spare time and thought, not much else to do, might as well save Fiona...again."

I giggle. "I know, right? I'm a bad habit you can't seem to break. I'm the least damsel of any girl I know, but you still keep having to swoop in to save me."

"Should I give the two of ye a minute?" Da asks.

I shake my head. "No, I *do* want to stretch my legs. I desperately need a trip to the loo."

Da backs out of the curtain, and Sloan rolls off the bed. He helps me over Manx, and I leave the sleeping mass of thick gray fur with my brothers.

Sloan sets me on my feet and holds me by the elbows for a sec to make sure I'm steady. When I'm good, I straighten and brush my hands down the collared jersey he gave me to wear last time when I flashed here to save Liam.

"Do I have clothes?"

"Yer wee bag is in there already, and I put out fresh towels and some toiletries same as the last time."

I hug Sloan and take a beat to catch my breath. "Thanks for the save and for everything you do between the saves. You're amazeballs."

"That yer here to say so is all the thanks I need."

I hug Da and kiss his cheek. "I love you, oul man. Thank you for being here."

"There's nowhere else I'd be, luv. Nothin' matters to me more than my kids, ye know that. The rest of the world can go to pot as far as I'm concerned, as long as my kids are good."

"I'm good." I say the words as a reflex but realize as I pull back, they're true. "Or at least I will be once I shower."

Sloan catches my wrist and stops me from getting away.

When he pulls my hand to his mouth and kisses it, I get a weird foreboding feeling.

"Am I missing something?"

He offers me a forced smile and my heart rate doubles. "There's one wee thing we need to tell ye before ye head in there."

"What?"

"It's nothing terrible." He squeezes my hand tighter as I try to pull away. "Or, at least, we don't think it's terrible. Yer up and strong and ye said yerself ye feel good."

"*Okaaay.*" My chest tightens and a chill snakes down my spine.

"Do you remember when we studied fae traits, and we talked about how some are determined at birth because of genetics, some emerge at puberty or in stressful situations, and some come from being exposed to high levels of power?"

"I remember." I blink against the sting of my eyes, tears building at the promise of what's coming next. "Sloan, you're scaring me. Tell me what happened."

"We don't know what it means, but you were exposed to an incredibly high level of magic and more stressful situations than one should have to endure."

"And I got a faery trait?"

I look at my father and see the worry in his gaze. "Show her, son. It'll be better than her worrying."

Sloan takes my hand and leads me into his ensuite. "Now don't freak out. It's fine. Everything will be fine."

"Screw that. Saying 'don't freak out' makes me wanna lose my shit." My breath rushes in and out of my lungs as I swallow against the scream pushing at the base of my throat. "What is it? For fuck's sake, just tell me."

He grips my wrists to stop the trembling and pulls me inside the washroom to face the mirror. "As far as we can tell, everything is all right. You're beautiful. Stunning. It's just that now—yer eyes are...different."

Different?

I stare at the ice-blue eyes, wild black lids and sockets, and figure it has to be a makeup prank. My irises are tiny black dots, and there's a black ring around the creepy, washed-out blue. It makes them almost look like they're glowing.

No. They *are* glowing.

"I look like Marilyn Manson."

"That's one opinion. It reminded yer brothers of a Husky dog one of yer neighbors had when ye were kids."

"Chimo," I say, my voice thready. "I don't want Chimo eyes. What does that mean? Are they going to stay like this? I don't understand."

"I'm afraid no one has those answers yet," Da says.

"But it's just the eyes, right? I'm not possessed or anything? You mentioned faery traits, but I didn't sprout wings, and I don't have gills or anything. So, I'm good right?"

"We must wait and see what the future has in store for ye."

I stare at myself in the mirror; only it's not me. It looks like me, but it's not. "How much more could the future have in store for me, Da? Gawd, when will enough finally be enough?"

"I don't know, *mo chroi*. I simply don't know."

By the time I have a long, ugly cry in the shower, the mirror in Sloan's bathroom steams up enough that I don't have to look at myself. I shut the water off and commit to facing the world. As much as I would like to, I can't spend the rest of my life hiding in a castle ensuite.

Even if it is a *very* nice ensuite.

"Let me know when it's safe to come in and tend to yer leg," Sloan says outside the door. "I need to wrap it before ye slide yer pants on."

I exchange the towel for my underwear and pull his jersey on over my head. It's long and too big, and it makes me feel like I can hide a little more than my fitted clothes. Padding over to the door, I open things up and usher him inside.

He takes one look at me and pulls me against his chest. "Och, Fi. I wish I could take the hits fer ye once in a while. It's too much, what this life puts ye through."

"I'm glad I'm not the only one who thinks so."

"Yer not. Yer da and yer brothers think the same. Now, come. Let's treat ye to a little TLC." He taps his hand on the granite countertop.

When I step over to him, he grips my hips and lifts me to sit on the bathroom counter. The granite is cold on the backs of my legs, and I hiss. "Here's a hint for you, Mackenzie. With me, TLC is warm...always warm."

"I'll make a note of it. Now, let me see if I can help with yer eyes. It'll not change them, but perhaps having things seem normal will help for a little." He places his palm over my eyes, and I feel the warmth of his magic tingling on my skin.

Irish eyes of brilliant blue,
Return to yer natural hue.
My glamor changes what is seen,
Fiona's eyes are what they've been.

When he's finished, he removes his hand and smiles. "There now. That'll do. We'll figure out the rest in time. We always do."

I twist on the counter and touch my image in the mirror. "There I am."

"Yer always there, Cumhaill. Whether it's yer skin tattooed and hard as bark, or a possessed dark book on yer leg, or yer eyes changing color and glowin' like the moon in the night sky, yer always there."

"Thanks for saying so. I'm still glad I look like me."

He tugs his medical kit across the polished surface and unzips the bag. After taking out a couple of bottles of salve and some fresh gauze, he sets things out on the counter. "Let's get yer leg sorted and get out there. Yer da and yer brothers need to get back to Toronto to work."

"You're leaving me? Have we been here for three days? Can you even portal back yet?"

"No on all three counts." He coats my thigh with his father's medicinal goop. "Yer under my da's care, and I'll not leave yer side for a moment. Nikon's here. He and Suede came to check on ye once they finished with the vampires. When they heard what happened, he brought Dillan, Aiden, Kevin, and Suede to be with the family. I couldn't portal everyone who wished to come."

I lean back and lift my leg so he can re-wrap the poisoned skin. It's still gray and disgusting, but sadly, I'm getting used to it. "Do you think this will heal?"

"I do. Once the tissue regenerates beneath, I'll work on getting it to look healthier. For now, I want all the cells to focus on healing."

That makes sense. "Your dad thinks I'm better?"

He tilts his head from side to side. "Optimistically hopeful that yer bond to the grimoire is severed."

"But there could be more. It might not be only the eyes, right? They're wondering if there's more."

"Wondering, yes. That doesn't mean there will be or that the eyes have a direct correlation to the grimoire. It could still be a fae trait evolving. Only time will tell. But if anything strange happens or if ye feel something comin' over yerself, ye must let me know."

"Okay."

He tucks his supplies back into his black kit and helps me off the counter and onto my feet. "All finished. Yer safe to get dressed."

He moves to step away, and I pull him back. Rising onto my toes, I hug him and breathe him in. Sloan always smells good. His scent is a mixture of the Irish countryside and a very expensive aftershave. It's quickly becoming a balm to the panic of my life. "Thanks, Mackenzie."

He presses his cheek to the side of my head and sighs heavily. "I'd say it's my pleasure, but it's not. I'd rather ye stop havin' these kinds of setbacks altogether."

"Yeah, you and me both."

CHAPTER FIVE

Sloan leaves me to finish getting dressed, and when I exit the ensuite, I'm surprised to find the room empty, other than Bruin and Manx awaiting my grand exit. My bear rears up onto his back legs, and I step into his embrace. His massive paws drape over my shoulders, and the warmth of his fur envelopes me. After a long bear hug, I ease back. "Any chance you'd like to merge? I'm shaky and could use your strength."

"I thought you'd never ask."

My grizzly dematerializes, and in a gust of wind, he enters my chest and settles inside me. I press a flat palm against my sternum and draw a deep breath. Much better.

"So, Manxy boy, where did everyone go?"

"There was talk of yer grandparents bringing honey cakes for tea. I think Sloan went and fetched them to have a wee visit before yer brothers pop off home."

Right. Home. Because my brothers have jobs that demand their time and attention.

Sometimes I envy them the sense of purpose. To know what your calling is and get paid for it must be nice. I honestly believe my calling is to be a druid. I've yet to figure out who wants to pay me to do it.

"Lead the way, furry fellow. Let's get there before all the treats are gone."

Manx takes the lead, and I follow him through the maze of stone passageways that make up Sloan's childhood home. I have to admit; it would've been cool to grow up here with my brothers. The challenges of hide-and-seek would've been raised to new heights. Endless rooms. No squeaking floors to give you away. And space to run and pass in the halls.

Century-old Victorians aren't ideally suited for six rambunctious kids.

Sadly, Sloan grew up here alone. It seems a wasted opportunity not to fill up these rooms and these halls with kids.

"Do ye want a brood of kids then?" Manx asks.

I blink. "Sorry?"

"Ye said it's a waste the castle wasn't filled with kids. Do ye want a large family yerself?"

I hadn't realized I'd been speaking aloud. Did I? Could he hear me on an animal frequency? Is this part of the effects of the dark book? Am I paranoid? I feel paranoid.

"Is it a secret then?"

I blink again. "No. Sorry. Um…yeah, I'd like a bunch of kids. Four. Five. Six. The best part of having a big family is growing up and always having someone to play with or to complain to or to back you up when someone comes at you. It makes me sad that Sloan never had that."

"He has it now. He enjoys spendin' time with yer brothers almost as much as spendin' time with a certain redhead lass that has him turned around."

"You're a sweetheart. I'm sorry he's spent so much time away from you. He mentioned bringing you to the city next time. I think it's a great idea. There are a few concerns, but I think we can make it work."

"I'd like that. He might be dry and a little repressed, but he's my human, and I do miss him when he's gone."

"Of course you do. We'll do better at not separating the two of you. *I'll* do better. I promise."

"Thank you, Fiona. I appreciate that."

Manx leads me into a dining room I haven't been in yet. When I was here when Granda was dying, Sloan and I ate sandwiches in the guest room they gave me. When I was here when Liam was shot, we ate in a smaller, less formal eating space. This dining room is quite grand.

"Fi!" Dillan breaks away from the chatter around the table.

I raise my hand to signal them not to all get up, but it's too late, and they swarm me. Not that I'm complaining. My brothers give the best hugs *evah*.

"How's things, baby girl?" Calum asks.

"You got the eye thing taken care of." Emmet points. "That's good."

Dillan whacks him, and Emmet stiffens. "Hey, what the hell?"

"The first thing you mention is the eye thing? Use your head, eejit."

Emmet frowns. "Sorry. I thought that was a compliment. I wanted her to feel better about things."

"It was, and I do." I go back for another hug from Em. "At least that's the way I took it. S'all good. Yes, the eye thing is the stuff of nightmares, but hey, Morgana's grimoire was the stuff of nightmares too. It stands to reason I couldn't get off unscathed. I'm sure Wallace will figure it out. In the meantime, Sloan taught me a glamor spell to conceal it."

Granda pats Sloan on the shoulder, a definite look of pride lighting up his face. "Good lad. Thank ye, son."

"My pleasure."

"So, are we hitting the ether then?" Nikon asks. "Niall starts work in an hour."

"Oh, Da. Did you get any sleep?"

Da purses his lips and grunts. "Don't ye worry about yer oul man. When you kids were teethin' and takin' bottles through the night, there were many a shift I worked without a wink of sleep. It won't kill me. That yer well and on the mend is all that matters."

I hug him tight and kiss his cheek as I ease back. "Love you huge."

"How could ye not?" He winks. "I'm pretty feckin' spectacular."

I'm still smiling when he steps back and taps my heart. "Take good care of my baby girl, Bear."

Rest assured, Da. I do so swear.

I smile. "He swears he will."

Before they leave, I hug Nikon and thank him.

"Fi, don't give it another thought. Honestly. If I had it in my power, I'd do more than taxi a few loved ones to help you. I wish I could fix this. It's just not in my wheelhouse."

"Thank you. And don't downplay the value of taxiing loved ones. For me, that's huge."

He dips his chin. "When you get back we'll do another big dinner. This time, maybe you won't fertilize the daisies with it."

"One could hope."

After one last round of hugs, my fam jam flashes out with a *snap* in the air, and it's me, Sloan and Manx, my grandparents, and... "Suede. Did you get left behind?"

"No. I mentioned to Sloan that it's been years since I was back on ancient fae soil. I thought I might stay a little longer and get back to nature for a few days."

"Awesome. I thought for a sec you stayed to babysit me."

She laughs. "Hardly. Most people think they need to babysit *me*. Although, I'd love to meet the elf that laid that kiss on you. A woodland elf who could favor others with the gift of fae sight is extremely rare. I'm very curious who he is and why he's hiding out in a druid grove."

"Tomorrow, maybe. Right now, if nobody minds, I think I'd like to go back and lay down. I'm a little drained, and it's a mile and a half back to King Henry. Sorry."

"Och, don't apologize, luv." Gran picks up the plate of honey cakes and hands them to me. "Forget about walkin' back. If yer tuckered out, Sloan here will take ye straight away, won't ye, my boyo?"

"Of course. I'll get Fi settled and be right back to take the two of you home."

A blink later, we're in Sloan's suite. He sets the baked goods on his table and escorts me back to bed. "I won't be long. Do ye need anythin' while I'm out?"

"Do you have ginger ale here? Some kind of bubbly soda to settle my tummy?"

"Are ye still nauseous?"

"Not much. It's probably more anxiety than upset."

He helps me into bed, covers me with the flannel sheets and coverlet, then presses his lips to my forehead as if he's assessing my temperature. "Close yer eyes, Cumhaill. And try not to cause any trouble while I'm gone."

I adjust my hair on the pillow and yawn. "Trust me. I'm not going anywhere. If trouble rears its head, it won't be my doing."

"It rarely is."

Lightning cracks and thunder rolls, jarring me from a deep sleep. I don't know if I cried out or the clap scared him awake too, but Sloan pulls me against his side and fixes the covers over us. My heart races and I'm glad not to be alone in a strange bed when I don't feel at all myself.

I realize I'm clinging to him like a scared koala and force myself to ease back. "I'm not complaining, but I thought you said you prefer to sleep on your own to avoid temptations."

He shifts my hair back and settles it over my shoulder. "I figured since yer half-dead, I'm safe to watch over ye without fear of ye tryin' to seduce me."

"I think your virtue is safe."

Another thundering crack rents the air and I jump out of my skin. "It's all right, *a ghra*. A storm is brewing, but we're safe from its ire here, together."

I'm acting stupid. Why am I so jumpy?

It's a freaking storm, and I'm shaking like a leaf. I snuggle closer and lay across his chest. "It offends my inner warrior to admit I'm scared by thunder but do you mind if I cling to you like scaredy-koala until I get back to sleep?"

His amusement raises my cheek in a gentle bounce. "I don't mind. Cling away. Ye've been through a lot. It's probably a delayed reaction to any of the traumatic events ye've survived lately. I won't tell if ye don't."

I blink against the pitch of night, and eventually, listening to the steady *lub-dub* of his heart beating beneath my ear lulls me to calm.

"This is nice," I say, as much to myself as to him. When he doesn't respond, I figure he's fallen back to sleep.

"Aye, it is."

With my smile lost in the darkness, I try to breathe to the depths of stiff lungs. It's only a storm. Everything is fine.

Maybe if I hold on tight, eventually I'll believe it.

"Fiona? Where are ye, lass?"

I follow the call of Patty's voice deeper into my subconscious mind. It's not everyone who can say their leprechaun friend taught them how to access a spiritual plane within themselves. I'm one of the lucky few.

When I open my eyes, I'm sitting in my wicker swing surrounded by the magic and wonder of my sacred grove. Brendan is here. I'm the custodian of his heritage spark and will always have a part of him within me.

I wave to him, lying along one of the widest branches. He's lounging beneath the speckled light of the canopy, his leg hanging toward the forest floor swinging lazily.

When he sees me waving, he winks and waves back. He's happy where he is and that makes me happy too.

"Fiona. There ye are," Patty says.

I turn to greet my diminutive friend and giggle at the flyaway frazzle of his puffy white hair. Jackson said he looks like a dandelion. I suppose, to a four-year-old, that's exactly what he looks like.

But while the hair of my Man o' Green might look like a dandelion gone to seed, Patty has warm eyes and a smile that twinkles with mischief. "Where have ye been, sham? I've been trying to contact ye."

I step behind the Shenanigan's bar that appeared in my imaginary happy place grove and pull him a draught. "Sorry. Long story short, I was poisoned by an evil grimoire and have been slightly possessed by Marilyn Manson. I'm on the mend now, but it kicked the snot outta me for a while."

His bushy eyebrows wriggle like two albino caterpillars. "I'm sorry to hear it. Are ye up and about yet?"

"I think today, maybe. I've been sleeping a lot, but something's still not quite right."

"I'm sorry to hear it—truly I am—but if yer able, I need yer help. Something has happened. Something I can't take care of alone. I need ye and bring yer Granda too. Hurry."

I wake with a jolt and sit up in bed. I'm alone, and something about that feels odd. No Sloan. No Manx. Scootching to the side of the mattress, I pull back King Henry's heavy drape and get a rush of cool air. Wow...privacy and thermal insulation.

The suite is empty, so I figure I'm on my own.

What's wrong, Red?

"I'm not sure. Patty needs us, and he seemed upset."

I text Granda, then shuffle across the stone floor and head to the loo. After closing myself in, I take care of things and dig into my suitcase where it's set on a spare counter by the Gothic arched window. I smile at the neat piles and grab a cotton stretch top, my beige cargo pants, and fresh socks and undies.

I wonder about unwrapping my leg and slathering on a fresh layer of Sloan's salve but decide against it. It'll take more time than I care to spend and he'll likely want to take a look at the progress and tend to it himself.

In five minutes I'm dressed, brushed, primped, and wolfing down a honey cake. My phone *bings* and I check the incoming text. "Okay, Granda's ready. I just need my ride."

At the knock on the door, I lick my fingers and turn. "Come in."

The door opens, and it's Sloan's mother followed by an extremely tidy blond man in livery carrying a tea tray.

She's tall, insanely fit, and walks with the same rod-straight gait as her son. Where his skin is the shade of a warm, mocha brown, hers is quite a bit darker, chestnut almost. I haven't spent much time with Janet Mackenzie, but from what Gran and Granda say, she's a good person and an amazing martial arts fighter.

I think it's awesome that there are no gender roles in the Order. Janet is the kickass warrior and Wallace is the caregiver. I like that.

"Fiona. Sloan asked me to check on ye and make sure ye eat

more than a fistful of yer Gran's pastries. Dalton prepared you a mushroom omelet with fruit. I'm told yer not fussy."

"No. I'm not." I smile at Dalton as he sets the tray down on the table. It has one of those metal meal covers over the plate like they use in fancy hotel room service. *Welcome to the Mackenzie's Stonecrest Castle. We hope you enjoy your stay.* "I appreciate it. Thank you."

Janet smiles—at least I think it's supposed to be a smile. It's more like her face is pinched, and she doesn't like it. "It's his job, dear. There's no need to thank him."

All righty then.

"So, where is Sloan?"

"Off somewhere with the silver-haired elf. He said he'd not be long."

Crappers. I check my watch and sigh. "Okay, thanks. I appreciate the message and the breakfast. I'm sure by the time I've eaten he'll be back and ready to start our day."

One manicured brow arches and that pinched face returns. "The start of day began hours ago, but your point is clear. Eat and perhaps when he returns there might be enough day left to do something productive."

Now it's me forcing a smile. "Perfect. Let's hope."

The two of them leave, and I sit at the table. First, I text Sloan to say I'm ready and we're on a mission. Then, I lift the lid to check out the offerings. Holy-schmoly the omelet is as big as my head, and there's a mound of hashbrowns and brown beans and sausage. There's no way I'm going to be able to eat all this. And yeah, there's a side bowl of fruit too.

I dig into my omelet and try to at least look like I'm playing the part of a good patient. Wow. The omelet is yummy, and I make a mental note to make sure Dalton knows it.

My phone buzzes back a reply text, then Sloan's standing next to me. I choke and swallow the breakfast bliss, pressing a linen napkin to my mouth. "Hey, you're back."

"I texted that I was comin'."

I open the text and nod. "So you did. But when the text and you arrive at the same time, it's not much good as advance notice."

"Ye said ye needed me so I came straight. If ye wanted lag time, ye should've said so."

I chuckle and take a few more bites. "No. You're good. Patty needs us to pick up Granda and come to the lair."

As I'm getting up, Sloan places his hands on my shoulders and holds me in place. "Finish yer meal. I'll check in with my father and be back in a flash. There's no sense leavin' food to go to waste when ye need the nourishment, and I need a moment anyway."

I chuckle and take another bite. "I'll *never* finish this meal but fine, if you promise to hurry, I'll do my best. Patty sounded upset."

He doesn't bother to respond before he *poofs* out.

I get another few bites down and realize there's no chance in hell. "Bruin, I need your help with something..."

By the time Sloan gets back, my plate is clean, and I'm popping pineapple squares into my mouth as I tie my boots.

"Ye gave it to yer bear, didn't ye?"

"I ate what I could."

"Fine, I'll not argue, but ye need to take better care of yerself. Even if ye feel better, it takes time to recover from the level of poison the book infected ye with."

I understand that. I'm the one with the evil residue feeling lingering in the background.

Straightening, I search the room, looking for my jacket. My suitcase is in his bathroom. My shoes are by the door, and my dishes are on his table. "Wow, I've kinda spread out and taken over. Sorry."

"Och, don't be. I've lived so long under the threat of spot

checks and bouncing quarters off my mattress it feels utterly rebellious to see disorder in the room."

I snort. Yeah, he's a rebel all right. "You're too funny, Mackenzie. Now, enough chit-chat. Let's roll. You get us to Granda's, and I'll take it from there."

CHAPTER SIX

After three failed tries to activate my dragon portal, I'm not sure what to think. Every time before, accessing the lair has been the blink of a thought and the work of a moment. Patty's worry about the queen might be more urgent than I first thought. Something is interfering with the magic.

With Sloan and Granda holding my free hand, I try once more. I grip the dragon infinity band on my arm and flash from my grandparent's kitchen to the ante-chamber of the ancient queen.

The lair of the Wyrm Dragon Queen is enclosed in a massive cavern deep in the rocky cliffside of the Cliffs of Moher.

The mid-morning sun outside spotlights the opening to the cliff edge, and I glance down four hundred feet to the white-capped water crashing below. The salty sea air lifts my hair as wind buffets against us, twisting and twirling at the opening to the outside world.

"The first time I was here, bodies and bones littered this whole area." I sweep a hand through the space and can see the horror of the original scene in my memory like it was yesterday and not four months ago.

"Come in, and I'll show you around. Oh... I don't have to remind you not to touch Patty's gold, right? He's quite protective of his cache of valuables."

Granda grunts. "Yer givin' me pointers on etiquette around a Man o' Green, are ye? That's ironic."

I chuckle. "Yeah, maybe it is. I don't want to see either of you eaten by the dragon queen. It's her privilege to chomp people who go for Patty's hoard."

"Noted and understood," Sloan says.

I lead the way deeper into the lair, and while our eyes adjust to the dim light, I give them a second to let the sight sink in. "This section of the cavern is where Her Exaltedness lives and sleeps. There she is."

A hundred feet from the opening where we stand the dragon queen lays coiled up, her eyes closed. Her muscular tail encircles her many times over and her scales glimmer in vibrant shades of red.

"Incredible," Granda says, his gaze fixed. "Ye told us about her magnificence, Fi, but it's not the same as seein' it."

No. It's not.

The torches are lit in the treasure area, and the reflection of light off hills and valleys of gold bathes the entire cavern in a glow of warmth.

"It's more treasure than could be held in a thousand druid shrines." Sloan stares across the vast space and shakes his head. "It's hard to grasp that this much treasure even exists."

Granda grunts. "Patty is a lucky man. Imagine the stories these treasures can tell. Imagine the history and the significance of the pieces. It's an incredible collection."

"I knew ye'd understand, Shrine-Keeper." Patty joins us. "Those who see gold as wealth and possession are missing the entire meaning of treasure."

Granda nods. "I couldn't have said it better myself."

I bend to hug my friend. He looks harried and tired. With his disheveled appearance and the worry lines under his eyes, he's barely recognizable as the playful Elvis dance partner I know and love.

"What is it? What's happened?"

He gestures at the queen. "Someone's done somethin' to her, Fi. She hasn't woken in over a week, and I was hopin' Lugh might be able to help on that front. The young are hungry, and they miss their mam, and I don't know what to do. I've done my best, but I can't watch them and feed them and get her the help she needs."

As if the mention of the young has called them, the rumble of an incoming horde of twenty-three baby dragons grows in the air.

"Brace yerselves, boys," Patty advises. "They're an energetic bunch, and they haven't eaten, so they might bite."

Sloan flashes a wide-eyed gaze and looks like he's fighting the urge to *poof* out.

I raise my hand. "It should be fine."

"Och, it might not." Patty makes a face. "I'll ask them not to nibble, but they're a hungry bunch."

Hells bells.

"Granda, you get in the pink Cadillac. The kids know they're not allowed near the queen's memorabilia. Sloan, you *poof* back to Gran and find us some roadkill quickly. Now that you've been here, you'll be able to get back."

"Unless the cavern is enchanted," he reminds me.

"Och, I'll clear your way, sham. Away ye go."

The two of them follow my plan and get to safety as my honorary children stampede me. "Dudes, hi. Yes, I'm here. I know, it's super exciting."

I don't need to bend to pat and stroke them this time. They come up to my waist now. Man, you blink, and they've grown. Time passes differently in the presence of creatures with massive power, and a mythical dragon queen certainly qualifies there. "Look at you guys. So many changes."

My blue boy, Dartamont, is the oldest and the first to transition into his adolescent form, but more of them have gone through puberty now.

I stagger to the side, swarmed by wyrms, wyverns, and Westerns. Scanning the jostle of wings, horns, and scales, I find my boy and smile. "There you are, Dart. Come here."

A quick scan of my baby dragon assures me that nothing much has changed since I saw him last. He's still cute as a button, two wings, three horns, four legs, and a goofy grin that probably only a mother could love.

And I do.

Sloan *poofs* in, kneeling over a dead cow, his hand pressed against its shoulder for transport. The moment the babies smell the meat, he abandons the carcass and materializes beside me. "It's a start. Lara is scrambling to find more. She's expanding the search across Kerry, up to Tralee, and over to Killarney. Farmers, municipal road clean up, and hunters without proper permits."

"That's a good start." In the time it's taken for Sloan to catch me up, the full-sized cow has disappeared in a bloody spray of savagery.

Sloan frowns. "*Shite.* But it's only a start. I'll be back."

It goes like that for the next hour, Sloan *poofing* in every ten or fifteen minutes with a cow, a deer, or a couple of sheep collected from towns moving out in the growing distance from our home base in Farrenfore.

With each offering, the dragons get less ravenous, and their manners improve. They're a disgusting sight, covered in blood and entrails, but at least they're not eyeing us up as the main course anymore.

After a huge black Angus bull arrives and there are only a couple of takers for the meal, I think the babies are sated to the point of safety.

Once Sloan returns, he'll be off the clock for a while.

"I don't suppose you have a power sprayer handy?" I say. "It seems our kids have made a bit of a mess."

Patty is all grins. "Och, I'll take a macabre mess over knowin' the young have gown hungry any day of the week. What would I ever tell Her Magnificence if I let something happen to even one of the wee dolls?"

Ha! The wee dolls are getting wilder and more vicious every time I visit. It won't be long before they're out in the world terrorizing flocks and villagers across the Emerald Isle and beyond.

That's a problem for another day.

I rest a hand on Dart's back as I navigate the plasma slip-and-slide and make my way over to where Granda is safely stashed in the King of Rock and Roll's Cadillac. The pink convertible sits with the top down, and Granda seems content to lounge on the white leather seats while watching the show.

My boots squelch in the ooze, and I try not to think about it. Druiding is hard on footwear. "Immediate crisis averted. The kids are fed. You are safe to exit the car."

Granda chuckles. "That was somethin' to see, I'll tell ye. When yer wee man was at our place, I thought I'd seen what it was fer a dragon to feed, but seein' two dozen of them consuming beasts in a flurry was somethin' else altogether."

I understand Granda's awe, but honestly, we don't have time to get caught up in it. On to the next problem.

"As a historian, what do you know about why the queen might not be waking up?"

Granda frowns. "That depends on what state she's actually in. To be still like this, she could be sleepin' as Patty said, or she could be sick or spelled or siphoned or a dozen other things."

"How can you tell?"

"Och, I can't. I'm a shrine-keeper, not a dragon keeper."

"What about Gran with her nature abilities or Wallace with his experience in healing?"

An alarm jingles over by Patty's Lay-Z-Boy station and he jogs over to shut it off. When he returns, he picks up a wide-headed street broom and starts scrubbing over the queen's scales. "They'll not be much help, I'm afraid. Dragon physiology is very different from animals and people of all species."

Granda nods, his attention locked on the queen lying there deathly still. "The knowledge is quite singular, I'm afraid, and it has fallen out of study with the disappearance of the beasts over the past centuries."

"So, what we need is someone ancient who's trained and dedicated to the care of dragons. Do either of you know anyone like that?"

"I don't," Paddy says.

"Nor do I," Granda says.

Och, but we do, Bruin says. *I know exactly who we need.*

After another half-hour, Sloan fails to return, so we decide to try the infinity band portal and not to wait. Almost all the dragons have returned to their nursery area. A couple chose to curl up next to their mama for a nap, and Dart stayed with me. They're content.

For now, anyway.

It's not like Sloan to flake, but maybe he got caught up with something and couldn't get back. Or, even more likely, it has something to do with the bizarre passage of time in the lair. Maybe it's as simple as that.

Whatever the reason, I hug Dart around the neck and scrub the spot between his horns with my knuckles. He lets out a contented purr. "For us to help the queen, I need to be topside to make a few calls. I'll be back, baby. Patty, have faith. I'm on this. We'll figure it out."

"Thank the goddess." Patty hops down from the rolling hills of the queen's scaly coils to fist-bump. "May the luck of the shamrock goose yer perky arse."

I giggle. "One can only hope. Oh, and if Sloan comes back here before we run into him, let him know we're at Gran's and Granda's place."

"Will do."

Dartamont makes a little snuffle sound and tenses with a look of sheer concentration. A moment later, a wisp of smoke rises from the two slits of his nostrils.

"Wow, you're amazeballs, dude. Next thing you know, you'll be blowing fiery streams of flame and be razing the countryside."

Granda takes my hand and scowls. "Ye realize that won't be a good thing, right?"

"Oh, I know, but I'll still be proud."

Gripping my arm where the dragon portal encircles my arm beneath my jacket, I picture the quaint country home where my grandparents live. The sprawling stone cottage built into the Irish hillside boasts an old-growth tree growing up through the center of the living room, arched windows, and undulating thatched roofs that sit atop the different sections like a gnome's floppy hats.

When nothing happens, I close my eyes and focus. I imagine the thick hedge that separates their land from the rest of the world, the training rings built into the dip of a small valley out the back, their grove...

Still nothing.

"This can't be good."

Patty's staring at me, his brow creased. "I'll help ye, Fi. Please hurry."

I close my eyes, focus once again, and sense the moment

Patty's surge of magic launches us through the ether. This time when I open my eyes, we're exactly where I expect to be.

Night has fallen, and the bite of late October is gaining strength. It's less disorienting to me now—the time gaps. We set off after breakfast around nine this morning, and three or four hours later, it's after midnight.

"Home, sweet home." I grab the latch to the front door, but before I head inside, I think better of it. "I think I'll hose off my boots first. No sense in tracking death across Gran's floors."

"A spark of wisdom, indeed." Granda follows me over to the hose bib.

The two of us make quick work of cleanup, then stomp off the excess water and head inside.

"Hellooo the house." I scuff the soles of my boots on the mat before leaning over to untie the laces. "A bit tired, quite smelly, but we're home all the same."

Gran meets us inside the main entrance, rocking a sixties-cut dress with wildflowers on it. "Oh, my poor dears. Yer hungry, I bet too. Come, grab a quick bite while I fill ye in on a few things."

I roll my eyes. Crap on a cracker. That can't be good.

What I wouldn't give to have a boring day with no disasters and no one needing to "fill me in" on things.

Gran hands Granda a sandwich and frowns. "There's been a development. Lugh, ye'll need to head to Ardfert straight away."

Granda scowls. "What's happened? Is it the shrine?"

"I'm afraid it is. Yer wards went off to signal a breach. Sloan left straight away, but I haven't heard back."

I wash the dragon crud off my hands and take half a sandwich to go. After jogging back to the front door, I put my boots back on. "Well, that explains why Sloan didn't come back to meet up with us."

"Oh, my sweet boy," Gran says. "I wondered about that. I secured two racked stags earlier this evening and hoped he simply went off to pick them up after checking on the shrine. If he didn't, and he didn't meet up with you, he's been gone a donkey's age."

When I straighten, Granda already has his keys in hand.

Without Sloan, it's either old-school travel or dragon lair-hopping. Only, dragon lair-hopping isn't a viable option right now. I need to make those calls about the wyrm queen, so twenty minutes isn't a bad thing.

Unless Sloan's in trouble.

I phone him, but he doesn't pick up. I text him next. *Heading to Ardfert. Let me know you're okay or meet us there. Worried about you.*

I rub the pressure in my chest. It isn't the usual, comforting pressure of my spirit bear making his presence known. This is the kind I hate feeling...

Someone I care about is in trouble.

CHAPTER SEVEN

The trip seems endless although it lasts less than fifteen minutes. Granda is quiet, focused on the road, and lead-footing it like an Indy driver. The best part of it being close to one o'clock in the morning is that there's almost no one on the road and we can gun it through the countryside.

While we barrel forward into the darkness, I try Sloan twice more, then call up the contacts list on my phone and work on the problem with the queen.

Straight to voicemail.

"Hey, Dora. It's Fi. I need your help. Something has happened to the Wyrm Dragon Queen, and I need your expertise. Call me back. Day or night."

Granda barely has the Land Rover pulled to a stop when I jump out. "Bruin, I need you to search the site. Sloan's missing and the wards went off. Let me know if you find anything."

On it. Locked and loaded.

I release him from his place within me and smile. He's been spending so much time with my brothers that he sounds more urban street than ancient warrior by the day.

Granda catches up to me as I close the distance.

The long, twisted shadows cast by the skeletal remains of the Ardfelt Cathedral seem extra eerie with my nerves on edge. Either that, or it's because I've never been here in the dark before. Either way, it's super creepy.

The first time I was here, Sloan told me this church was built-up, marauded, burned, and rebuilt more times than I could imagine. It makes me wonder...

"Are ghosts a real thing?"

"That's a discussion for another night."

Okeedokee.

He's by the parish entrance, Red.

"Thank goodness. Bear, can you keep watch?"

On it.

"Bruin says Sloan's by the parish entrance."

Granda changes course, and I jog to keep up with him. Apparently, with druids, sixty-five is the new forty.

While much of Ardfelt remains a massive framework of gray stone ruins, there is a Gothic section that houses a small parish church still in use.

"There you are." I rush him and punch him in the shoulder. "Why didn't you respond, dumbass? We were worried."

He rubs his shoulder and scowls. "Don't worry. I'm fine."

"What about the breach?" Granda asks. "What did ye find when ye got here?"

"Nothing. Everything looked fine. Ye'll want to check yerself, though, I'm sure."

"Go ahead." I pull out my phone. "I'll only be a minute."

"Take yer time," Sloan says.

Granda lifts his chin and pegs me with a scowl. "When has leavin' ye alone in a questionable moment been a good idea?"

Whatevs. "I'm capable of making a phone call without getting kidnapped or killed."

"Good enough." Sloan gestures toward the door. "She seems

confident in her ability to remain unscathed. She knows the way."

Granda frowns. "Make yer call, *mo chroí*. It won't take more than a minute."

I narrow my gaze at them both and dial Pan Dora a second time. Still no answer. "I'll try again once we check out the shrine issue. We can only put out one fire at a time."

Granda takes the lead, unlocks the front door to the parish church, and takes us through reception to the end of a private hall. We stop in front of a solid stone wall, and he presses his palms flat on the surface. In response, a doorway appears, and we descend a set of circular stairs.

"Oh, the memories," I say as we cross the damp, crumbly space and close the distance between the Shrine-Keeper and the shrine he keeps. "It was right here that I first told you that your head is stuck up your Irish ass. Do you remember?"

Sloan frowns. "I remember we're here because of a shrine breach. How about we remember that?"

"Rude. Well, I remember. You said you're better than me because you have mold and stink in your basement."

"Uh-huh."

He turns away, far more interested in what my grandfather is doing than what I'm saying. "Hey, what's with you?"

He shrugs. "I've a lot on my mind."

I watch the golden trail of magic illuminate as Granda draws sigils on the stone wall with his finger. The power he emits makes the hair on my arms stand on end.

Then the shield on my back lights up.

"Wait!" I hold up my hand and try to grasp what's setting off my early warning system. "My shield's going bananas. Let's take a step back."

I meant that figuratively but Granda retreats a couple of feet. I do the same.

Sloan holds his ground and sighs. "What's the problem?"

"I don't know. I was getting a warning."

"Was?" Granda asks.

"It eased once you stopped the spellwork."

"So, may we continue?" Sloan asks.

I peg him with a glare. "Who pissed in your beer, surly? Instead of getting hostile with me, why don't you portal in and see if you can figure out what the warning is?"

He closes his eyes and sighs. "Fine. If I apologize, can we let Lugh finish removing the security measures?"

A niggle of warning flares when he says that and I realize something about this is way off. On a hunch, I grip the lapels of his wool peacoat and pull his mouth to mine.

The realization occurs at the same moment as his shock sets in. I push back and call Birga to my palm. Stepping back, I swipe his legs out from under him and poise my spear's razor-sharp Connemara marble tip against his chest.

"Who are you and what have you done with Sloan?"

The Sloan doppelganger wipes my kiss off his mouth and scowls. "It didn't have to be this difficult."

As we watch, the visage of Sloan Mackenzie morphs, and we're left staring at a woman with fire-orange hair.

Awkward.

That dirty grimoire residue I've been feeling grows thicker around me, and I swallow. It tastes like ash on the back of my tongue. I'm not sure what this aftereffect is, but it's dark and unwelcome.

It does, however, sense the darkness inside this woman and recognize her as a kindred spirit. No. I'm nothing like her.

I advance my stance and grip Birga, ready to plunge. "If you know what's good for you, witch, you'll give me back my boyfriend."

"You're outmatched, druid. We've got you and the old man over a barrel. Finish removing the wards and give us what we want, and we'll let your man go. This doesn't have to end in bloodshed."

A shuffle behind the shelves of the musty stone cellar brings two brunette witch bitches into the mix. One has the pursed scowl of a person who drank orange juice after brushing her teeth, and the other has the small, darting eyes and pointy face of a fox.

I've still got Sloan's impersonator pinned down, but when I assess where Granda is to me, I don't like our position.

Bear, I need you in the basement. I call him on our private bonding frequency. *We have hostile witches down here.*

On my way.

"Let me guess," Granda snaps. "This has something to do with the Narstina Cup and Moira's coven."

The orange juice pucker bitch laughs. "Oh, this is bigger than our coven. This is about raising the level of all Wiccan power. Things have been set in motion, and you're going to help ensure our success."

"I'm not," Granda says. "If ye think ye can blackmail an Elder of the Druid Order to betray an oath, ye don't understand what it is to live to a code of honor."

She pulls a jeweled athame from the leather sheath hanging from her hip and frowns. "Moira said you were a frustratingly righteous old windbag. Perhaps a little persuasion is in order."

When she purses her lips and whistles, the dark pull of my grimoire possession flares. As the melodic pitch carries in the air, the dagger lifts and hovers, its pointed tip threatening to pierce Granda's chest.

My blood grows hot in my veins. They've taken Sloan, and now they threaten my grandfather? They haven't seen the high-light reel of what Bruin and I have done when cornered.

"Think twice about threatening people I love, bitch," I snap, my voice threaded with the promise of violence. A searing burn rims my eyes, and I blink against the discomfort.

I breathe a little easier as the fire burns away. "By the wide-eyed stares and looks of shocked horror, it's clear the glamor on my eyes burned off. I'm more than what I appear, and certainly more than Moira warned you about."

My hair kicks up as Bruin arrives on a gust of musty basement breeze. *Perfect timing, buddy. Get that dagger away from Granda.*

With his maw open wide, Bruin materializes between us and them, his roar echoing off the stone walls. He smacks the dagger with such force that it shatters, and metal shards rain to the stone floor.

The sudden appearance of my massive grizzly has the women stumbling back. "Last chance, ladies. Give us Sloan."

"Not our call. We were sent for the chalice and instructed to use whatever means necessary to secure it."

"So, you triggered the ward and waited for Granda to show up, but he wasn't the one who responded."

"Not that it mattered. Moira was more than happy to claim your boy as a personal project. Unfinished score to settle was what she said. While she has her fun, the rest of us have been charged with gaining possession of the chalice."

Granda presses his hand against the wall, and a surge of druid magic builds in the air. I'm both proud and saddened that he re-established the wards. I would never want him to succumb to the threats of a faction of evil, but we're talking about Sloan's safety.

"Then it's a standoff," Granda snarls. "Get off this property and tell yer witch friends that attempting to steal from the druid shrine is a direct violation of our accord terms. Consider yerselves suspended from the magic alliance."

"It's time you let Genevieve go," the brunette fox-faced woman says. "And if you ever want to see your apprentice again, you'll consider a trade."

My urge to rip these women to shreds is almost uncontrollable. I can feel my fingers tightening around their throats. I can see their blood spraying the stone as I impale them with Birga's spearhead. I can hear their pitiful pleas for mercy as they realize they're about to die.

"Fiona? Are ye all right?"

I follow Granda's voice and see the concern in his eyes. "Let her go, Fi. We can't be reckless with Sloan's life."

No. Of course not.

Releasing my call on Birga, I return her to the tattoo on my right forearm and grip Granda's wrist. Then I pat my sternum and exhale. *Time to leave, Bruin.*

Leave? But we didn't get to kill anyone yet.

Not tonight, buddy.

Can I stay and kill one or two of them? I'll be quick, I promise.

They have Sloan. We can't risk triggering their pique any more than we already have.

That's no fun at all.

Sorry. When he vanishes, and I feel the flutter of him settling in my chest, I grip my infinity tattoo and focus on being in the dragon lair.

Nothing happens.

I try a few more times, and I've got nothing.

Awesomesauce. So much for our dramatic exit. "He told you to get the hell gone, witches," I shout, waving at the door. "And if you ever play Sloan clone again, blood will be shed."

CHAPTER EIGHT

"I'm sorry, Granda. Witches be bitches is a saying for good reason. I want them dead for taking Sloan. We need to go after them hard. They're up to something underhanded and for some reason, they think the chalice in your shrine is the key to getting what they want. I get that they can't have it, but how do we find Sloan and get him back?"

Granda's gone into silent mode, pegging the oncoming center line of the highway with a murderous glare.

My phone rings, and it takes my hamster a moment to get in the wheel. Right. "Dora, thank goodness."

"Fiona. I'm sorry for the slow reply, girlfriend. I'm having a bit of an emergency myself."

Oh, no. I was hoping to have her undivided attention for the dragon queen issue. "I'm sorry to hear that. Is it anything my family or I can help you with?"

"You won't tell the Guild?"

"Of course not. I don't tell them a quarter of the things that happen in *my* life. I do not need to tell them about what's happening in yours."

There's a deep, bass grunt of agreement at the end of the line before she continues. "Something valuable of mine was taken. I've spent the better part of two days tracking the magic signature of the guilty party and just had a nasty run-in with a bunch of out-of-town witches."

"You're kidding." My shield tingles and a shiver runs the length of my spine. "Granda and I just faced off with three witches trying to rob the druid shrine. What's with the witches this week?"

The line goes very quiet. When Dora speaks again, her voice has shifted from being harried and annoyed to being laced with concern. "What were they after, Fi? Do you know?"

"Hold on one sec." I mute the call and swivel in the shotgun seat. "Granda? Dora was robbed by witches too. She wants to know what they were after. Can I tell her without breaking any non-disclosure issues on you?"

He casts me a sideways glance. "Fiona, considering yer friend's first life, you have my permission to speak freely with her about anything."

I take the call off hold and put it on speaker. "Sorry about that. I'm putting you on speaker. My grandfather's here. He's the Shrine-Keeper for the Druid Order."

"It's a pleasure to speak with you, sir," Dora says, genuine respect in her tone. "Your granddaughter speaks highly of you and your wife."

"Och, well, I can say the same."

I realize the pleasantries of introductions are all good, but honestly, I'm not in the mood. I want Sloan home and safe. "You asked what the witches were after...yeah, they want something called the Narstina Cup."

"Is it a gold chalice by any chance? Maybe with an interesting base?"

"It is at that," Granda says. "How'd you know? Have ye come upon it over the years?"

"I haven't. It's a long story. Did they get it?"

"No, the vault is locked down tight. It seems they expected to force me to open the shrine. When I didn't, they slithered off to regroup."

"But they have Sloan," I say, hating to imagine where he is or what they'll do to him to try to get him to open the vault. "We have to get him back. They want to force a trade, and I'm trying to figure out how to work that to our advantage."

"Fiona—listen to me, girlfriend—no matter what, no matter who they have or who they threaten, you must ensure they don't get that chalice."

"Why? What's so special about the Narstina Cup?"

"I need to check in person, but I think it might be part of the key to access the Cistern of The Source."

"What's The Source?"

"It's the source, Fi. The source of all fae prana."

"I thought that was the ley lines?"

"Picture it like the ley lines being rivers flowing off a vast lake of power. The Source is...well, it's the source. Look, it's complicated, and like I said, a long story. Now, tell me about your dragon queen."

I recap what I know about her lethargy and what Patty told me. "When it rains it pours. Witch thieves, kidnapped boyfriends, and ailing dragons."

"I think, in this case, that's less about bad timing and more about things being interconnected."

Granda frowns and turns from the main road to take us off the beaten path to his property. "How are they interconnected?"

"Yeah," I say. "What do thieving witches have to do with sick dragons?"

"I have to examine your dragon to be sure, but if I'm right, she's not sick. Dragons are the oldest of the fae mythological creatures. The fae prana of her life force comes directly from The Source. If I'm right, the witches are draining her magical strength."

"That sounds bad."

"It is, and it'll only get worse. I need to get there. Let me check the availability of flights and get back to you. Whether they're connected or not, we need to address both situations immediately."

"Maybe I can do one better than searching for flights. Let me make a call. Do you know Nikon Tsambikos, cute blond Greek, looks like he's almost old enough to drink in public?"

"Nikon, from the Isle of Rhodes. Yes, when you've lived as long as we have, you tend to cross paths with others in the same circles."

"If you have no objection, I'll call him and see if he can taxi you here."

"No objection. I'll pack a bag."

"Perfect. And Dora...thanks for jumping in and helping. This is bigger than me."

"Fi, if this is what I think it is, it's bigger than all of us."

Ten minutes later, the beams of illumination from Granda's headlights swing across the front lawn of their home and wash over Nikon, standing with Dora, Emmet, and Dillan on the stone walkway in front of the house.

"That was fast." I jump out of the Land Rover and join them. "Thanks for dropping everything and coming."

Dillan side-hugs me and stiffens when he sees my eyes.

"Sorry. I know they're freaky."

Emmet waves that away. "Totes not your fault, Fi. We'll get used to it."

"I hope not. Sloan taught me a glamor spell. I'll fix them as soon as we get sorted."

Dora frowns when she sees my eyes, and I shrug. "A side-effect from the grimoire. Sloan said his father thinks he's broken the bond, but apparently, I'm a little tainted."

"About Sloan," Dillan says. "Calum, Dad, and Aiden wanted to come too but are on shift. They're on standby, though. If we need them to get him back, they'll be here in two snaps of a Greek immortal's fingers."

I smile at Nikon. "Thank you for your help. You're much more than a transporter. I'm so glad you're here."

Nikon flashes me a genuine smile. "I told you, Red. I enjoy Team Cumhaill. And hey, we need to get Sloan home and back into the net. He's the only chance I have to score this season."

"He's the only chance *she* has to score this season too." Emmet flashes me a teasing grin.

I chuckle, but honestly, I'd rather cry or kill someone. "There's nothing wrong with being selective about who you get naked with."

Emmet adjusts the strap of his duffle on his shoulder and smiles. "Nothing wrong with it, no, but certainly less fun."

Dillan squeezes my shoulder and winks. "We'll get him back, baby girl. We might give Irish a hard time, but whether or not you two are canoodling yet, he's good people, and he's one of us."

Emmet hugs Granda and heads inside. "Besides, no one gets to torture him except us. Sorry, Granda, but if your glamoured witch-bitch ex Moira is taking a run at us and ours, she miscalculated. She's going down."

"Hells yeah, she is." I toe off my shoes inside the door.

Granda places a finger over his lips, and we tiptoe past where Gran has fallen asleep on the couch waiting for word. Granda pulls a throw blanket off the couch's back, covers her, and points toward the office.

Dillan flicks on the light and hands his bag to Emmet, who takes their stuff to the spare room.

Granda rounds his desk and plunks down in his leather seat. "What a night."

"So, what do we know about what's going on?"

Dora starts us off. "Have any of you ever heard of Gobekli Tepe?"

"Gesundheit," Emmet says while joining us.

Dora chuckles. "Gobekli Tepe. It's an ancient ruin site discovered and being excavated in Turkey."

I check the expressions around the room. It's a solid blank from Team Cumhaill, but Nikon seems to recognize the name. He also doesn't seem pleased to be discussing it.

The Greek frowns. "What about it?"

Dora looks at Granda and me. "It's where the Cistern of The Source is. It's the ancient birthplace of fae prana."

For my brothers' benefit, I give them a quick recap of Dora's lake of power analogy and how the fae ley lines we believed to be the source of all power are the runoff distributaries from the mothership of power.

Dillan pulls the hood of his cloak up, and I'm glad to have him and his gift here to help me find Sloan. "The witches found the ocean of raw fae power that feeds the ley lines?"

"That's my guess."

"And the Narstina Cup?" Granda asks. "How is that a key for them to access it?"

"The legend states that the reservoir of the ancients was located deep beneath an ancient city. Modern civilization recognizes the Greeks and the Romans for their innovations. The Ottomans, etc...but Gobekli Tepe existed thousands of years before any of that."

"How long before?" I ask.

"From the carbon dating and what archeologists have found in the city digs, ten thousand BCE."

My mind spins out on that one. "Is that even possible?"

Nikon nods. "Not only possible, but it's factual. People of modern society make up myths and educated guesses to explain Atlantis, Easter Island, and many of the civilizations that came first. The truth is advanced civilizations existed long before the periods when modern society credits their arrival. Gobekli Tepe is one of them."

"You sound like you know a fair bit about this, Greek," Dillan says.

"I guess I do. My grandfather was a general in the Macedonian Wars and discovered the cistern while invading Melitene in the third century BCE. It's because of the cistern's raw prana that my family possesses such a focused level of power as well as immortality."

Hubba-wha? "Okay, that's good to know. You never mentioned that before."

"My papu vowed never to divulge the source of our gifts or the location lest a horde of power-grubbing empowered folk gets the bright idea to try to gain from it."

"Imagine that," Emmet says. "Evil is as evil does even thousands of years later."

Granda frowns. "Well, yer family secret is safe here, son. The Ancient Order of Druids is specifically tasked to protect nature and fae power. We have no intention of making it known where the mecca of magic is."

"Did this advanced culture know there was a giant cistern of fae power beneath their city?" Dillan asks.

Dora shrugs. "On a whole, no, but some of the upper echelons of government and society knew and accessed it through a maze of underground passages that led deep into the earth's crust."

"When you say accessed it, what do you mean? Skinny-dipping and lake-sipping?"

"That would be a safe bet," Dora says. "It's said that some of the people with access began to show signs of change. Some altered physically, while others developed heightened mental strengths, and still others learned to access and utilize the energy in the water."

I frown. "And the birth of magic and fae creatures had begun."

Dora nods. "Exactly."

"You think the witches found this source of power and are siphoning it somehow?"

"To affect the dragon, they must be draining one of the primary distributaries, but if the dragon queen's been sleeping for a week—and given how time works in a lair, that's a month—they don't have access to the cistern itself."

"Because they don't have the key," I say.

"Right. It's said that once the first fae species developed, they realized not only the gifts the pool offered but also the danger of that level of power falling into the wrong hands."

"How do you close a lake?" Emmet asks.

"They used their powers of stone manipulation to seal off the tunnels from the inside and left only one locked access point."

"The chalice is the key?" Granda asks.

"Part of it." Dora steps up to the desk. "Do you have a sheet of paper and a pencil?"

Granda provides the requested materials and Dora bends over to draw. "The key was broken into three pieces: the base of a chalice is the disc plate, then a brooch with matching striations will fit into it, and a dragon-bone dagger pierces an opening in the other two pieces and links them all together to form the key."

Dora straightens, and we look at what she's drawn.

I look at the three components and my focus locks on Dora's sketch of the dragon-bone dagger. "I've seen that dagger before. I know where the third piece of the key is—or, at least where it was."

It takes us a few tries to get to the lair of the dragon queen. My portal power is seriously on the fritz and Nikon wasn't keen on guessing where the cavern lay beneath four hundred feet of rock. In the end, Dora gives me a power boost, and we hot-wire my transport method.

"Remember, don't touch Patty's treasure."

Nikon snorts. "It's cute you think you need to school the two of us on the dangers of pissing off a member of the Tuatha De. You've been at this what now, four months?"

I shrug. "Fine. I'll let you get chomped next time."

Nikon flashes me a crooked grin and grabs my arm as I breeze past him. "We'll get him back. Lugh and your brothers are working on how. I'm sure they'll have a course of action by the time we get back."

I sigh. "Sorry. Not your fault."

"No problem. I've got your back, Fi. Even snippy and looking like Marilyn Manson."

I try to laugh, but I don't have it in me. If any emotion leaks out, it's more likely going to be tears.

He raises his hand and presses it over my eyes. In most instances, I feel the tingle of magic as people access their powers. Not so with Nikon.

When he lowers his hand from my eyes, he looks at me and smiles. "That's better. Now, let's see a man about a knife and save Sloan. It's been too long since I've seen you smile. Believe it or not, I've become rather addicted to your infectious humor."

I squeeze his hand and head into the main chamber. "Patty? Are you here? I brought reinforcements."

I take Dora straight to the queen to let her get started assessing her theory on whether or not she thinks it's the witches siphoning The Source.

"Wow." Nikon's eyes lock on the glistening scales of Her Reptileness. "See, it doesn't matter how long you live. You can always learn or see something new."

"You've never seen a dragon, Greek?"

He chuckles. "Almost no one alive has, Fi. Your normal isn't normal even in empowered circles."

Now it's my turn to chuckle. "Okay, then you're going to love this." Pressing my finger and thumb together, I push them under my tongue and let out an ear-piercing whistle. "Come on, babies. Mother of Dragons is in the house."

Nikon's eyes pop wide as the thundering footsteps and rustling of scales and tails builds in the distance and rush through the darkness of the corridor that leads to the nursery. "Shit, Fi. What did you do?"

I giggle as my twenty-three children rush out to meet us. "Hi, guys." I reach for as many as I can, scrubbing scales and massaging horns and wings. "Don't look so scared, Nikon. It's only been like twelve hours since we fed them close to bursting. They won't eat you."

Nikon chuckles. "The fact that you have to qualify why they won't eat me now but they might at another point in time isn't comforting."

Patty follows in the wake of the brood, and I gasp. "Oh, Patty, you look so tired."

He scrubs a hand over his face and scowls. "Och, I'm at the end of my tether. Please tell me ye have good news."

I introduce Patty to Nikon and Dora and explain to him what we think is going on. "When Dora drew this, I recognized it. This is part of your treasure, isn't it? Didn't I use it to open the Amazon order when I was here?"

Nikon's mouth falls open. "You used an enchanted dagger made from the talon of the first dragon as a box cutter?"

Patty shrugs. "The talon dagger is wicked sharp and indestructible...and Amazon box tape is savage strong."

"Do you still have it?" I ask. "Could the witches have gotten in here and taken it?"

Patty closes his eyes and raises his hand. He can call his treasure like Thor calls Mjolnir. When the dagger fails to come, he frowns. "They must've come when I was distracted with tendin' to the kids."

"Damn it. That puts them one step closer."

"The witches, then." Patty's sparkling blue gaze hardens with murderous intent. "It's good to have an enemy in my sights. I'll make them sorry as soon as we get things handled here. First, they attack Her Grace, then they invade our sanctum and steal from us. They will rue the day."

"I have no doubt."

"What's our next move?" Nikon asks.

"Can you sense the dagger's whereabouts?" Dora asks.

"Within a certain radius but not from here, I'm afraid. I'd need to be above and have access to ambient magic."

"Then Nikon can snap us back to Granda's, and we'll get my brothers and go from there. There's a good chance if the witches took the dagger to their headquarters of evil, Sloan might be there, or someone there might know where he is."

Nikon nods and holds out his hand. "It's worth a try."

"I can't leave." Patty frowns at the chaotic tumbling and jostling of the baby dragons. "The kids can't be left unattended. They're a mischievous bunch, and they haven't been taken topside for over a week."

"I'll stay with the young," Dora says. "It has been too many centuries since I've spent time caring for dragonborn. You go and do what you need to do, and I will tend to the queen and her young."

Patty looks hesitant, so I intercede. "It'll be fine. I promise. I'll vouch for Dora. This ain't her first dragon rodeo."

Patty nods. "Very well. Give me one moment to grab my weapons holster and my hat."

When Nikon snaps Patty and me back to Granda's, it's midday, and the October light wraps me in a cold and dreary blanket. As much as I loved the warmth and greenery of Ireland in the summertime, it's not nearly as warm and welcoming now.

Or, maybe it's my mood.

I want Sloan home.

"Tell me you figured out where to start looking for Sloan." I stride into the house from the side door.

Gran's pouring coffee for my brothers and Granda as the three of them pore over materials on the kitchen table. "What have we got?"

"Not enough, I'm afraid. There are six covens in Ireland and over forty registered between here and the area in Turkey where the Gobekli Tepe archaeological site is being excavated."

Gran makes a grumble grunt and slams the coffee pot back into place. "Och, well ye know feckin' well where to start and if ye'll not say it, I will. We need to track down that loose-moraled hussy and make it plain we want our boy back, or we'll be takin' it out on her wrinkled hide."

Granda frowns. "It's not that simple, Lara. There are certain levels of diplomacy between the Order of Druids and the Guild of Covens—"

"Fuck diplomacy," Gran snaps.

Lightning strikes close to the house, and we duck as the crack shakes the house. The lights flicker and flash as my heart races.

The only person standing straight is my Gran. "Kids, it seems yer with me on this. I'm not a feckin' Elder of the Order, and I'm not held to any kind of asinine protocols. We're takin' that bitch down. If she doesn't have my Sloan, she knows who does."

"Go, Gran!" Emmet cheers. "We're with you."

I nod at Nikon and hold my hand out. The boys pile their hands together like a sporting team getting ready for the big game. When Patty and Gran join in, we're ready. "Take us to the Regent House in Dublin."

CHAPTER NINE

Moira Morrigan lives a block away from Trinity College across from the Regent House in Dublin. When Sloan portaled us here, we materialized in the shadows of the back stoop to keep from being seen *poofing* in out of nothing. Nikon doesn't do that. With him, we appear among the scattered students and locals beginning their day.

"*Dude.*" Dillan looks at the oblivious people passing. "Do you have a cloaking component to your transport or a horseshoe up your ass?"

Nikon chuckles. "I forget you guys are so new to this. We don't need rectal horseshoes when we're in the presence of a Man o' Green."

Emmet frowns and looks at Patty. "That keeps us cloaked how?"

Patty grins. "Luck-o-the-Irish, my boy. A stroke of serendipity when ye need it. Yer welcome."

I'm not a hundy percent sure what that entails, but if good fortune is with us, I won't complain.

"The cloaking luck is over," Dillan says. "We're gathering the attention of rubber-neckers now."

We're quite an entourage storming up Grafton Street. As we cross at the lights and head toward the row house that belongs to Moira Morrigan, we draw more than a few curious glances.

Gran is a stylish lady in a fifties circle dress, stockings, and a chenille wrap. The *clack, clack, clack* of her druid staff marks each angry step toward facing off against her nemesis.

Patty has transformed from the jovial wee Man o' Green of lore to a white-haired angry leprechaun. Granda warned me never to piss off a leprechaun, and I see why. This version of Patty is scary—and not only because he's choking the neck of a hatchet and whistling an eerie tune.

Yep, we're a sight.

A Greek immortal, a leprechaun, and four pissed-off druids closing the distance to get my boyfriend back from power-hungry witch bitches.

"Let them stare," Gran snaps. "Actually, they should follow us. The show is about to get better."

"Dayam, Gran." Emmet grins from ear to ear. "You're on fire tonight, warrior woman."

Nikon chuckles. "Your maiden name wouldn't happen to be Croft, would it, Lara?"

I get a kick out of that one. "Patty? Do you sense anything on your dagger tracking?"

"No, but that's fine. We'll take them down one at a time if we have to. The result will be the same."

All righty then. It's good to have goals.

Moira lives in a historic brick building that runs the length of the block. It's a three-story rowhouse with arched windows and neoclassical lines and architecture. If I didn't know the woman who lives inside, I'd think it's charming.

"Can Bruin get in there to search for Sloan?" Dillan asks.

I shake my head. "Not until there's an opening. Moira has extensive wards, and I don't want him caught in one of her witch's traps."

"I doubt she'll just open the door for us," Emmet says.

"Agreed. When Sloan and I picked her up last month, she said she takes every precaution."

Patty snorts. "Every precaution *she* thought of. I've never met a practitioner yet who could anticipate the kinds of attacks I can come up with."

Emmet's brows arch. "A fellow prankster. Nice. Do your worst, sir. I look forward to seeing what you come up with."

"Is it too obvious to suggest we knock first?" Dillan holds his hands up in surrender as Gran, Patty, and I weigh in on that. "Just fielding all the options. I love an offensive as much as the next guy."

I stop on the walkway that leads up to Moira's unit and point. "This is it."

Dillan pulls up the hood of his cloak and nods. "So, who wants the first crack at getting us inside?"

I turn to Gran. "Could you call another bolt of lightning to get us started?"

"To burn her house to the ground, ye mean?"

I blink. "No. I thought we'd start by hitting that power transformer there to give us the cover of darkness."

"All right, we'll try your way first." Gran turns her full attention to the power box, and another strike of lightning hits the ground. The block goes dark.

I nod to Patty. "Do your worst, my friend. Bring her wards down."

"Wait here." The five of us watch him climb the stairs leading up to the enclosed breezeway. He's a wee man, so he uses the handrail to help pull himself up the six steps one by one. When he gets to the top, he raises his hands and presses them to the front door of the house.

The crashing inside starts instantly.

The screeching starts a moment after that.

Patty holds his hands toward the house and swings his hands

from left to right and back again. The crashing calamity continues inside, following Patty's orchestrations.

When he straightens, he throws both hands over his shoulders toward us, and I tense. The windows on all three floors blow out in a violent explosion of glass.

Shattered window panes rain into the flowerbeds below.

It seems everything in the house made from a precious metal has responded to Patty's call. Silver candlesticks, a massive golden dragon figurine, a compass, several heavy door-knockers, a gem-hilted sword...

"He's a treasure whisperer," Emmet says.

I chuckle. "Moira didn't ward against being attacked by her keepsakes? Seems short-sighted."

"Lazy, actually."

When the front door flings open, Moira storms onto her closed porch, sees us, and starts casting.

I pat my sternum and release my bear. "Go find him, buddy." There's no swirling breeze of comfort this time. Bruin launches from me and is gone like a shot fired from a gun. "Please be in there."

Moira spots Patty on her porch and goes for him. Gran counters. "*Gale Force Gust*." She swipes her hand through the air and Moira is thrown back inside.

"Don't let her close us out," I shout.

Nikon grabs my arm, and the boys join in for the ride inside. With a magical *snap*, the four of us find ourselves in Moira Morrigan's posh living room. It's lit by floating globes of magic burning in the corners along the roofline, and Patty's treasure redecoration process leveled it.

The moment we appear, we fall under attack.

A bolt of magic catches me in the shoulder and knocks me twisting into a mahogany sideboard. The surge of magic tingles over my skin. Whatever *oomph* powers the spell triggers the grimoire's residual darkness.

I roll to my feet, my eyes burning with fury.

Emmet has confiscated a wicker bowl filled with decorative marble balls, and he's whipping them. He cracks one of the witches in the back of the head, and she faceplants onto the plush ivory area rug.

He cackles with glee and grabs another.

Dillan cuts the air with his daggers and deflects another barrage of magic bolts. He sends one into the wall, shatters a mirror, and dives behind an overstuffed sofa. He catches the cushion with his blade as he cartwheels over the backrest, and the thing splits wide, barfing stuffing from the cut.

All we need to do is stall them long enough for Bruin to figure out if Sloan is in here somewhere. Three more witches fly into the room.

"Incoming," I shout while calling Birga to my palm. I catch one of the women rushing me in the thigh and swipe left. As she buckles to the floor, fountaining blood, I spin the enchanted spear and catch the next one with the staff.

On one of my spins, I catch sight of Gran and Moira in a showdown and smile. Gran has stripped the witch's glamor and is bitch-slapping her like you read about.

A shamrock *shuriken* whistles past my head and I duck.

The breathy cry behind me has me spinning to watch an Asian woman flip back, her feet flying into the air at the force of the hit. I turn back to catch Patty whipping more of his weapons from his shoulder holster: a pink heart, yellow moon, orange star, and more green clovers.

I bark a laugh at Patty being a Lucky Charms warrior. Then the wind picks up around my face, and I feel Bruin's presence.

He's in the northeast corner in a locked cell in the basement. One guard on the outside of the door.

The moment Bruin speaks the words, I repeat them internally to Nikon. *Get him. Help him, Bear.*

When Nikon flashes off, I get a boost of energy. Bruin and

Nikon can take care of one guard and get Sloan home. All we have to do is distract them long enough to get it done.

They'll get him. I know they will.

An orange star *thwacks* a brunette in the side of the head, and she goes down like a felled tree.

When Bruin comes back, he materializes and roars a deafening roar. "Got him. The Greek is taking him to Lugh."

"Thank you, baby Yoda." I face off with an ebony-haired woman when a crystal vase catches her square in the back. She goes down, and I smile at Emmet. "Thanks, bro."

"No problem. I like redecorating. Gran, wrap it up..."

Gran plants her staff, launches her feet in a swinging kick, and catches Moira solidly in the crotch.

"Yes, she *did*," Emmet shouts. "A solid crotch shot."

Dillan snorts. "And that, my friends, is what we shall forever call an Irish boxty."

I snort and catch the surprise on Nikon's face as he flashes in to join us. "Did your grandmother just give that witch a cooter-booter?"

"Hells yes, she did." Emmet beams. "A well-deserved one too. Good job, Gran."

I roll my eyes. "Okay, bring it in, people. I want to go home and see Sloan."

Patty agrees. "I don't sense the knife, so it's not here. I don't think the brooch is either, so we might as well regroup."

Nikon flashes us into the living room of my grandparents' home, and I rush around the trunk of the tree to find Sloan sitting on the couch with a rubber bin in his lap. I've almost closed the distance to pounce on him and give him a hug when he doubles over and hurls.

"*Snap.*" Emmet laughs. "You almost wore that, Fi. Back away from the splash zone."

I sit on the edge of the couch beside him and lean in to get a better look at him. His usual warm, brown skin is pasty and dotted with perspiration. "What's wrong? What did they do to you?"

Gran takes his other side and presses her wrist against his forehead. "Och, my poor boy. What did that bitch do to ye?"

"A spell...to keep me from portaling...so dizzy."

Gran looks up to me and frowns. "Bring me my basket of gemstones, luv. We have to re-establish his equilibrium. Once his world settles, maybe the nausea will too."

I hurry over to where Gran keeps her woven basket on the shelf by the television and take it back to the couch.

By the time I'm boomeranging back, Patty's there and scowling. "No offense meant, Missus, but I believe I can do more for the lad faster if ye don't mind me interferin'."

Gran sits straighter and waves that away. "If ye can help, yer welcome to try."

"Have ye a spare amethyst geode?"

Gran nods and I return to the shelf, grabbing a chunk of raw stone that fits into both my hands cupped together. "Do you want it or should Sloan hold it, Patty?"

"Yer man should hold it."

I take his puke bucket and give him the amethyst. It seems to me he got the much better end of the trade, but whatevs. Oh, my poor, surly.

"Focus on a thing that centers yer soul, lad. Picture yerself in a place of calm and welcome the healing power of the crystals."

Sloan closes his eyes and Patty places his stubby fingers at the base of his throat. I feel the magic in the air being drawn to Patty's command.

I rub the ache in my leg and scowl. Why is Patty's healing making me feel off? Sympathetic spell poisoning? Is that a thing?

I shake myself inwardly and focus on Sloan. "Something's not right." I press my fingers to my mouth. "There's a darkness to this. I feel it."

"Aye, there is." Patty frowns at me. "Apologies, my boy, this won't be pleasant. Fi, hold the bucket for him. There's something inside him, and I need to get it out. Missus, if ye wouldn't mind, may I squeeze in beside the boy?"

Gran gets to her feet, and Patty slides around to press his free hand at the small of his back. "All right then, give me two more minutes, and this will be over. Fi, yer up."

I'm still trying to figure out what that means when Patty strokes his hand up Sloan's back. As his hand rises, so too does Sloan's discomfort. When that hand gets to the back of Sloan's neck, he lets out a pitiful groan and doubles over.

Having five Irish brothers, I've spent more time than most holding buckets or standing witness to the violence of reject and eject, but this isn't that.

This is vile and painful.

Sloan's whole body shakes as his body ejects the aftereffects of Moira's spell. He's not only hurting. This is hurting him. I blink at the sting of tears and switch to kneel in front of him. Gran takes my spot and grips him around the hips.

I feel her healing energy and hope it's helping him in some way. It's hard to tell.

After one final choke, he gags, and it's over.

His muscles relax, and Patty nods. "All right. Let the boy lay down for twenty minutes. In the meantime, Fi, you and I need to kill that festerbug."

"That what?"

Patty tilts his head to the bucket, and I look in. Wriggling in the pool of Sloan's stomach contents is a spiny blue beetle. "Okay...you earned an Oh! Henry for that, Mackenzie. That is officially the grossest thing I've ever seen."

Dillan and Emmet close in and look into the bucket.

Dillan winces. "Yep, I may never sleep again."

Emmet nods. "Agreed. Consider this my new worst nightmare. Worthy of a chocolate bar for sure."

"Question one, what the hell was that? Question two, where the hell's Granda? And question three, what the fricky-frack is a festerbug?" My voice gets screechy at the end, but I don't care. It took Patty and me five minutes to kill a freaking barf beetle, and when we did, somehow, I felt the evil intent of the thing. Okay, question four, how is that possible?

No one has any answers for me though.

After the bug was dead and he checked on Sloan, Patty flashed back to the lair with Nikon and the two racked bucks Gran found for the dragon babies to eat.

"Fi, slow down. Yer makin' me ill."

I spin to check on Sloan, but no, he's definitely better. His skin has returned to its rich, mocha color and his eyes are clear.

When he holds out his arms, I give in without a fight and join him on the couch. "Are you feeling better?"

"Much, thank you. Give me five more minutes, and we'll see if we can track down Lugh."

"The boys went with Nikon to Ardfert to check at the shrine. It's the only place we could think of that would draw him away when he knew we were going after you."

He leans back, and I let him pull me with him. "Yer shakin', Fi. Are ye all right?"

I shake my head. "Not even close."

He leans sideways, rubs his shoulder with mine, and laces our fingers. "Yer accustomed to bein' the victim, not the one standin' by holdin' the waste bin."

"I prefer it that way."

He chuckles. "I don't. Yer gettin' a taste of what it's like bein' me. I hate it when ye suffer."

Gran comes in with a serving tray and sits it down on the coffee table. "Mashed with ginger sauce. Ye always loved it when ye were a wee boy, and yer tummy hurt."

"Thanks, Lara."

When he leans forward to collect his plate, she leans in and kisses his forehead. "Yer welcome, my wee man."

He sits back and casts me a shy, sideways glance. "What's the smile for?"

"Nothing."

His brow arches in disbelief. "Are you laughing at me?"

I lay my cheek on his shoulder and close my eyes. "Wouldn't dream of it. Now, eat your mashed potatoes. The boys will be back at any time, and I'm sure we'll be on the move again. No rest for the weary."

I wake disoriented to the gentle shake of my arm and an apologetic smile from Dillan. "Sorry, baby girl. You two are gonna want to be awake for this."

My brother straightens, and I extricate myself from where I'm tucked in against Sloan's side on the couch.

"Sorry, we must've fallen asleep."

"That's a good thing. You both deserved a time out."

"You woke me up, so something is happening?"

He nods and glances behind me to the couch. "Sloan will probably want to be part of this too."

"I'm awake." Sloan's voice is deep and graveled. "Just contemplatin' stealin' yer sister and portaling back to my bed for a solid sleep. Maybe shut out the world for a while."

"I hear you, my man, but the world already busted in on us, I'm afraid."

Sloan opens his eyes and sits up. "All right, I'm up." When he looks at me, he raises his hand over my eyes and the tingle of his magic soothes their evil appearance. "What did we miss?"

Dillan's frown doesn't bode well for any of us. "While we were in Dublin, the witches destroyed the shrine. Granda is sorting through the rubble, but the chalice is gone. The witches have all three pieces of the key."

"Shit. If they could destroy it in the first place, why take Sloan and try to force Granda to open it?"

Dillan shrugs. "Nikon says he can sense Source magic in the aftermath of the destruction. We figure when they realized they'd never get the shrine open through Sloan or Granda, they harnessed the power of the prana and went for 'blowed up, real good.'"

I sigh. "Yeah, I suppose wards won't keep things safe if the entire building is destroyed."

"Guess not. Whatever the reason, we gotta boogie."

CHAPTER TEN

"Google says it's springtime in Turkey in October." I close the search window and grab a couple of outfits to stuff into the bag we're taking. "Long-sleeve temperature for Emmet and me. T-shirt temperatures for you, D."

"I'll have my cloak if I get cool, anyway," Dillan says.

I giggle. "I have no doubt."

The three of us have put our stuff on the bed in the spare room and are moving in the organized, chaotic way that only happens when you spend your life with people. I give Emmet my stuff, and he adds it to the backpack.

Gran comes in with an insulated cooler and hands that to Dillan. "A little something to tide you over on your travels."

Dillan tosses the strap of the bag over his shoulder and gives me a nod. "I think we're set."

I glance around and frown. "Sorry to leave such a mess, Gran. Just leave it and close the door. We'll clean up when we get back."

"Och, don't give it a thought, luv."

"Speaking of messes," I say. "How's Granda doing with the shrine disaster?"

Gran frowns. "I'm sad to say that he doesn't think they can

save the parish cellar. Brian Perry and Evan Doyle are helping him gather the relics, but they'll have to figure out another place to store them."

"He needs an underground cavern with a dragon, like Patty has. If he needs a guard dragon, I can hook him up."

Gran chuckles. "I'll be sure to mention it. Now, have ye got everything ye need?"

I glance at the boys, and we all nod. "Yep. We're good. Once Sloan gets back, I'll take you to the dragon cavern and get Patty and Dora. Then we'll go."

"Sloan is back," he calls from the hall. He fills the doorway a moment later, and I smile at how strong and healthy he looks once again. "I apologized to Suede for abandoning her at the Doyle grove for two days, but she doesn't seem at all put out. I think she and the kissing elf have been doin' some puttin' out of their own."

"Noice," Emmet says. "Suede's a cutie patootie. Did you know elves don't believe in mating and monogamy? They're a free love race."

I blink at my brother. "I *didn't* know that. How do you know that?"

Emmet's cheeks flame red, and he clears his throat while glancing at Gran. "It may have come up in conversation over dinner the other night."

I wonder if that was before or after she asked me about them in the washroom. Not that it matters at this moment. "Okay, Gran, are you sure you want to do this? Twenty-three baby dragons can be a lot."

Gran waves that away and pats the carpetbag hanging over her shoulder. "We'll make do. No need to fret. I'm looking forward to it. Sloan, dear, could we make a stop at the O'Leary meat plant before we go? Someone brought in a cow that was struck on the road. I thought it would be a nice snack for the little ones."

Ha! Little ones. "Speaking of dragon snacks, are you taking your pet skunk?"

Gran casts me a humoring glance. "I thought he'd be safer staying here."

"Are you trying to avoid him being a two-bite badger?" Emmet asks.

"I thought it prudent." She holds out her hand. "Shall we?"

Getting Gran settled in the dragon lair takes less time than I expect, but then, I'm not sure why that surprises me. Gran is a superhero in her own right.

"I want ye all to behave yerselves while Lady Cumhaill is carin' for ye." Patty addresses the masses. "She'll tell me when I get back if ye've been naughty, and I'll not be happy. Understood?"

Twenty-three dragons stare at him, doing their best to look angelic.

"Don't worry, guys." I scrub the glittering scarlet scales of a wyrm girl that looks like her mama. "If all goes well, the queen will wake up soon."

Dart pushes between the red dragon I'm petting and me and gives her a huff of smoke. "Easy, dude. I can give attention to all your brothers and sisters, and it doesn't take away from you. Don't get testy with your siblings."

Dart doesn't seem to care about that. He snuggles in and rubs his cheek against my chest. I scrub the line of spikes developing along his spine. It runs between his little wings and is so cute. I wonder how much longer he'll be cute before he becomes a scary, fire-breathing dragon of legend.

"Off ye go." Gran slides her bag off her shoulder, drops it on the area rug of the Lay-Z-Boy lounge area, and steps over to the gramophone. "Och, I haven't seen one of these since I was a wee girlie in pigtails and spent time at Granny's house. Do ye mind if I play music while yer went?"

Patty gestures at the antique machine and gives the handle a crank. When the turntable is spinning, he puts the needle on the record. "We have an extensive Elvis collection, but there are a few others as well."

"The King is fine with me. Now, go stop those witches and right the wrongs of the world."

"Will do." I kiss Gran on the cheek and hold my finger out to point at the kids. "Be nice to my Gran. I mean it. I'll only share her with you if you're good. Remember, she's the one who's been arranging for all your food...so don't bite the hand that feeds you."

I hug Gran and Dart and join Patty and Sloan over by the queen. "How is she?"

Dora straightens from whatever healing spell she's casting and shakes her head. "We need to figure out where they're siphoning the prana that powers her lifeforce or she won't last much longer."

The six of us materialize on the north boundary of the excavation site of Gobekli Tepe. We're on a rise above the discovered city and take a moment to assess our surroundings. Because Sloan has never been to Turkey before, it's Nikon who brought us on this leg of our adventure. The Greek's ability to transport isn't hindered by the internal GPS restriction Sloan works with. Nikon can focus on a point on a map and get there.

Besides, although Sloan's putting on a good front, I don't think he's as fixed up as he's letting on. I totes get that and let him fake it without questioning him. After all, I'm doing the same thing, aren't I?

"Well, done, Greek." Dillan pulls his hood up. "Right where we need to be."

"Yeah, Google Earth street view was a game-changer for me. I can pretty much go anywhere with pinpoint accuracy."

"Ah…where are ye, my precious?" Patty's eyes narrow behind his round spectacles, and he does a slow, runway turn. It's night-time here, and hundreds of lit torches outline and highlight the scene below us. Patty searches the darkness in every direction before turning back to us. "Och, I feel her. My wee dragon dagger is close."

"Where are we headed?" I call Birga forward.

Patty frowns. "She's under us, but I don't know how to find her."

"Give me five minutes," Dillan says. "I'll figure it out."

"Cool," Emmet says. "I need to piss anyway."

"Ye didn't go before we left the house, did ye?" Dillan asks in his best impression of our father's accent.

I roll my eyes. "Okay, regroup in five. Bruin, would you like to come out and play?"

I thought you'd never ask.

The pressure in my chest builds until my bear pops free and materializes at my side. "Hey, big guy."

"Hey, Red. Let the games begin."

Dora strides away from the group, pulls up a standing torch, and spins it in her hands like a Hawaiian flame juggler. The fire screams against the blackness of the night sky, letting off sparks of fire in its wake. After dazzling us with her dexterity and testing its weight and balance, she roots the staff against the grass.

Her call to nature tingles across my skin as the torch staff thickens and twists around her hand as a protective guard. Dora is more than a druid. She has huge roots in the traditional wizarding world too.

It's such a kick to watch her work.

Bruin and Nikon strike up a convo so I take the opportunity to check in on Sloan. "You okay? How are you feeling?"

"Fine. I could use a day or two in bed sleeping though."

"I hear you. Between the portaling and time spent in the

dragon lair and chasing down witches, I've lost two or three days. I'm not sure how many hours I'm behind on sleep."

He leans closer and squeezes me in a one-armed hug. "You're officially invited to join me."

I chuckle. "You're taking advantage of my weariness."

His cocky smile is too cute. "Whatever works. A good guy can still be a bad boy."

"Mmm...that's a good thing. I likes me a bad boy."

Dillan jogs back, his footsteps silent against the brittle grass of the excavation site. "All aboard. The witch ass-kicking train is leaving the station."

We fall into formation, and I call forward my body armor. As I connect with the *Tough as Bark* gauntlets gifted to me by my ancient ancestor, Fionn mac Cumhaill, the intricate inking of trees takes root on my arms. Branches and leaves twine over my skin moving upward and outward from my shoulders, neck, and chest, while roots snake down my arms, fingers, and down my body.

A month ago I was horrified by the inking of the spell. Then it saved my life. Then it saved me again.

I would've been dead four or five times over by now if it wasn't for this armor. Funny how opinions change when held in a new light.

"We're getting closer." Patty maneuvers through the rocky terrain like a spry mountain goat. I thought his short stature would make hiking through the rough landscape in the dark a slow and tedious process. Nope. He's remarkably sure-footed and adept. "I feel my girl callin' to me."

When we come to a rise in the landscape, Dillan signals for us to stop. He flashes hand signals of what's happening over the rise. Emmet and I nod.

We're both well-versed in the unspoken language of the police raid. Hell, Da taught us as kids, and we used that as the basis for all our childhood games. Over the years, we adapted and added some signals.

It dawns on me that the others are lost.

I raise my finger for everyone to hold position and speak to Bruin and Nikon. *There are two guards, two hundred feet to our right. We need them taken out with no chance to sound an alarm. Do you think—*

Consider it done, Bruin says. He looks at Nikon. *On one, Greek. Five. Four. Three...*

Nikon frowns at me when Bruin disappears. *Damn it. He ditched me.*

I meet the curious gazes of the others and shrug. A moment later, Nikon snaps back. "All clear. And just an FYI, your bear is a greedy fighter."

"True story. He loves to maim baddies and doesn't share well with others."

"It doesn't matter who took them out." Patty steps over the rise and heads toward the opening of a cave. "Two fewer witches to block us on our path of vengeance."

I rub my hands over my sleeves and shiver.

Justice is what I'm looking for...isn't it?

The fact that I'm not one hundy percent sure ignites a dull ache in my chest. The druid I want to be stands solidly in the "good guy" column.

Yes, I'm angry about Sloan's suffering and what they're doing to the queen dragon in their quest for power dominance, but if I lose track of who I am in these battles, aren't I as much of a problem as the people I'm trying to stop?

We trudge toward a rocky outcropping, and Dillan points at a hole in the ground. "It's a forty-foot drop straight down, then into the maze of corridors we go."

Emmet, Dillan, Sloan, and I call on *Feline Finesse* and step off, landing soundlessly on the balls of our feet at the bottom. When we get there, Dora is already standing there, her torch lighting the small space. I have no idea how she managed that so quickly, but really, what do I know next to her?

Diddly-squat.

Once Nikon sees where we are, he flashes Patty and himself down to join us. "Thanks for the light."

Dora nods. She's been unusually reserved since we picked her up at the dragon's lair. Other than the time we spent back in Carlisle Castle, I've never known her out of drag. I'm not sure what to think about her sedate black outfit, her lack of an outrageous wig, or her subtle mannerisms.

"I hope being here with us isn't asking too much of you," I whisper as we navigate the maze behind Dillan and his cape of knowing stuff. "I know your magic side is something you try to keep in the past."

She makes a wordless noise of dismissal and shrugs. "Destiny has other plans, girlfriend. You gave me the brooch for safekeeping long ago, and I failed to secure it. I'm a Keeper of Dragons and failed to connect with your queen when you told me she exists. I took an oath to safeguard magic, and I've failed that too. I won't fail again. All or nothing isn't working anymore."

"I'm sorry."

"It's not your fault. The way your family has embraced your gifts makes me ashamed of how I've ignored mine. Not to worry. I'll figure it out."

I squeeze her arm and smile. "I have no doubt."

The torchlight from Dora's staff keeps everyone in a tight fighting party. Patty's pace has been increasing as we go, to the point that now he's moving at a lope. Dillan and Sloan are with him in the lead. Nikon and I are next, and Emmet and Dora are behind us.

When the Fianna shield on my back tingles to life, I adjust the straps of my pack and reach out with my senses. "On your toes, everyone. Something wicked this way comes."

Dillan calls his daggers forward, Patty draws his hatchet, and I call Birga once again.

"I need a druid weapon," Emmet says. "I know the universe chose to give everyone else a physical offensive power, but if we get close enough, I'm going to drop a coin into the Prana Lake of Ultimate Power and make a wish."

Nikon shakes his head. "You need to steer clear of the waters in the cistern. It's raw power, and it alters people. My papu wasn't alone when he discovered The Source. Two other men from his cohort were there. He said they rushed forward, drank from it, then waded into its waters."

"Your grandfather didn't?"

"No, he dipped his finger into the lake water, and the moment he touched it, he felt the power start to work inside him. It's ley line power in its purest form."

"What happened to the other two?" I ask.

"He said they writhed and screamed and transformed into fae beasts right before his eyes. He was terrified."

I bet. "Okay, Emmet. That's good enough for me. Steer clear of The Source."

Emmet frowns. "Says the girl with all the powers. How about I toss my coin from far enough back that it won't splash me? No harm in that."

"You're a dumbass," Dillan says.

"No. I'm a smartass."

I'm about to interrupt the convo and explain to Nikon that it's impossible to herd a jumpy cat when the ground trembles beneath my feet. Slowing to a stop, I glance up and down the rocky passage. "Did you guys feel—"

An eerie creak resonates through the corridor, and the passage floor is suddenly insubstantial. It's as if I've gone too far out on a thinly frozen lake and it's fissuring under my weight. Frozen in place, I hold my breath...

The stone collapses, and I fall.

CHAPTER ELEVEN

"Fi!" Someone shouts behind me.

My stomach plummets as I drop into the crevasse. Emmet dives. The grip that clamps on my arm is bruisingly tight. The bones in my wrist grind together as he grapples and clutches my hand. It's pain with a purpose because it saves me from dropping into the abyss below.

His hold is tenuous at best.

Dillan vaults over my head in a somersault and dives for my other hand. "Someone reform the stone beneath her feet."

Sloan drops and plants his palms flat on the edge of the crumbled ledge. He casts enough spells near me that my senses recognize his magic signature.

It's strong and precise—like him.

A moment later, my feet find purchase on solid stone and I rise out of the ground.

Jell-O legs don't hold me. I stumble forward, and Dillan pulls me to his chest. His heart races under my palm as I close my eyes. Emmet brings it in hard and crushes me from behind. I'm the creamy filling in the sibling Cumhaill Oreo.

"They need a 'watch your step' sign there, eh sista?"

I chuckle. I can always count on Emmet.

I haul in an unsteady breath and squeeze them both again before reclaiming my independence. "Okay, s'all good. No harm done."

Nikon lets out an exasperated chuckle. "Yer a nut, Cumhaill. No harm done? You nearly plummeted to your death. You get caught in a witch's trap and nearly bite it, and your first response to that is no harm done?"

"Infuriating, isn't it?" Sloan slides in for a hug and squishes the breath out of me. "She's a 'pint half full' kind of girl when it comes to minimizing her peril."

I shrug. "Can't a girl be optimistically cynical?"

Sloan frowns. "Not usually, no."

"All right, enough about me. The show's over." I brush the crumbled debris off my palms and frown at the dim corridor. "How did a witch trap ignite under our noses without warning? Why did none of us pick up on that? My shield didn't even let me know I was walking into a situation."

Dillan grabs his backpack and slings the straps over one shoulder. "Could the excessiveness of the magic filling the air cancel out our early warning systems?"

Dora raises her torch and takes a closer look at the stone walls. "That's more probable than the witches having the strength to silence all of our instincts to coming dangers."

"Is there a way to stop that and detect traps as we continue?" Emmet asks.

"Maybe a divining rod?" I try to stifle my laugh and fail miserably.

Emmet flips me the bird.

"Sorry, bro. You getting dragged along on Mr. Toad's Wild Ride was one of the funniest moments of my life."

"Yeah, yuck it up, asshole. Poison ivy is no laughing matter. You try working a street beat with your junk on fire."

I wave away his annoyance and square off with the corridor.

"Okay, speaking of working the beat, break time is over. Let's getter done."

The seven of us meander through the warren of underground tunnels, and I wonder how many times the witches got lost before they found their way. Hopefully a lot. Then we won't be too long behind them. Do they have someone in their coven that acts in the same capacity as Dillan does for ours?

Dillan is our stealth fighter and with his hood up, our ranger. The knowledge that comes to him from wearing his cloak hood up is both astounding and vital.

Without him and his strategic instincts, it would take us days to find the main chamber. That's not a bad thing. The longer it takes the witch bitches to find the access point for the key, the better. Although, if the queen dragon has been ailing for weeks in real-time, they likely already found it.

They just couldn't access it without the key.

"Shh...is that water?" Emmet stops and looks around as we arrive at the junction of several tunnels.

We all stop, and the corridor goes quiet.

"I don't hear anything." I check with the others.

"No, he's right." Dora shifts her torch to light the mouth of one of the off-shoot branches of the tunnel. "I hear it."

I focus and close my eyes but get nothing back. "I'll take your word for it. Does anyone else hear it?"

Blank faces stare back at me. "Okay, so why can only Emmet and Dora hear it?"

"I'd guess that maybe only Emmet and Dora are meant to hear it," Dillan says.

"Thank you, oh wise one, and what celestial message are you getting for our path now?"

He shrugs. "I've got nothin'. Maybe we're supposed to follow the call of the babbling brook. Maybe that's why Emmet heard it. Destiny is calling, and it sounds like the flow of the mighty river of power."

"Hello? Where did Dillan go? Give a guy an enchanted cloak of concealment, and he starts waxing philosophical."

Dillan's mouth lifts in a crooked grin, and he shrugs. "I'm an evolution in progress. Have you got a better answer?"

I study the offshoot corridors and consider that. Searching them all will take too long. Splitting up is a bad idea. I still don't hear anything, but I've got nothing else.

"I guess this is literally a case of go with the flow. Lead on, you two."

Patty moves up to take the lead with Emmet. Between my brother hearing the call of the prana distributary and Patty being drawn like a magnet to the dragon claw dagger from his hoard of treasure, we delve deeper into the bowels of the Gobekli Tepe underground.

We march on, each of us keeping to our thoughts for another fifteen minutes before Dillan breaks the silence. "How far do you figure?"

"Not far now, lad," Patty says. "In fact..." His hand comes up to stop our progress.

I follow his pointed finger to a Wiccan disc secured to the rough stone wall. The size and thickness of a dartboard, the disc's face depicts a three-part labyrinth design. I trace the fluid lines of the maze's branches. They pulse with a pink glow, and the ambient power they exude is incredible.

Emmet pulls up short and frowns at the thing as if it might attack him. "What exactly are we looking at here?"

"That's Hecate's Wheel," Sloan says.

Emmet frowns. "And for the noobs, can we get a CliffsNotes version of who that is and why it matters?"

"Hecate is the goddess of magic, witchcraft, and crossroads." Nikon steps forward to take a closer look. "In my days in Greece, she was named the chief goddess presiding over magic and spells. She's also a total bitch."

"Sounds like the mighty witch goddess served the Greek sour grapes." Dillan waggles his ebony brow. "Let's file that away to circle back to at a later date."

Nikon grins. "Circle all you want. You'll never get the story behind why I despise Hecate."

"Challenge accepted."

"So, what's with her dartboard?" Emmet asks.

"Right?" I chuckle and hold up my fist for a bump. "That was my take on it too, bro. Nice one."

Dora leans in to examine it and frowns. "It's a power disc. I'd wager there's a ley line stream on the other side of this wall and this disc is draining and collecting its source power."

"So, this is what's drainin' my queen's energy?"

Dora frowns. "There has to be more than one to affect the dragon queen."

"Then we keep looking," I say.

"And now we know what we're lookin' for," Sloan says.

"Should we split up?" Emmet asks.

"No!" Dora and I say together.

"All righty then, the ladies have spoken." Dillan gestures forward. "Lay on, MacDuff."

Emmet takes his bow, adjusts the strap of his backpack, and strides off again.

As I pass the power disc, I stare at the swirling Barbie pink glow flowing like liquid energy through the pathways of Hecate's Wheel. My shield flares hot and itchy against my back. Awesomesauce.

I love it when it does that.

Over the next five minutes, we come across three more witch discs but not much else. Dora wants to leave the discs in place until after we face off with the witches because we still don't know where the lake of power is, and the element of surprise is our only advantage.

As anxious as Patty is to remove them, he agrees.

When we get close, we go silent.

It was a boring trudge before, and now, without having Emmet's chatter or Patty's whistling to entertain us, it's an all-out yawnfest.

Hold up, Red. I smell something.

I stop walking at Bruin's request, and Sloan smacks into me and knocks me stumbling forward. "Dude."

Sloan rolls his eyes. "Yer seriously blaming *me* for that?"

I wave that away. "Bruin wants us to hold up. He says he smells something."

Emmet scowls. "If he smelt it he dealt it and man, seriously? We're all trapped in here."

I roll my eyes and release my spirit bear from our physical bond. He pops out of my chest in a swirl of bear breeze and does a quick lap around the group.

Give me one minute.

"You got it, buddy." I scan the tunnel we're in and wonder what he smells. "Does anyone smell anything alarming?"

The members of the group lift their noses, but no one seems to share my bear's olfactory concern.

Emmet shrugs off his backpack and unzips the top pocket. "Anyone want a Gran-wich? They're cut in those cute triangles, so we have time to pop a few in and fuel up."

I take ham and swiss, and true to Emmet's theory, it's gone in a flash. "It's strange," I say while reaching for the next one. "For an all-Wiccan event, you'd think these corridors would be crawling with witches working to secure their big find."

Dillan shoves a triangle in his mouth whole and starts chewing. "You sound disappointed. Considering how long we've plodded along in here, I'm glad we don't have witches up our asses every fifty feet."

I reach for another sandwich triangle and catch a glimpse of Dora's brow knit with worry. "What is it?"

She places a hand against the stone wall and scowls.

My stomach twists around my snack as my shield starts to tingle. "Put the sandwiches away, Em. We need to be locked and loaded."

"Why?" Sloan searches the rocky cavern. "What do ye sense?"

The cavern we're in is wider than a tunnel but narrower than a cave. It's about the size of our family room.

"I don't know yet. It's faint but unmistakable." On a hunch, I slide my hand into my pocket and find the smooth green stone Patty gave me.

Next, I take Sloan's hand in mine and run my thumb over his bone ring. It's the enchanted ring from the Fianna fortress that allows him to see the unseen. He gets the gist of things instantly and laces his fingers with mine.

I close my fist around my gemstone and call to the natural enchantment on Sloan's ring. Something is blocking its sight, and I have a sinking feeling I know what it is.

Sloan's back stiffens the moment I feel the magical block. Good, he feels it too.

I tighten my fist around my gemstone as his magical signature tingles in the air. As he casts a spell, the deception lifts like a thick drape raised at the beginning of a musical.

Our vision is no longer clouded by the illusion the witches are projecting on us—the witches wearing black fatigues and lining the rocky walls of this cavern like unwelcome wallpaper.

"Shit. We're surrounded."

The force of a magic bolt hits me squarely in the chest and knocks me stumbling back toward the waiting arms of the enemy. I grit my teeth, but it's all fury and no pain.

Tough as Bark wins again.

What the hell is happening? With their ambush discovered the glamor drops, and our group gets all caught up on the status of things. The little cavern explodes into the blinding pyrotechnics of witch magic, the sounds of close-quarters combat, and the smell of burning hair.

That last one makes me turn and yep, Dora is shooting fireballs out of the end of her torch.

"You go, girl!" Emmet dances around, boosting Sloan's casting and Dillan's accuracy.

A spinning green clover flies past my head and catches a witch in the throat. Nasty. I evade being struck by an electric blue witch ball and dive behind one of her teammates.

Friendly fire. *Sorry, not sorry.*

I scramble back to my feet and call Birga and rise to face the bitch. It's the redhead, Genevieve, from the shrine cellar.

Her face splits into a wide grin. "We meet again."

"Too bad for you."

She thrusts her hands forward and another energy ball forms between her palms. When she throws this one, I choke up on Birga. "Batter, batter, *swing* batter."

Right before I connect, I push her energy orb with a counterspell of *Protection from Energy*. The incoming danger is now an outgoing attack.

While she scrambles to defend, I harpoon-throw Birga and catch her at the same moment her spell boomerangs home. Unable to defend on two fronts, her cocky grin shifts to a look of horror.

Birga impales her chest, and her body explodes in a burst of power. I shield my face with my arm as rock explodes and the cavern wall crumbles behind where she stood.

I call Birga back as a vibrant pink glow fills the room.

Crap on a cracker.

Will the ley line spill into here? No. Thankfully, the surface of the distributary lays below the remaining wall.

"We've got open access to a ley line, people. Be careful."

I duck the next incoming hit and press my hands against the stone floor. *Shape Stone.* Focused on the feet of the foes in the cavern, one-by-one, I command the stone at their feet to swallow their legs and harden.

The distraction is effective, and the witches are sitting ducks. Two more are ended and explode the same way as the redhead. Twice, the explosion releases more power than I can brace for. The blast of energy knocks me off my feet and sends me flying backward.

Emmet's thrown too.

My pulse thunders in my ears as I track my brother's trajectory. He's flying straight at the breach in the stone wall. I reach, but momentum is carrying me in the wrong direction.

"Sloan! Catch him..."

It's too late.

Emmet is hurled through the gaping hole in the cavern wall and drops out of sight.

CHAPTER TWELVE

"*Emmet!*"

Nikon is the closest to get to him and leans over the crumbled wall into the darkness. "Dora! We need your torch. I can't see a thing."

Dora backhands her opponent and knocks the woman spinning into a spear of stone jutting up from the ground. When she hits the jagged peak, she's impaled and collapses in a limp heap.

Oh, my heart. "Do you see him?" I finish my opponent and leave the last three to Dillan, Patty, and Sloan. "Emmet!"

"There." Dora points her staff out over the swirling pink river, and the light catches on the current flowing beneath the surface. "He's on that jut of rock. Do you see him?"

I'm the third man in so no, I can't see him. Still, I'm not the one who needs to see him. "Nikon, can you get him?"

"I don't think so. My gift doesn't turn around on a dime. I'm liable to get caught in the current and pull us both in."

"Sloan? Can you see him? If you see him, you can get him, right? Your gift is fast."

"I see him...I'm just not sure I can get him without—"

"Please try," I beg, tears stinging my eyes. I know it's unfair to ask him to put himself in danger, but this is Emmet. He's my partner in crime—my purest joy.

And, I know without a shadow of a doubt, Emmet wouldn't hesitate to try to save anyone in distress.

"Please try," I say again, my words clogged in my throat.

Sloan flashes out, and my bowels practically liquify.

What did I do? What if I lose both of them—

Before my mental tailspin gets its groove on, Sloan is back, and Emmet is coughing and sputtering.

Dillan and I are on the ground with him in a flash, and I'm gripping his hand. "Are you okay? Did you swallow?"

Emmet's choking takes on another wild round of coughing, and he shakes his head. "How am I supposed to answer that with a straight face?"

The stress of the moment is too much, and the three of us crack up. I fall forward and hug my brother, and Dillan folds over me and the terror of the moment subsides.

After I calm a little, I pull back to check him over. "Are you okay? Are you tingly like Nikon's granda? Do you feel like you're transforming?"

He studies the scrapes on his hand. "Yeah. I feel something. I'm sure it's okay, though. Despite me being a smartass, I tried not to swallow. I went under and got caught in the flow right after. When I broke back to the surface, I saw the rock and scrambled out."

Shifting his attention, Emmet holds up his fist to bump Sloan. "Thanks for fishing me out of the river, bro."

"My pleasure. I'm glad it worked."

My mind catches up with my emotions and my tears return. "I'm so sorry. I shouldn't have begged you to do that. It was selfish and... I wouldn't want anything to happen to you either. I hope you don't think—"

Sloan presses a finger over my lips. "Breathe, Cumhaill. I

didn't risk it because ye asked me. I risked it because it was Emmet and the right thing to do."

I swipe my cheeks and hold out my hand. He helps me off the hard ground, and I hug him tight. "Thanks for being your wonderful, heroic self, surly."

"It's weird that you're not even wet." Dillan helps Emmet to his feet.

Emmet shakes his head. "Yeah, it looks and acts like water, but it's not. When I pushed up and broke the surface, it felt more like an energy cloud—an intelligent energy cloud. Does that make any sense?"

Dillan pats him on the chest. "Not much, bro, but it's you talking, so we're used to it. Did you at least make your wish?"

Emmet frowns and stares at the pink glow. "Dammit! I was too busy trying to escape the water before I turned into a fae beast that it totes slipped my mind."

I smile. We tease Emmet about being a goof, but he's the most loveable, dependable goof ever. "Well, since you're not sprouting antennae, horns, or wings just yet, I take it we can continue?"

Emmet brushes himself off, grabs a triangle sandwich out of the backpack, and shrugs. "Yeah, s'all good. No harm done, right?"

Nikon rolls his eyes.

Sloan grunts. "Yeah, they're all cut from the same cloth. No harm done."

Nikon frowns and mimics, "I just took a flying leap into a pool of untold power. No harm done."

Glancing back at the glowing pink river of intelligent energy, I wonder about that.

I hope he's right.

We leave the fallen witches in the small cavern, and Patty leads the way toward the magnetic pull of the dragon claw dagger. At the edge of a turn, he raises his hand to stop our procession. He nods and points to indicate around the corner.

When we stop, I notice the scuffle and shuffle of movement in the distance. There's also the distinct sound of grunting. What the heck is around there?

Patty unsheathes his hatchet from his weapons belt.

I call Birga. *Bruin, would you mind taking a quick recon run so we know what we're dealing with?*

Happy to, Red. BRB.

BRB? I chuckle. My brothers have to stop influencing my ancient warrior bear. I'm still thinking about that when Bruin returns and lifts my hair to tickle my face.

We hit the motherload on this one, Fi. The door is unlocked and open, the witches are inside the lake area, and the two guards aren't paying any attention. The only questionable foes are the three fae mutant monsters between them and us.

Awesomesauce. Somebody sipped the water, I take it.

Looks like it.

I relay that to the others in a whisper, and Bruin, Sloan, and Nikon lead the offensive to take out the guards. After the three of them flash off, I signal for Dillan and Dora to round the corner and assess the mutant witches.

The two of them possess the best stealth abilities, and I'd rather not alert the witches to our presence yet. Dillan flashes me a cocky smile, adjusts his hood, and strides off like the badass he is in battle now.

I shake myself inwardly at that. When did I start admiring my brother for being a lethal assassin? Life is cray-cray.

All set, Red.

I nod when Bruin gives me the all-clear, and Patty, Emmet, and I move around the corner.

This cavern is double the last one's size and has lit torches affixed to the stone wall at regular intervals. The door, if you can call it that, is a gaping opening beside a carved circle housing the key made out of the base of the chalice, Morgana's brooch, and the dragon-claw dagger.

Two downed witches lay unconscious on the ground beside the opening into the Cistern of The Source.

Obvi, I didn't give Dillan enough credit for his restraint.

"Druidsssss," a lizard creature hisses.

The three mutants move to block our access to the pool of power. It's unnecessary. Having one of us take a dip directly in the ley line current is quite enough. We have no intention of rushing them to claim the prana for our own.

The fae-mutated witches scramble to attack. Eight against three is hardly worth our time. Bruin, Dillan, and Dora face off to put them out of their misery while the rest of us move in on the door to the cavern of the cistern.

Unfortunately, the battle alerts the others.

A brunette witch I recognize as one of the women from the shrine cellar sees Sloan, and her gaze tightens. "How did you get free? You should be curled up in a ball by now. How did you exhume my festerbug?"

On a list of things not to say in front of the darkness-possessed, pissed-off girlfriend, those sentences get the highest possible marks. I harpoon-throw Birga, and my spear is as ferocious and blood-thirsty as I am at that moment.

The witch bitch's expression morphs from arrogance to surprise to horror in the span of a fleeting heartbeat. The force of Birga's momentum pins the witch to the stone wall and the dark film coating me rejoices.

"Anything else you'd like to say about my boyfriend's suffering, bitch?" I move in close, adrenaline pumping hard in my veins. I grip Birga's staff and pull her free. "Yeah no, I didn't think so."

"Well then," Emmet says, his emerald green eyes blown wide.

"In case anyone's wondering how Fi is dealing with the stress of the past few days. I think it's fair to say she's working through a few personal issues."

"Moira should've killed ye from the start as we all wanted," another witch says while coming out of the cavern.

"Then why didn't she?" Sloan snaps. By the storms shadowing his gaze, he recognizes this one. "Why the games?"

"Ye embarrassed her. Had ye traded the chalice for our help protecting the groves as ye negotiated, none of this would be an issue. Instead, ye made her look bad."

"Boo-freaking-hoo. She was lying about her motives, and we saw through it. No deal. The end."

The witch tips back her head and laughs. "If ye thought that was the end of it, ye don't know Moira. She wanted to watch ye suffer. She wanted to compromise Cumhaill's morals and bring him down a peg."

Dillan barks a laugh. "If she thought that would work, she doesn't know our Granda."

"Yeah," Emmet says, his voice tight. "Moira wouldn't know honor if it punched her in the witch's tit."

Something in the timbre of Emmet's voice catches my attention. He's got the same pale complexion as I do, so the mottled patches climbing his neck and spreading across his jaw are both noticeable and worrisome.

He swipes a hand across his forehead and blinks. "FYI, your thieving pissed off some very powerful fae."

Nikon points at the silver casks stacked near the door. "Going to a magic kegger?"

"That's none of your business, little man. Run home before mommy realizes you're out after dark."

Nikon doesn't seem amused. "My family vowed to keep the secrets of this cistern a secret millennia ago. There's no way I step aside and watch you carry these out of here."

"Then don't watch," a crone with straggly silver hair and jaundiced yellow eyes says. "Problem solved."

Something about the old witch brings forward a surge of dark yearning. I stretch out my neck and adjust my grip on Birga's staff. "What? You're banking on those waters being a fountain of youth? Have you been drinking it?"

"Chugging it, I'd guess," Nikon says.

"That won't end well for you, oul girl. Sad face."

Red. Something's wrong with Emmet. He's lookin' a little green himself.

Emmet is standing with a hand propped against the stone of the cavern wall. *When this fight starts, keep him safe, Bear.*

Like he's my cub.

This mission has suddenly become a whole lot less interesting. I want to end this and have Wallace check Emmet over. "All right, moving along. Bad guys stall and overshare. Good guys won't stand for it. Now we're at the part where the fight breaks out."

The old hag shoots me with ocular daggers.

"Sorry. We're on a bit of a time-crunch here."

"I'll start things off, Fi." Patty fires a few lucky charms across the cavern and catches the two witches in the forehead. "That's for the suffering of my queen and the kids."

Yep...that certainly kicks off the battle in a big way.

Wands appear at an amazing speed, and I take a step forward to position myself closer to Emmet. Dillan does the same thing from the other side of our group.

I'm busy focusing on the group's front-runners when a massive white wolf barrels through the crowd. Snout open, teeth exposed, it charges at me with a snarl.

Where the hell did White Fang come from?

I poise Birga and brace for the impact. Before the weight of the wolf strike hits, Bruin takes form, looses a wild roar, and guts the beast. Its momentum carries its body into a collision course with him, but Bruin barely shifts.

He catches the animal and throws it to the ground with a bloody *thud*. I draw a deep breath. No matter how many times I see Bruin in action, he's breathtaking.

Crack.

The sharp snap in the air hurts my ears and fogs my mind. I fight the brain blur of confusion. Sloan has hit me with enough spells like this in training for me to recognize the sensation and how to defend.

I counter the spell and the fog burns off.

A large woman is advancing fast.

"*Wind Wall.*" As my spell picks up and gains momentum, I send twisters at the two witches pointing wands at Sloan.

Another witch sends out an arching spray of white light. It bounces off the rock walls and ceilings and splits into round, silver projectiles. Suddenly we're being pegged by possessed pinballs of pain.

Damn, they hurt even with my armor.

Dora slams the end of her torch staff against the ground in an ultimate Gandalf the Gray move.

You shall not pass, motherfuckers!

The satanic orbs drop lifelessly to the ground.

"Emmet? Are you okay, dude?" Dillan's voice has me spinning to cover my brother.

No. Emmet is not okay.

Dillan looks at me. "Is it his dip in the river?"

I rush to them. "Sloan? We need you."

"Little busy, *a ghra.*" He deflects a barrage of magic bolts being hurled at him by two witches at once. He sends most of them down the corridor from the direction we came, but one makes it through his defenses and catches him in the chest.

With a grunt and a curse, he's knocked to the side. When the bitch witch that cast it leans in to grab him, I run and do a flying leg lariat. In an aerial leap, I wrap my legs around her neck and take her to the ground.

Dillan snorts. "Such a lady."

I roll to my feet and give my brother a dainty curtsy. "Better?"

A curse behind me cuts off the shenanigans.

My mind short-circuits as Emmet groans. Then his form shifts. One second he's an ebony-haired, emerald-eyed hottie, and the next he's a—

"What the fuckety-fuck!" Dillan shouts.

Sloan turns. "Where'd the kangaroo come from?"

I duck a flying rock. "That's Emmet. Everyone, Captain Jack is my brother. Don't kill him."

I don't even know what to do with that, but in true Emmet fashion, he takes a few tentative hops. Then he leans back on his tail and kicks the shit out of witches. Front paws up and clenched; he's an Evander Holyfield with fur. Fine. There's nothing to be done about it now.

I get back to it. There's still a lot of wand-flicking going on, but thankfully, in such close quarters, the witches are at a disadvantage. If they try anything too big, they're liable to take out their own.

An explosion of rocks behind me sends Patty flying through the air.

Bruin rises on his mighty back paws and plucks the leprechaun out of the air before he hits the wall.

"Good catch, Bear."

A blonde witch yelps as Nikon backhands her and her wand flies free of her hand and lands out of reach. He makes a quick grab for the twined twig and comes up smiling. Gripping it tightly in one hand, he holds out his other hand, and a steady stream of magic arcs from his palm.

"I can play that game too." Nikon's arcing stream takes her down in a fit of convulsions.

Dayam, the Greek's got game.

Out of the corner of my eye, I catch someone moving in on Bruin hard and fast. I spin Birga in my palm and swipe low, catching her across the back of her ankle and severing her Achilles tendon.

She goes down like a rock.

An energy blast hits me in the chest and throws me back. The next thing I know, I'm staring up at the rock ceiling of the cave. I cough, and blood washes my throat. Turning my head to the side, I spit scarlet.

The straggly-haired old witch with yellow eyes leans over me and lets a gob of loogie drop from her mouth. I can't get up or out of the way. Her spit lands on my face and slithers its way down my jaw and into my ear.

Um...nasty.

The whistle of air as Bruin line-drives the old girl into the wall is satisfying—but not as satisfying as the crunch of prehistoric bones.

"Fiona, shitshitshit." Dillan drops to his knees beside me.

The weighty shuffle and hop of two small and two large paws and a tail follow his arrival. I can't help it. When Emmet-roo leans in and looks down at me with his little snout and ears, I start to laugh.

I regret it immediately. The blood in my mouth makes me sputter and graduates to a full-on coughing spell.

"Sloan, we need you," Dillan says. "Okay, Fi. I'm going to finish off these assholes and tag out your boy-toy so he can heal you, yeah? Hang in there."

"Don't panic," I wheeze. "S'all good."

"Shit yeah. I can tell by the blood you're coughing up. You're aces."

I let him have that one.

"Och, Fiona, yer gonna be the death of me, I swear." Sloan kneels beside me and presses his hands on the scorch mark on my shirt. As he runs his hands over my chest, the warmth of his healing energy seeps into my body.

Telling him I'm good won't fly any better than it did with Dillan. Tough crowd. "How's your chest? I saw you get pegged by a magic bolt too."

"Close yer eyes and focus on healing. Yer the one with internal bleedin'."

"So you can worry but I can't?"

The tension in his brow eases. "I'm sorry. I'm fine, Fi. Thanks fer askin'. I'll be pleased to let you play doctor and give me a thorough examination later."

I fight not to laugh. The last thing I need is another blood-horking coughing spell. "Did you see Emmet in action?"

Sloan cants his head to the side. "It's hard to miss an eight-foot kangaroo power-kicking witches into the walls."

I blink up at Sloan and see the concern in his eyes. "It's temporary though, right? A side effect of his swim?"

"I expect so."

"More words, please. Elaborate."

"Ye do realize that I'm healing yer internal injuries after both of us were recently struck down by a witch's spell, yes?"

"What? You can't do that and elaborate? Communication is key to a lasting relationship."

He rolls his eyes, finishes with my chest, and lifts the hem of my shirt to get a visual of my ribs and tummy. When he resets the position of his hands, he meets my gaze. "Yer ridiculous. Yer lucky I've learned to find it endearing."

"Such a sweet-talker. Back to Emmet being a marsupial."

"Wildlife Transfiguration is a common advanced ability of Druids. I'm sure that's all it is. I highly doubt yer brother will be hopping long."

As good as that is to hear, it would be better if I didn't hear the lie in his voice. He doesn't have a clue and doesn't want to scare me...thus the original evasion.

"Are you done yet?"

"Not quite."

I close my eyes, but that's a major mistake. Without my sight set on a focal point, the world spins, and the squirrels nesting in my stomach go nutty.

I open my eyes again and smile at Emmet. "Hey, bro. What do you call a lazy kangaroo?"

Emmet-roo tilts his head to one side, and I can read his thoughts as clearly as if I could truly read his thoughts. The way his mouth falls open and his little black nose twitches, he's saying, "Seriously, Fi? I'm a freaking kangaroo, and you're going to tell jokes?"

"Any guesses?"

Dillan chuckles, joining in. "I give up, Fi. What do you call a lazy kangaroo?"

"A pouch potato." Ha! I crack me up.

Emmet looks far less amused.

I tweak his shiny black nose and giggle. "Seriously, Em. This is temporary. You wished for an offensive weapon, and now you have an advanced ability to transform into animals. That's super cool."

"Is it different animals or kangaroo-specific?" Dillan asks.

Sloan's healing energy stops tingling, and he sits back on his heels. "Wildlife Transfiguration usually starts with one dominant form, and as the warrior grows more accomplished at shifting forms, it expands to other animals."

I hold up my hands for Dillan and Sloan to help me to my feet. The shift in position gives my stomach a slosh, but I swallow back the burn of bile and fake it.

All is well. Look away. Nothing to see here.

After checking that I'm steady on my feet, I take a look at the carnage. "Yay team! Did we get them all?"

"No," Nikon and Dora both say at once. "The witches that were here weren't coven leaders or high priests or priestesses. These were minions."

"Yeah, but we kicked their minion asses. Still a win. What's next?"

Nikon points at the shiny steel kegs. "I vote we return the magic waters to the lake and seal this baby up for another two thousand years."

"Agreed," Dora says. "And we'll do better at safeguarding the three key components this time around."

The mention of safeguarding magical components reminds me of the *Eochair Prana*. I still have to come up with a better solution for Morgana's answer to all evil than buried in the cemetery behind my house. That's straight out of any paranormal tv show.

I collect Birga, clean her, thank her, and return her to her inked form on the inside of my forearm. She's always quite content after bloodshed.

It's the necromancer enchantment on her.

Meh, everyone has their thing.

With that done, I head over to help empty the kegs.

"Let us take care of it." Sloan frowns. "It'll take an hour or two until yer strength is restored, and I'd rather ye not spill a keg of magical energy on yer foot."

"Irish has a point, Fi." Dillan points at where Patty sits on a rock next to Bruin. "Take a load off until we're ready to roll. Once we get things restored, Sloan and Nikon can *poof* us home."

I want to argue, but honestly, if they want to do all the grunt work while I recoup and eat the Gran-wiches, who am I to argue?

Despite Sloan's prediction, it only takes Nikon, Dillan, Sloan, and Dora slightly longer than one hour to return the water to the cistern. They're super careful about making sure not to get splashed, and after seeing Emmet scratching his furry ass, I think that point has hit home even more.

It's back-breaking work, but they never complain.

Sloan steps through the opening to the prana lake and sets down the last empty keg. "This is the birthplace of fae power and should've been left undisturbed."

"Since that ship has sailed, the least we can do as guardians of nature is restore it." Picking the last triangle sandwich from our Gran care package, I hold it up for Emmet to munch.

"Well done, boys," Dora says. When the four of them exit the lake area, Dora activates the key, and the stone wall seals off the cistern behind them. "Take no liberties. Leave no trace."

Dillan sighs and perches on a rock. "What about dead bodies and captive criminal witches? Can we leave those? Because I'm beat."

"I shall take care of the misguided ones, my child."

The eight of us stiffen as a woman walks through a shimmering spot on the stone wall. The white glow coming off her is blinding. When the brilliance dims, I lower my hand shielding my eyes, and try to make sense of this.

She's a healthy-looking, plus-sized woman wearing overalls and lady-bug print gardening gloves. The knees of her pants are dark with dirt, and the soil matches the smudges on her cheek.

Her skin is the warm, chestnut brown of Bruin's fur, her hair black as night and hanging in long, lazy curls, and her eyes are the stunning turquoise of a Caribbean coastline.

She's utterly resplendent.

Her beauty isn't so much what we see but what I feel inside when I look at her.

She is home.

Sloan, Nikon, and Dora drop to one knee and lower their gaze to the ground. I blink at the coordination of the act and if we weren't in the presence of the woman I think is the goddess of nature herself, I would've cracked wise.

Instead, I join them.

Patty and Dillan kneel beside me and Emmet bows.

"Such a welcome. Thank you. It's been a great many years since visitors wandered these corridors, and after bearing witness to the behavior and motivation of these women, it disheartened me. Then you arrived—my beloved guardians—and restored my faith."

Yay team!

She walks forward and scrubs the fur of Emmet's cheek. "Yes, sweet boy, you are whole and well and will once more be the male you are. Your body is simply adjusting to the power you were exposed to. There's no need to be afraid. All will be as it's meant."

Emmet thumps the stone floor with his tail.

I draw in my first deep breath since his transformation.

"Now then," Mother Nature says, "as much as I value what you all have done already, there is a task I must ask of you. A task of vital purpose."

CHAPTER THIRTEEN

Our entire group *poofs* into the dragon lair, directed by Sloan and power-boosted by Nikon. The night's been a team effort all around. "Hello, the lair," I call out as we all stride toward the dragon queen. I catch a glimpse of our group, and it strikes my funny bone. "A kangaroo, an immortal, and a Man o' Green walk into a dragon lair."

"Funny girl," Nikon says.

"Yer back." Gran looks up from where she's reclining in the chair Patty added to the seating area during my stay. She looks whole and relaxed and not at all as harried as poor Patty did when he oversaw the kids on his own. "What's the craic, kids?"

I giggle at her question. She's lounging in the chair with a scarlet dragon head in her lap while twenty-two other dragons are piled and overlapping on the area rug around her. "We got the job done, and everyone has their fingers and toes. Emmet gained a tail but still has his fingers and toes. What about you guys? Everyone seems to be behaving well."

"Every child loves storytime, luv."

Sloan's expression breaks into a wide grin. "Did ye tell them the one about the wolf riders?"

"I did."

"And the sprites getting trapped in their home tree?"

"That one too."

Sloan catches me smiling at him and shrugs. "What? She's a great storyteller."

I hug his arm and push up onto my toes to kiss his cheek. "By the look of this contented crew, I have no doubt."

Dart straightens from where he's curled up next to the gramophone, checks out the cluttered heaps of sibling dragon bodies between us, and grunts.

My jaw drops as he launches into the air and with a few awkward flaps of his wings crash-lands next to us. Swishing his tail, he pushes the scaled appendage between Sloan and me and pulls me against him.

I hug him and scrub my knuckles between his horns. He lets out a contented purr, and I kiss his snout. "That was amazing, baby. Good job."

Dillan smacks Sloan on the back and laughs. "That's classic. You just got cock-blocked by a dragon. Dude, that's gotta be a first."

I straighten and catch the triumphant glimmer in Dart's eyes. *Oh, dear.* I don't want my dragon jealous of my boyfriend. That can't be good on any front.

"Fi, luv. Ye still haven't told me what went on."

I snap out of my mental musings and catch Gran up on Gobekli Tepe and the Cistern of The Source and the witches. "Then we spent the next hour removing witch discs from the offshoot tunnels and corridors of the underground passages. We hope that's all the queen will need to revive."

I look over at where Patty and Dora are examining Her Scaliness. "Any change?"

Patty runs his stubby fingers over his white beard. "It's hard to say. I think her breathing is deeper, but she's not waking up yet."

Gran shoos a few dragon babes away from the base of the

chair, lowers her footrest, and joins us. "Och, I'm sure it's a matter of a moment, and she'll revive. It sounds like ye had a grand adventure."

"Also known as a day in the life of yer granddaughter, Lara." Sloan laughs when I throw him a look, but he's not wrong. It seems the Fianna crest on my back is still working its magnetic magic to draw all of life's whacked and weird adventures to me.

Gran wraps an arm around my shoulder and kisses my cheek. "They're only coddin' ye, luv. Yer meant fer great things. I knew that the moment I met ye."

I stick my tongue out at Sloan, and the bastard only laughs harder.

"And what's this? Ye picked yerselves up a kangaroo along yer travels—och, good gracious." She looks at me with a knowing look, and I nod. When she returns her attention to Emmet-roo, she cups his pointed jaw. "What happened, my sweet boy?"

"The battle took a turn," I say. "He ended up taking an unexpected dip in a primary ley line. It's okay, though. Mother Nature said all is as it's meant to be and he'll be fine once his body adjusts to the exposure to the power."

"Mother Nature?"

"Yeah, we met her. She came to praise her guardians for doing what's right for the natural world."

Gran looks at me, her eyes far too glassy. "My word, ye make me so proud I could burst at the seams, I swear."

I hug her from the side, and we look at Emmet. "I'm sure you'll be back to normal soon, Em. I have a good feeling."

Gran scrubs the tips of her fingers under his chin. "Well, if the goddess says it's so, then it is. Chin up, son. Ye still have three days before yer due back to work. I'm sure ye'll be sorted by then."

Dillan flashes me a private look. Yep. We need him sorted because he's the new kid on the beat. He can't miss shifts this early out of the gate. Deciding there's nothing to do about that but wait and see, I head over to join Dora and Patty.

"Anything?"

Dora is straddling one of the queen's tail coils, her hands pressed to her chest, her hands glowing gold. "It won't be long now. I think it might be best if we leave. She doesn't know us and will likely wake disoriented and defensive."

"No argument here." Nikon takes a step back. "I'm all for avoiding angry dragons."

I rub my hand over Patty's back and stand staring at the queen. "Are you okay to wait alone? I can stay if you want. I think she'll recognize me as a friend."

Patty's furrowed brow relaxes. "I'm certain she would, lass, but no. We'll be fine, and there's still much to do. If I can be of assistance, let me know. Otherwise, ye know when to come and get me."

"Yep. The moment we find the witches responsible for what happened, I'll let you both know. You have my word."

Patty lifts my knuckles to his lips and gives me a mischievous wink. "And yer word is as good as gold in my estimation."

After dropping Gran and Emmet off in what I like to consider Granda's Shire, Nikon takes Dora home to Toronto, and Sloan and I go back to his place. I've lost track of the passage of time, but Wallace was very clear about checking on my leg at regular intervals.

I'm not about to complain. The idea of spending a little downtime with Sloan is better than what the doctor ordered.

"Shotgun on the shower." My bag flops on the floor of his bedroom with a weighty kerflop. I trudge over to sit at his dining table and unbuckle my boots. "Do you think your dad can look at my leg tomorrow? I'm done like dinner, baby."

Sloan unlaces his boots, sets them on the rack by his door, then picks up my bag. "I'll check it tonight and arrange for him to set aside time in the morning."

Awesomesauce. I drop my boots and glare at the door to the loo. "Your bathroom's so far away."

Sloan picks up my boots and chuckles as he sets them neatly beside his own. "Come, *a ghra*. Let me help you."

At first, I think he's going to *poof* me to the shower, but he surprises me by scooping me out of the chair and carrying me across his suite.

"I'm not a damsel you can sweep off her feet."

"Never thought it for a second."

"You can only carry me because I let you and because I'm too tired to resist."

"Understood."

When we get into the ensuite, he sits me on the counter, starts the water in the shower, and takes out two puffy towels. "Anything else I can do? Do you need a hand with your clothes, maybe washing your hair?"

"That's a tempting offer."

"It was meant to be."

I chuckle and tilt my mouth up to accept his kiss. As tired as I am—and I'm bone-achingly exhausted—I consider his offer. "No fair. With a kiss like that, my thought processes go all warm and fuzzy."

"Then my evil plan is working."

I press a hand against the scorch mark on his shirt and smile. "Raincheck. But after I clean up, maybe we could snuggle to sleep? I'm too beat to do much more."

"Snuggling to sleep sounds heavenly. Don't forget to let me see yer leg and wrap it before ye put on yer Pikachu PJs."

"Promise."

———

Morning comes too soon, and Wallace is pleased with both the regeneration of the dead skin on my thigh as well as the lack of evil intent trying to possess me. Little does he know about the urge to kill that witch that infected Sloan with her creepy blue beetle and how satisfying it was to peg her to the wall.

"Now, would ye like to tell me what yer not tellin' my son?"

I blink at the man's knowing smile. "Clever man."

He has the same crooked smile as Sloan. I've never noticed it before. I don't know that I've ever seen Wallace smile before. "It hardly takes a scholar to figure it out. Ye sent him off on a food errand to have a private minute, didn't ye?"

"I'm sure it's nothing, but I don't want Sloan to worry." I confide in Wallace about the evil filmy residue I sense and how when I get angry, my eyes burn and flip to the creepy ice blue. "I understand the bond I made with that level of evil is bound to leave a trace, but I thought someone should know."

"Has it gotten worse or stronger as time passes between healings?"

"No. It's just sorta there and flares under stress."

"Well, yer daily life seems to bring more than yer fair share of stress."

"True story."

"All right. I'm glad ye told me, but let's not worry about it. There are bound to be aftereffects. We knew that comin' into yer recovery. Monitor things. As long as it doesn't get worse, or nothing else comes of it, we'll take that as good news."

"Good news?" Sloan strides in with Manx. "I like the sound of that. So, yer healin' up well then?"

"She is." Wallace offers me a slight nod. "And yer free to go start yer day. What's on the agenda?"

Sloan shrugs. "We have an errand to follow up on for the goddess. I expect we'll be gone most of the day."

"Uh-huh, fine."

I hop off the exam table and slip on my shoes. Really? Sloan mentions working for the goddess and doesn't even rank a follow-up question.

"Try not to come home bleedin', you two."

I snort. "That's always the plan. It's when the world doesn't follow the plan that things go to hell."

When no response comes back, I find Wallace's attention engrossed by something in his medical cabinet.

Sloan takes my hand and leads me out. "Sorry about that. When things stop being medical, Da tends to lose interest."

I swing the door open to Gran's and Granda's house and cup my mouth. "Hello, the house! Anyone home? Granda? Gran? Brothers o' mine?"

Gran comes out of the back room with Emmet hopping along behind her. "Lugh and Dillan went to finish up with the restoration of the parish. Yer brother said to fetch him when yer ready to leave."

"Cool, thanks. Emmet, are you ready to roll?"

Leaning back on his tail, he raises his hands.

"Of course you're coming, dude. There's no way you're missing out on the second half of this quest. We're only getting to the good stuff now. And hey, Mother Nature said you're one hundy percent good, so you might change back at any time."

I look over at Sloan and frown. "Okay, weird thought, but when he changes back will he have clothes on or be nakey man? Ohmygawd...is that why his statue was a nakey man? Do you think he was a Wildlife guy?"

Sloan sneaks a bunch of cookies off the plate in the living room and starts in on his stack. "Clan Cumhaill has the strangest preoccupation with nakedness. Ye realize that, don't ye?"

I snort. "Nice try, Mackenzie. When it comes to the whole

nakedness thing, the Cumhaill preoccupation falls solidly in Goldilocks territory."

"Which means what exactly?"

"Not too much. Not too little. We're *juuust* right."

Sloan rolls his eyes. "Says you."

I shrug. "Well, I'm not taking any chances with my brother's junk. I'll pack you a change of clothes, Em. I got you covered. Ha...see what I did there?"

Sloan waves a hand in the air as he leaves the room. "Get yerself sorted, and we'll meet up with Lugh."

I leave Sloan and Emmet to do their thing and head into the spare room to grab some clothes for Emmet. His bag is open on the dresser, so I help myself.

"Fiona, dear." Gran joins me. "Can I have a quick word?"

"Sure, Gran. What's up?"

"Honestly, I'm not sure if I should say anything at all, but since we love ye both so much, yer granda and I feel it best to err on the side of caution."

I roll a pair of boxers inside a t-shirt and a pair of sweatpants and grab some socks. "Sorry. I'm not following. What side of caution?"

"I know ye grew up without a mam, luv, and forgive me if I'm overlooking, but it's plain that yer spendin' a great deal of time with Sloan. While I love him like he's my own, I know he's had a few indiscretions with the ladies."

Oh, lordy. It dawns on me too late what this is.

I look at the door, but there's no way to escape.

Gran is giving me the talk. "Oh, Gran... I, uh..." My cheeks flush hot, and I swipe my hair away from my face. "Enough said. We're good. Sloan and I... Well, you don't need to worry. We're good."

"Ye know what they say, dear. Safeguard yer hearts and safe-guard yer parts."

Oh, gawd. Yep, this is happening. I force a smile. "Understood.

We're not rushing into anything, but if and when Sloan and I get there, we'll be careful."

"When we get where?" Sloan strides in, loose-limbed, and smiling. "What are my two favorite ladies talkin' about?"

"Your penis, actually."

Sloan chokes and spits cookie across the rug.

Could it get any more awkward? "Gran is reminding us to glove the love."

Sloan's footing falters, and I swear it's one of those cartoon moments when the character looks back at the way they came and *zoom*, speeds off in the opposite direction.

I raise a pointed finger. "Don't you dare *poof* out on me. If I'm enduring this, so are you."

Sloan swallows and takes an extremely long time to set down his cookies on the dresser. When he turns back, he lifts his chin and smiles. "All right, Lara. Ye've never had any interest in my affairs before, so I assume it's Fi yer worried about."

"Not just her, son, but I worry. Raised in the house with six men, she might need a woman's guidance."

Emmet-roo arrives, and even in his 'roo form, I can tell he's busting a gut. Yeah, yuck it up, asshole.

I rub the fire burning in my cheeks, but there's no hiding my reaction. "I'm fine, Gran. Really. I got the whole female lowdown from Auntie Shannon when I was twelve, and Da is frank with all of us about what it means to be an adult. There's nothing to worry about."

"Even so." She reaches into the pocket of her apron. "Granda and I thought it best to pick ye up somethin' while yer here...ye know, to tuck in yer bag. Things sweep ye up more often than not, and we want ye to be prepared."

I stare at the cardboard box, and I can't feel my limbs.

My grandparents bought me condoms.

"Now, it's been a few decades since yer Granda and I bought things like this, but Erin at the counter says these are especially good and the girl in the queue in front of me agreed. She likes the ribbed ones herself."

Oh. My. Gawd. I grab the box and shove them in the bag with Emmet's clothes. "Thanks, Gran. Message received. Before we get spunky, we'll cover his monkey."

Sloan makes a pitiful noise, which I expect is the sound a man makes as his testicles climb up inside to hide forever.

I take Sloan's hand and grab Emmet's ear. The stupid kangaroo is doubled over, shaking in racking fits of what I can only guess is laughter. "Love you, Gran. Thanks. Bye."

I send a pleading gaze at Sloan and thank the goddess, he portals us out of hell.

"What the fuck just happened?" Sloan snaps the moment we materialize in the cellar of the parish church of Ardfelt Cathedral. The place looks like it's been completely restored to its condition of two days ago except the shrine wall is gone, and the shelves of the shrine are empty of treasure. "Since when do Lugh and Lara feel the need to pep talk my cock?"

"How do *I* know? I've never had grandparents before, and they've been your pseudo-family longer than mine."

"In my house, we don't talk about such things. Sweet mercies, that was mortifying."

"Ye *think?*"

Emmet flops onto the cellar floor and slaps his tail on the ground. "Shut up, Emmet. You are *soooo* not helping."

"Not helping with what?" Dillan says.

"Nothing!" Sloan and I shout at the same time.

Dillan throws up his hands and takes a step back. "Message received. Sorry I asked."

I rub my hand over my face and try to recover some vestige of calm. Today started so well too. "Sorry, D. Trust me, once

Captain Jack over there recovers from his trip to the Outback, you'll hear all about it. I'm sure everyone will. For now, I'd rather stick my head in the sand and pretend the past ten minutes never happened."

"Me too." Sloan strides into the empty shrine. "Wow, ye got a lot done. Ye've been busy. Where's Lugh?"

The idea of facing my grandfather right now makes me want to hyperventilate. "Not that we need to see him. In fact, we have our mission to worry about. I'm going to text him that we're off."

"Great idea." Sloan points at my phone as if that will hurry things up. "Tell him we'll check in once we get things squared away with the goddess. It could take days."

"Hopefully, weeks."

Dillan snorts. "Are the two of you on something? You're talking a million miles an hour and acting weird."

"Less talky, more do-y, Dillan. Now, shut your yap trap and put your hand in." I grab the flailing foot of an extremely annoying kangaroo and reach out for Sloan. When he has hold of Dillan, he *poofs* us out.

CHAPTER FOURTEEN

The first stop on the goddess's task of vital importance is for the four of us to go to Blarney Castle, a medieval stronghold in Blarney, near Cork. To track down the witches involved in siphoning from the lake of fae origin, we first have to find out who the players are and where they've taken the casks of prana they made away with before we got there to stop them.

We know Moira is involved. She's either running the show or one of the key players running the show, but beyond her, we don't know anyone else.

We also know that Moira hasn't been back to her rowhouse in Dublin since our battle to rescue Sloan, so trying to catch her there or through that place is futile.

Since Sloan is by far the most knowledgeable in matters of sects and witches and the like, we let him take the lead on this.

"So, we're going to talk to a witch about how to catch the witches involved?"

In the distance, a gray stone castle stands against the horizon. Sloan points across the grounds of the grassy estate to a wooden bridge crossing a small stream. "We'll speak to a white witch I know, Sarah, and ask her what she knows about who's dabbling in more harmful forms of magic, yes."

Dillan and Sloan are taller than me so I have to jog to keep up with their long strides. I'm not sure if Emmet is hurrying or not. It's hard to tell with him springing and sproinging along beside us.

"Your friend Sarah. How well do you know her? Anything I need to know ahead of time so I'm not blindsided?"

Sloan casts me a sideways glare. "Why would you ask?"

"Because you portaled us straight here, so I'm assuming you have some familiarity."

Dillan chuckles. "Is it true what they say, Irish? Once you go witch, you never switch?"

Sloan scowls at both of us. "Sarah's a volunteer tourism guide here. I don't know her biblically. I know her through my visits as a druid. Blarney Castle is a historic site for witches and druids alike. As well as the castle, there's also the Druid Circle, the Witch's Kitchen, the Wishing Steps, the Badger's Cave, the Battlements, and I assume ye've heard of the Blarney Stone?"

I study his expression and frown. "I can't tell if you're shitting me right now or if that's a genuine question."

He casts a sideways glance. "I take that as a yes."

"You *do* know we're Irish too, right?"

"It may have come to my attention once or twice. My point is, this site is a magical place for more than witches. There are history and lore here."

"Which is why you like it." I look at Dillan and shrug. "He has a thing for crumbling stone and long backstories."

"I find history interesting, yes."

"I know you do. I'm just razzing you. Back to the part about this being the home of the Blarney Stone. That's cool. I want to kiss it."

"Me too," Dillan says.

"Emmet does too. Don't you?"

Dillan looks over at our goofball brother, and the kangaroo thumps the ground a few times. "Are you even trying to get back to your human form, or are you in there having fun? Try another animal or something. If you're all hopped up on prana power, maybe there's more you can do besides carrying your cellphone in your pouch."

I snort. "No. Seriously? You put his cell in his pouch?"

"I would have, but male kangaroos don't have a pouch."

I sigh. "That's so sad. I was already coming up with so many cool things we could do with his pouch."

Dillan shrugs. "Maybe he'll be an elephant next, and we can ride him. Or a hyena."

I nod. "A hyena for sure. He's always laughing."

"Right? He'd be a great hyena."

Sloan gestures to the right and reaches for the gate of a garden.

I read the sign and hesitate. "The Poison Garden. Not real poisons though, right?"

He holds the gate open for me. "Yes, Fi. Real poisons. Wolfs-bane, mandrake, ricin, opium, and other medicinal plants, even cannabis."

I glance at the withered plants. Maybe in the summer they're full and green, but now they're wilty. "At least they labeled them. I hope no bunnies get in here."

"Bunnies on edibles might be funny."

I giggle. "It would be. Remember how funny it was when we had to babysit Kevin's big black cat after the vet, and it was all wonky and banging off the walls?"

"Loki. Yeah, that was hella funny."

Sloan leads us to the back of the Poison Garden and points out a bench hidden under the curtained drape of long, hanging vines. As we slip inside the shelter of the tree, he checks his watch. "We're early. She'll be along shortly."

"Okay, you guys wait and do the witch meeting thing," Dillan says. "Emmet and I are going to go find the Blarney Stone. We won't go far. Send Bruin if you need us back."

"Have fun, kids." I wave my brothers away and wander around the interior of our tree enclosure. "So, Sarah, eh? How'd you contact her? If she's a volunteer you met, I'm surprised you had her number."

He arches a brow and smiles. "I never pegged ye for a jealous girlfriend. I kinda like it. Are ye stakin' yer claim? If ye'd like to torture the details out of me, I won't object."

I roll my eyes. "No. I'm asking a question. If you have her number, there'd be a reason. If she's not a person of interest romantically, then maybe there's a story there about how you know her. A project you asked her about? I don't know. I was making conversation."

He joins me at the wide trunk of the tree. "If it makes ye feel better, I found her number on Witchipedia."

Hubba-wha? I peg him with a look and wait for him to crack a smirk. He doesn't. "You're *not* serious. Witchipedia?"

He nods and circles his fingers in the air, prompting me to say something. "Go ahead and make yer jokes. I know ye can't help yerself. Get it out of yer system."

I wave that away. "*I* didn't make that funny. It *is* funny."

"It's also a valuable search engine when ye want to find something about witches. I simply typed in Sarah Connors and searched the profiles that came up and gave her a call."

"Sarah Connors?"

"Yes."

Oh, this is getting better by the moment. "Does she know she has the same name as Linda Hamilton's character in *Terminator?*"

"I expect it's been brought to her attention more than once. Perhaps we can make it through our meeting without bringin' it up at all."

I make a face. "I can try, but I can't make any promises. And if my brothers get wind of it, nothing will stop the outpouring of questions and comments."

"It might serve the Cumhaills well to realize that not every impulse needs to be acted upon."

I jump to grip a sturdy branch over my head and swing with my feet off the ground. "Well, it would serve you well to realize that not every impulse should be weighed and measured."

"What then? Should I forget we're on a quest fer the goddess and run off with yer brothers to kiss the stone?"

"No. You should wait for me because after we're done with Sarah Connors, I'm kissing the stone."

"Seriously? Now? Can't I bring ye back when we're not set on a task?"

I drop to the ground and brush off my hands. "You could, but I believe in living in the moment. Any goddess of mine will understand who I am and want me to seize the day. *Carpe diem*, broody. You seriously need to take your foot off the brake once in a while. All work and no play makes Jack Nicholson ax murder his family in a mountain lodge."

He blinks at me, and I know I've lost him.

"*The Shining*? No? Okay, we'll circle back to that another time. The point is you gotta give in to impulses once in a while, or you'll spontaneously combust."

"I'm sure I won't."

"That's your parents talking. Come on. Live a little. If you could do anything right now, what would it be? Do you know?"

"Och, I know."

"Is it something you really want?"

"It is."

"Then you should do it. No apologies. No hesitation. Just go for it—"

Faster than my mind can track, Sloan rushes me and pins me against the trunk of the tree. Gone is his guarded reserve. At this moment, Sloan is raw instinct.

His mouth moves over mine without restraint as one hand tightens in my hair and the other burrows into the open flap of my jacket. Splayed fingers slide up the ridges of my ribs and stop beneath the swell of my bra.

The bark is rough against the back of my head, but I don't care. I told him to seize the moment, and he is.

It suits him.

It suits me.

With my senses heightened, my awareness of him is intense. For once, the alertness has nothing to do with fight or flight and everything to do with being kissed senseless by the sweet and salty Sloan Mackenzie.

Never have I been kissed like this before.

Annnd that makes it all the more painful to be the one to put on the brakes. Yeah, I urged him to go for it, but we're in a public garden, and my brothers are here somewhere, and Sarah Connors is coming.

I break from the kiss and drop my head back to catch my breath. He takes my cue and slows things down. As I get reacquainted with oxygen, he nips the tender flesh of my throat, sending a zing of pleasure through me.

"Holy hell, Mackenzie. Where did that come from?"

Warm breath washes my neck as he chuckles. "Och, it's been below the surface of courtly manners for some time. Ye asked me to let loose a little. Now ye know. I told ye before that ye just need to say the word, *a ghra.* Until then, it'll keep."

He eases back a step, and I press my palms against the rough bark. I'm not sure my legs will hold me so I use the solid support to keep from melting into a puddle at his feet. "You call that letting loose *a little?*"

"Och, there's plenty more where that came from."

I swallow. How can my throat be dry when I'm salivating? "Good to know. You get an A-plus by the way. Full marks for seizing the moment. That was quite a moment."

His cocky chuckle is too damned sexy. "Agreed. It was at that."

I've never been that girl, the one who gets swept away by a chiseled jaw, a husky voice, or a set of rippled abs. I thought being raised surrounded by men exempted me from that batting of the eyes, girly gene. Wow. Big hells no on that one.

Sloan Mackenzie proved that.

As the two of us step apart, I fight the mighty pull of magnetism and settle. I'm glad to see that I'm not the only one affected. I've had a few steamy moments, cute guys, the bad boys, the musician—Da hates the musician—but this is different.

I'm not naïve enough to get swept away by a kiss and think it's true love, but this is more than a casual affair of the heart. I might be in big trouble here—my heart anyway.

Maybe Gran was right.

Guard yer hearts, guard yer parts.

My mental musing is interrupted by a gentle tap on the forehead. I blink up at Sloan and draw a deep breath. The cocky gleam in his eye has dimmed, and his brow is pinched. "Where'd ye go just there, *a ghra?* Did I overstep?"

"No. That kiss was perfect." I run my fingers through my hair and try to clear the cobwebs. "I just didn't realize we'd become so..."

"Incendiary?"

"...deeply affected by one another."

His gaze narrows. "Is that a bad thing?"

"No. It caught me off-guard, but it's good. I think it's good. It's scary because it matters. To me, anyway. Sorry... I'm scattered."

He gathers me close. "No apology. Take yer time. When ye've sorted through yer process, I'll be right here."

I open my mouth to say something and change course. "Someone's coming."

After a quick squeeze, he steps back. "This will have to wait, but yer right, it matters. Perhaps it's grown to be more than we realized but yer right again, it's good."

With that doozy floating in the air between us, I draw a steadying breath and turn toward the approaching footsteps.

The hanging tendrils of willow leaves sweep apart of their own accord. The opening breaks the privacy of the world Sloan and I shared, and a ponytailed pretty blonde girl about my age walks through to join us.

"Am I interrupting?" Her brow arches.

Sloan straightens beside me and presses a hand against the small of my back. "No, yer right on time. We appreciate ye makin' the trip. It's important, as I said on the phone."

"That's all ye said. I should tell ye that I'm not keen on the cloak-and-dagger routine."

"I thought it best to get into it face-to-face." He gives the shield on my back a gentle pat. "Any tingling? Any itching?"

"Nope. S'all good."

"In that case, we'll get to it." Sloan goes on to inform Sarah about the dark witch covens banding together to steal raw prana from the ley lines. He doesn't mention the Cistern of The Source or Gobekli Tepe but instead keeps the deets to the information we can share without fear of repeating the past week's events.

"How much prana did they make off with?" Sarah asks.

"The goddess said nine casks. She's tasked us to track them down and return them to the source as well as find out who's responsible and bring them to justice."

"This is more involved than I expected. The kind of people yer talkin' about can be dangerous and cruel."

I nod. "We know that firsthand, but Sloan thinks you being a white witch makes you different, an ally in this. I admit I'm not sold. My experience with witches so far has been hostile at best."

She scowls. "We *are* different. White is not gray, and it is certainly not dark."

"Sorry. I didn't mean to piss you off."

"How did you like bein' lumped into the same pot as the Barghest druids?"

"You heard about that?"

"There are no secrets among the empowered ones of the Emerald Isle. What ye did at Ross Castle when ye rescued the fae from bein' siphoned is well-known and respected. Some think it was a druid mess to clean up in the first place because the Barghest are yer own sect."

"The Barghest aren't druids. They pervert everything we stand for and try to pass themselves off as druids."

"Ye mean like gray and dark witches pervert what true Wiccans stand for and call themselves witches? It offends us as much or more as it did you to be guilty by association."

I get that. "All righty then, consider me set straight. Do you have a way to help us find them?"

"Perhaps. I'd need to speak with my coven and get the approval of our Magis to get involved. If you're telling the truth and this is a direct request from the goddess, we are bound and honored to serve."

Sarah pulls her phone from the pocket of her long, peasant skirt and steps outside the drape of willow leaves. I strain to hear what she's saying, but she must have lowered a cone of silence around herself because there's no sound.

"So, Sarah. She's a very pretty girl."

Sloan blinks down at me and shrugs. "I hadn't noticed."

I roll my eyes. "Liar."

He chuckles. "All right, I might have noticed, but she never caught my interest. Face it, Cumhaill. Ye knocked me for a loop from the first time we met."

"I nailed you in the nuts, you mean."

He winces. "Don't remind me."

"The second time too."

"I recall."

"Huh, so maybe that's the trick women have been missing all these years. If you want to get a man's attention, bag-tag him from the start."

"That's poetic." Dillan sweeps open the leaves of the tree behind us and saunters in.

"You should write for Hallmark, Fi," Emmet says, swaggering behind him buck naked. "Speaking about man junk. How about those sweats you brought for me? Good call on that, by the way."

I hustle over to the tree trunk to get those. I dropped the backpack when Sloan laid one on me and forgot all about it. "Oh, and I should warn you. We're still talking with—"

"Oh, my," Sarah says, eyes wide. She saunters back into the convo with amusement plain on her face. "Who have we here?"

Any sane male would cup his junk and step behind the tree. Emmet isn't that guy. "Emmet Cumhaill," he says while striding straight toward her, hand extended. "Had a bit of an issue with my first animal transformation. Sorry for the nudist routine."

"No apology necessary." She eyes him up and down. "Ye know how to make quite a first impression. I'll give ye that."

"He makes an impression all right." I hand Emmet the bundle of clothes and point at the trunk of the tree. "Could you at least pretend to have an ounce of modesty?"

"Yes, ma'am."

Emmet struts off, putting a little extra sway in his stride, and I giggle. "You'll have to excuse my brother. He used to climb out of his crib as a baby and fell on his head one too many times."

"Hello...I can hear you."

"Yeah, yeah, put your pants on, Magic Mike." I gesture at Dillan. "This is another of my brothers, Dillan. D, this is Sarah Connors."

"No shit!" Emmet jogs out from behind the tree. "Sarah Conners? Hasta la vista, baby. I'll be back. You're terminated, fucker."

She rolls her eyes. "Whatever quip ye come up with, I've heard it. It's old."

"Challenge accepted." Emmet holds up his fist for Dillan to bump.

"It's better if you don't engage." I flick my hand to shoo them away. "So, what did your coven say?"

"Oh, right. Sorry, I got distracted by the naked bit."

I hold up my finger as Emmet opens his mouth. "Not a word about your naked bits. Focus."

Emmet chuckles. "Cranky pants."

"Sorry, Sarah." Sloan shifts to turn her away from the chaos. "Ye were sayin'?"

"The coven will gather. First, they'll test that yer tellin' the truth about the goddess and her wishes. Then, if that checks out, we'll help ye all we can."

"Excellent. We're glad to have yer help." Sloan holds his hand out to me, ready to leave.

Emmet does the same and holds out his hand to Sarah. "Sarah Connors, come with me if you want to live."

Sarah shakes her head and looks at me. "Is there an off switch?"

I laugh. "If there is, I've never found it."

CHAPTER FIFTEEN

"Blarney Woolen Mills. With every stitch comes a story." I scan the sweaters in the display window as we head past them and groan. It's a shame we've got places to be. "These sweaters are so beautiful. Look at that one. Stunning."

Sarah smiles. "A family business since 1823. Aran sweaters are an Irish treasure. They were originally knit for the fishermen to keep them warm and dry during their days out on the water. Each stitch pattern holds a distinctive interpretation. They're knit in Kilcar, County Donegal, and are all one hundred percent merino wool."

I want to stop and press my nose to the window. I would if we weren't trying to track down power-hungry witches. "Well, they're beautiful. Oh, look at the button collar on that one. It's long and has pockets."

"Yes, the coatigan. It's very popular."

Dillan chuckles. "Are we here to save the world or buy Irish knits?"

I stick my tongue out at him. "Fine, but the next time you want to stop and look at a motorcycle parked outside the pub, I'm going to remind you of this moment."

"Forewarned."

Sarah gestures farther down the walkway, and we carry on. Her coven doesn't meet in the mill store itself but in a private room of the building's hotel. I nod to the ladies as we step inside, surprised at how normal they look.

No pointy hats or cloaks or besoms in sight.

They represent an eclectic array of appearance and personalities from elegant, older ladies, to mom types, to a lively bunch of twenty-something girls, to a mousy redhead in the corner with her nose in her book.

"*Dia dhuit,*" Sloan says as we join them. "It's good of ye to have us. We appreciate ye comin' together to hear us out and hopefully help."

One of the elegant older ladies, a tall woman with cropped brown hair and questionable fashion sense, gestures at the large wooden table in the room's center. "When we heard yer claim that Our Lady asked it of ye Herself, it seemed too important to ignore."

"And too wild to believe," one of the younger girls adds.

"Fair point, Delia."

Sloan pulls my chair out for me and takes the seat to my left. Emmet sits on my right, and Dillan stands behind us. He may not have his cloak on, but he's always ready to be called to arms.

When we're seated, Sarah gestures at the brunette woman who welcomed us. "This is Shona Fraser, Magis of our coven. Magis, this is Sloan Mackenzie, and Fiona, Dillan, and Emmet Cumhaill."

"Yer Lugh Cumhaill's kin, aye? The Americans?"

I shake my head. "We're Lugh's grandchildren, but we're Canadians. We live in Toronto."

"Same thing. Isn't it?"

Emmet chuckles. "No. We're the ones who live in igloos with our pet moose and eat poutine, eh?"

I bite the inside of my cheek to keep from laughing.

Shona waves that away but by the look on her face, she's not sure if he's joking or not. "But yer the druids that live in the city. The ones causin' the stir."

I'm not sure what that has to do with anything, but who am I to diss the small talk? "I suppose that's us, yes."

She gives us an assessing glance. "Interesting."

I'm not sure how.

Sloan folds his hands together on the table and flashes her a winning smile. "Sarah mentioned ye'd like to test us to ensure our story rings true before we get into the meat of things. Are we ready to do that now?"

"In a bit of a rush, are ye lad?"

"Ye could say we are. When the Grand Mother sets ye on a path of importance, expedience seems prudent."

"I suppose that's true—*if* that's true."

I glance at Sarah across the table, and she sends me an apologetic smile. "The sooner we confirm it, the sooner we can make a decision, true?"

The coven Magis taps a glossy nail against the surface of the table and purses her painted lips. "*Maith go leor.*"

Sarah nods. "All right. Good enough."

The white witches of Blarney escort us to the next room. It's empty of furniture and has a closed pentacle painted on the floor. They sit the four of us in the middle on our knees and light a different colored candle at the five points of the elements.

Sarah steps outside the circle once we're settled and accepts a staff. "Witches and druids alike share a reverence for the five elements. In this casting circle, we have the quarters marked as well as the ether. To the east, the yellow candle represents air."

She turns in a quarter turn and points at the next candle. "South is represented by the red candle and corresponds with fire. At the west point, the blue candle represents water, and to the north the green candle is earth."

Emmet points at the white one at the top of the pentacle. "That makes that one spirit, right?"

Sarah nods. "Spirit, or ether."

The coven draws around us in a circle, each of them holding a wooden staff. Thirteen women lay their wooden lengths on the floor around the outer edge of the pentacle, crossing end over end until a continuous circle surrounds us.

"This is a circle of truth," Shona says. "Once we cast our spell, there will be no way you can lie to us. We will know the truth of things discussed and all will be revealed."

I see the frown clouding my brothers' gazes, and I agree. That sounds sketchy. I raise my hand and wiggle my fingers. "So when you say we won't be able to lie, do you mean about what happened with the goddess, or is this a blanket *carte blanche* kinda thing that gives you access to our personal business?"

"Do you have things you wish to hide?"

"Of course. Don't you? Doesn't everyone? Do you want to be questioned about secrets you vowed to keep, people you're protecting, or artifacts you don't want falling into the hands of others?"

The witch smiles, but there is no humor in her expression. "You mistake us for the dark practitioners you seek. We are white witches, women of our word, women of honor living our best lives in harmony with the earth and all her bounties."

"Fiona meant no offense, Magis." Sloan lays on that deep, silky tone he saves for calming females.

Come to think of it; he uses it on me quite often.

Am I being tamed?

Rude.

"If yer honest with yerself, her question is valid, and with what little experience she's had with the empowered community, quite understandable."

The mousy redhead has traded her book for a tray of tiny china teacups. She doesn't speak, nor does anyone pay her any attention. She sets down the tray on the sideboard outside the circle and retreats to her corner.

Sarah lifts her hand, and the cups rise into the air. When she gestures toward us, they float into the circle and hover in front of us. While that's happening, two younger witches set votives between the pillars burning at the main five points.

When all the candles are lit, Shona gestures to the teacups. "Please drink, and we'll begin."

Being a druid, magic in our everyday lives is kept to a minimum. To these women, wielding magic seems effortless. It makes me wary of what else they might be able to do.

Witches be bitches, after all.

I pluck my cup out of the air and study the floaties bouncing on the surface of the oddly champagne-colored tea. "What is in this mighty veritas serum we're drinking?"

"It's a mixture of China black tea, lemon balm, eyebright, mugwort, and rose hips," Sarah says. "It's commonly considered a divination tea, which simply means it stimulates the third eye chakra and opens the gate for honesty. You will be completely aware of what you say and remember everything. We're not trying to trick you in any way."

"We have your word you'll stay on the topic of our experience with the goddess and nothing personal, or things we've taken oaths not to repeat?"

Shona's gaze blazes fire as the lines around her lips crease. "Asked and answered. That's twice you've implied we share traits with the witches you seek. We may believe in harm to none, but we won't stand to be insulted."

"It really will be fine, Fiona," Sarah says. "I respect what yer family has done here in Ireland. I gave ye my word and brought ye here in good faith. Ye'll have to trust me."

I sense no deception, and since neither my Fianna shield nor my evil film of darkness weighs in on the matter, I lift the teacup to my lips and down it on a oner.

The tea is warm, thick, bitter, and tingles on my tongue. While it won't win any awards for taste, over the past few weeks I've been forced to drink far worse.

When the boys have finished their truth potions, we each set our cups on the floor before us and look around.

"What now? How long does it take to work?"

The two younger witches who set up the extra candles step away from the circle and return, each of them carrying a weighty black velvet bag in her hands.

They retrieve several beautiful stones and set them carefully around the perimeter of the circle. Each of the stones is the size of a chicken's egg and a rich, blood red.

Dillan's eyes widen as he glances down at the stone closest to him. "Those aren't genuine rubies, are they? Because *hello*, they're huge. They have to be worth a fortune."

A brunette witch in a long green smock nods. "The Rubies of Ravenhurst have been part of our coven ceremonies for centuries. They're star rubies, which are an especially strong stone when used to call the elements to aid in our workings."

With the rubies in place, one of the girls takes a large iridescent orange-gold opal out of the bottom of her bag and hands it to Shona. As she passes her Magis the stone, its surface glimmers with fiery flashes as it catches the light of the candle flames.

"This is a copper sunstone." Shona strokes its smooth surface with a lover's caress. "It's an exceedingly rare type of feldspar found in a remote part of India. Sunstone heightens intuition and allows a person's true self to shine through. Which of you will hold it while being questioned?"

Since I'm the one with the early warning system stamped onto my back, I raise my hands and accept the stone.

The gemstone fills the cupped palms of my hands and is

warm against my skin, warmer than it should be considering it only just came out of its holding bag.

As it sits in my palms, I stare at it and frown.

"Is it supposed to do that?" I study the stone, wondering if this will turn out to be a Wiccan game of hot potato.

"Do what?" Sarah asks.

"Heat up in my hands. I'm not sure why, but it's getting really hot."

Sarah's flaxen eyebrows arch and she looks at Shona. "I don't know of anyone outside the Wiccan sect who can feel the fire within a sunstone. You are a remarkably interesting woman, Fiona."

I shrug aside the discomfort of the heat of the stone seeping into my skin. "Just being honest. That's why we're here right? Are we ready to roll on that? I'd like to getter done and give you back your pretty rock."

Shona pegs me with a quelling look, but I don't give her the satisfaction of backing down.

"We're wasting precious time here, and I don't know about you, but I don't want to be on the goddess's shit list."

"Neither do we."

"Well, when she asks us how the dark witches managed to slip into Satan's ass crack, I don't want to throw you under the bus and say the white witches of Blarney were too busy playing supernatural parlor tricks to help us."

"Parlor tricks? You think we're wasting your time?"

"Yeah, I do."

"Do you also think fledgling druids we welcomed into our sanctum should blackmail us into doing what you need us to do?"

"No. That's not what I'm saying. I think you should *want* to help, but you're acting intentionally difficult. I'd think serving your goddess should be something you embrace. I don't get the hesitation. I also don't get that blouse with that skirt. Do you have a mirror in your bedroom?"

Sloan hisses and clucks his tongue beside me. "Fiona has a tendency not to filter, Magis. Apologies."

Yeah, okay, maybe I shouldn't have said that.

Come to think of it, why did I say that?

The tingling in my tongue is making my throat feel thick. The hot rock in my palms is making me sweat. "I need some air. I don't like this."

"You okay, Fi?" Emmet asks. "You look weird."

"She looks beautiful," Sloan says, his gaze far too heated for public view. "And all the more beautiful because she doesn't realize it and doesn't care."

"Such a sexy, sweet-talking stud," I say, a heavy sigh escaping my lungs. Wait. Why did I say that? Why am I here gushing over my boyfriend when there's danger approaching and work to do?

I rise from my knees and turn full circle. "I've had enough. Sarah, I appreciate your intention to help, but some people are talkers while others are doers. No amount of girl talk and rock-holding will fix what your bad apple witch cousins are doing. We've gotta move on."

Shona frowns. "What now? You're confident you'll find the witches on your own?"

"That's the plan. It would've been great if you could've helped, but hey, you do you. I'm not sure how we'll find them, but Sloan is really smart, not to mention the best kisser *evah*. He'll figure it out. He gives me the credit for most things, but he's too modest. He's a rockstar."

"And what happens when you find these witches?"

"We take them down or take them out, whichever gets the job done. The goddess made that clear. We recover the stolen prana and return it to its source at all costs. It wasn't meant to be taken and used the way they intend."

"You still profess this is the will of the goddess?"

"I don't *profess* anything. The goddess, Our Lady, Mother Nature, whatever you want to call her, stood ten feet in front of us and gave us our mission. Since you weren't mentioned in the debrief of what needs to happen, your reputation isn't on the line. We, however, took an oath, so thanks for the tea. It's been a slice. Druids are leaving the building."

I gesture for my brothers and Sloan to get up and make a dramatic exit with me. When the four of us are on our feet, Shona holds out her hand.

"Well done, Miss Cumhaill. You can give me the sunstone now. It has done its work."

I shake my head wondering what she's talking about. This woman is infuriating. She talks in circles and plays games when lives are at stake.

I hand her the rock and point at the circle. "If you don't mind, I'd appreciate it if you close the circle so we can leave. If not, Sloan can simply transport us out. Did I mention that? More than a pretty face and a sexy bod, this one. He's so freaking talented it blows my mind. I heart him, hard."

Sloan chuckles behind me. "I think ye drank yer tea too quickly. Yer a bit love-drunk. They get the picture. The goddess set us on a task, and we have to get the prana back before the dark witches do something terrible with it."

I swallow as he pulls me to his side. He's so pretty. "You smell *reeeally* good, Mackenzie."

Sloan and my brothers chuckle. "Nice of ye to notice."

The effects of the witch's divination tea wear off over the next half hour and if I could shrink into the shadows and disappear into the corner, I would. It's not like I can be mad at the witches either. Shona may have been subtle about seeking her truths, but true to her word, she never asked me about anything other than what we came here for.

I am the weakest link.

Loose lips sink ships and all that.

"Och, stop lookin' so scarlet." Sarah pulls out the chair opposite me and sets down two pints of Irish stout. While the boys fill the witches in on the details of what we know and care to share, Sarah has excused the two of us to give me a little distance from my heart's desire before I make more of a fool out of myself than I already have.

I take a sip and let the strong taste of roasted malt soothe my rough edges. Unfortunately, the alcohol content in a stout is low. Maybe I could get her to give it an infusion.

Yeah no, who am I kidding. There isn't enough alcohol in Ireland to make this better. "Any chance someone could hide in this room for life and join the coven? I'm asking for a friend."

Sarah's laugh is bubbly and makes me smile. It's similar to the giggles I get from my little niece, Meg. "Ye did fine. Honestly, that was one of the more reserved truth sessions. Ye did well."

"*Reserved?* I don't think anyone has ever used that word around me before. Certainly not after I gush over a boy in front of a room full of strangers."

Sarah runs a finger down her glass and draws a line through the condensation. "Not just strangers. The good news is that yer brothers were there too."

I meet her gaze over the rim of my glass. "How is that good news?"

"Emmet seems to have moved on from tormenting me with *Terminator* quotes and is now solidly ready to start coddin' ye about yer affections fer Sloan. Thanks for that."

I hold up my glass and cheers her. "Glad you benefit from my humiliation."

She lifts her beer in response. "However long the day, the evening will come."

I take another couple of sips. "Hey, and you never know, maybe Emmet will streak again and take the torch of embarrassment from me."

"Only, he didn't seem all that bothered."

I chuckle. "Emmet's a nut. I'm sorry your first meeting was a full monty howeyah."

She leans back in the ladderback chair and smiles wide. "I'll not complain about gettin' a gander at the cut of his jib. I expect there are a good many ladies back home who want to spend an hour or two with that fine thing."

"He is popular."

"And yer fella is no slouch either. So, no one was surprised ye think highly of him or that ye find him attractive."

I roll my eyes. "He'll be impossible to live with now."

"Nah, he seems solid. Ye've nothin' to stew over."

I wish that were true. Only I don't have time to sit here and stew. "Okay, pity party is over. Let's get in there."

I find my guys milling around the table in the first room we came into when we arrived an hour ago. Several witches are working diligently, assembling cuttings, wooden bowls filled with water, candles, etc.

"What are ye usin' in yer smudge wands, Ginny?" Sloan leans in to watch the process.

A middle-aged ginger in a blue smock lifts her hand to show him the sprigs of plants she's binding into six-inch lengths. "I chose white sage, sweetgrass, palo santo, dried orange peel, and lavender for the cleansing. Then, I added ague root and mallow for protection in case they're using black magic. If they're cloaking their location, there will be spells set to stop prying eyes from finding them."

Emmet lifts a wooden box off the floor, and the brunette witch who talked about the rubies selects a few candles from within. "This close to Samhain, the energy will be strong. That might help."

Sloan looks up and winks at me. "Hiya. Come see what we've

done."

I exhale most of my anxiety and join him at the table. "We're settin' up for a scryin' ceremony. Three of the coven will work the bowls while the others work the spell."

"I think we're ready." Ginny turns to the other girl at the table. "Brigid, tell the others to come in, will ye?"

When the witches return, the four of us step back from the table and let them work.

A hundred white candles are set up and glowing warmly on the sideboard, window ledges, fireplace hearth and mantle, and shelves around the room. Three women take their places centered on three sides of the square table. In front of them sit wooden bowls filled with water.

The rest of the coven fills in around them.

Ginny and Brigid hand out smudge sticks to the others, and they tilt them into the candle flames until they catch. Smudge sticks don't burn like a match. They smolder and give off smoke like incense.

In a slow exploration of the room, a half-dozen women move mindfully in a clockwise motion whispering a mantra chant in Latin. When they pass behind and in front of us, the smoke ascends, and I breathe it deep into my lungs.

The energy it gives off is a pure delight and raises the hair on my arms.

Ting.

Shona raises a chunky wand from the rim of a singing bowl and draws the wand's surface around the top edge in a slow, even movement.

The sharp sound of her striking the side is swallowed by a harmonious sound flowing over us like a gentle vibration of calm. I close my eyes and try to find my Zen.

When I tried to use my singing bowl at home, it sounded more like the shrill pitch of playing wine glasses. This song is much more hypnotic. It makes me feel floaty.

That may or may not have something to do with the drugging tea and the pint of stout I downed.

Shona walks one full circle around the table moving wither-shins—counter-clockwise—until she returns to where she began at the fourth side of the table. "Ladies, your crystals have been cleansed."

"Blessed be, Magis." Each of the three women at the scrying bowls reaches forward and chooses a quartz crystal from inside the singing bowl. In unison, they place them in the water before them, then extend their right arms back toward the center of the table.

Shona holds her arm out too, and their hands stack much like the boys do when transporting with Sloan. From Shona's hand, a long black chain with a pendulum dangles over a map.

The three witches tending to the scrying bowls focus only on the water's surface while Shona focuses on the map in the center of the table.

Goddess of the sun and earth,
We hear your plea and prove our worth.
Unseen and unknown the enemies be,
Their place of hiding reveal to me.
To reclaim the prana, of which you asked,
Location revealed, and foe unmasked.
So mote it be.

Shona's words hang in the air like the suspended pendant crystal as the pendulum begins to sway. After a few seconds, the sway becomes a swing.

At first, I'm totes thinking this is like the seventh-grade sleep-over when Gabbi Clarke brought out her Ouija board and we all knew she was pushing the hand guide.

Yes, I know magic is real now, but after living twenty-three years as a skeptic, it's hard to believe the things I see.

Goddess of the sun and earth,
We hear your plea and prove our worth.
Unseen and unknown the enemies be,
Their place of hiding reveal to me.
To reclaim the prana, of which you asked,
Location revealed, and foe unmasked.
So mote it be.

The second time Shona recites the spell, my shield wakes up. It's not an itch or a burn so much as a niggle. For the eleventeen-millionth time, I wish there was an owner's manual on my Fianna shield.

What's the difference between a niggle and a tingle? A tingle and an itch? An itch and a burn? A burn and a flare?

No idea. Thankfully, this is only a niggle.

"It's working." Sarah smiles over at us. "Everyone, stay focused. Let's all say the spell with Magis the third time through."

I know from my days watching Prue, Piper, and Phoebe on *Charmed* that the power of three is important to witches. And yeah, as they start the chant the third time, my shield gears up from a niggle to an itch.

Goddess of the sun and earth,
We hear your plea and prove our worth.
Unseen and unknown the enemies be,
Their place of hiding reveal to me.
To reclaim the prana, of which you asked,
Location revealed, and foe unmasked.
So mote it be.

The pendulum swings in an unnaturally jerky motion as if two opposing forces are battling for control. Do the witches we're after know we're searching for them?

Is that what my shield is trying to tell me?

I wince and shift in place, my back's reaction growing uncomfortable. Dillan notices me squirming and shrugs. I point at my back and Emmet and Sloan both catch on. Sloan presses a hand on my back and sends me healing energy.

It does nothing.

Should I stop the ceremony? We're so close.

But if I ignore the danger to innocent witches to catch a group of monster witches, doesn't that make me a monster too? I frown and step forward. "I think we need to stop. I sense danger, and I don't want to see you hurt."

"We're close," Shona says. "If I can stabilize the pendulum we'll have them."

Emmet strikes off across the floor as silently as a cat. "I'm a buffer. I can boost your power if that helps." He stands directly behind Shona, and when she gives him her approval, he clasps her shoulder.

The pendulum's battle is won within minutes.

The tip of the shard locks onto the map, and Sarah smiles. "Got them! They're in Limerick."

Sarah's words are barely spoken when my shield flares hot. I launch forward, rushing to intercede. "Stop! Back away from the table. We need to shut this do—"

An incredible force bursts through the center of the table.

The *crack* is deafening.

Wood splinters.

Witches are thrown.

The force of the blast hits like a wrecking ball and knocks me off my feet. Bodies fly, and arms and legs flail through the air.

I can't make sense of it.

I hit the floor as the world explodes.

Then I black out.

CHAPTER SIXTEEN

I wake in darkness, and every part of me is screaming for attention. My chest is crushed, and I can't breathe. My legs are pinned, and I can't move. My head is pounding, and I can't think. What. The. Fuck. Stupid witches.

Not the white witches—the other ones.

Through the distant buzz fritzing in and out of focus, I hear my name...and crying...and growling.

"Sloan? Fi? Would one of you please fucking talk to us?" The panic in Dillan's voice hurts my heart.

I try to speak. Dirt and bits of debris coat my tongue. I taste copper pennies. Shifting my tongue around the filth in my mouth, I find the raw flesh on the inside of my lip where I must've bitten myself.

Either that or something slammed me in the face.

"Fiona Kacee Cumhaill, where the fuck are you?"

Where am I? I don't know. Where *am* I?

Something about the worry in my brother's tone keeps me fighting against the undertow of oblivion. "*Mar...co.*"

"Polo. Thank fuck. I'm coming, Fi."

I wake a second time when Dillan excavates me from the rubble of the explosion. He pulls off the building that fell on me. No. Wait. The weight crushing me isn't a building. It's Sloan. The building was on top of him.

"Is he alive?" I roll to the side but can't get up.

Emmet lays him out and checks for a pulse. They're both covered in blood, and I'm not sure which one of them looks worse off.

"Emmet? You hurt?"

He offers me a forced smile. "Not as much as most. I was behind Shona and sheltered from the brunt. I lived."

I hear his meaning. Others didn't. Someone's dead. Maybe several someones. "Who?"

"Later." Dillan scoops under my knees and lifts me free of the wreckage. "Let's get you two into the other room so we can see what's what."

My head lolls to the side and rests against his arm. I'm looking at cars in the parking lot. Where did they come from? "Where's the wall?"

"Mostly on top of you two."

"*Oh*, that's what that was."

When he sets me down in the next room, the world spins, and I hang my head forward. "For a minute there, I thought a hurricane hit us, and the mill decided to touch down on my chest."

"Nope. Mostly that was Sloan."

"How is he?" My heart races with all the emotions I never wanted to feel again. After losing Brendan, I swore I would keep everyone safe. I'd bundle my entire family in bubble wrap and cotton and Kate Spade micro-plush blankies if I had to, but nobody else would die on me.

I like to think that I'm a strong woman.

I'm not. I hurt and bleed and feel a loss as deeply as anyone else, if not more.

"Hey, now." Dillan wipes my tears. "It's okay, Fi. Sit here with Sarah, and I'll check. Emmet and I will bring him right out, I swear."

Sarah squeezes my shoulder, and everything about this feels wrong. These women were hurt because of us, but she's comforting me.

I give myself a shake and smile at her. "What happened? I get the part about the explosion, but what was it?"

"As near as we can tell, it was a reversal on our tracking spell. I've never seen so much power harnessed to a reversal, but from what ye said about the stolen prana, I suspect they're puttin' it to good use."

"Or bad use in this case."

She sinks into the seat beside me and runs her fingers through her matted blonde hair. "Bad use fer sure."

Dillan returns with Emmet, the two of them each tucked under one of Sloan's shoulders. I launch to my feet, but I'm as unsteady as a drunken fifteen-year-old and pretty much plow into them.

"Wow, okay Fi." Emmet scrambles to catch me with his free hand. "Good job on testing our strength and reflexes. Gotta keep us on our toes."

I focus on locking my knees and pulling my shit together. "Sorry, I'm a bit wonky."

Sloan straightens in their arms and flashes me an uneven grin. "Weak in the knees from heartin' me hard or from the kiss I laid on ye?"

I exhale a huge sigh of relief. "Dream on, Mackenzie. It takes more than a stolen moment of hot and heavy to turn this girl's head."

"As yer brothers say, challenge accepted."

When the boys set him down on a chair, I drop to my knees

and hug him around the waist. "Thanks for not being dead on me."

"Ditto."

I squeeze his hand and stand to check on my brothers. "That goes for you too. No more losses. Not now. Not ever."

Dillan and Emmet both smile and hold out their pinky fingers. I link mine with theirs, and we make it official.

"What are we dealing with?" I look at Sarah and honestly, I don't know what to say to her that will help. "I'm so sorry. If I had any idea that this would happen, we never would've involved you."

She wipes her damp cheeks, her tears smudging the silt and debris across her face in black swipes. "This doesn't fall on you, Fi. If it weren't fer yer warning more of us would've died. If it weren't fer yer brother takin' me to the floor, I'd likely be one of them."

It doesn't surprise me one bit that Emmet is a hero. It's too bad she learned about it this way. "What can we do?"

Sloan sits up straighter and scowls. "We do what we planned to do. We take the location of the witches, and we track them down and end this. As much as it pains me to have played a part in the suffering here, letting the witches responsible get away serves no one."

Sarah nods. "Come with me. I'll show you where we can wash up so we can be on our way."

Emmet cants his head and regards her with a gleam of admiration. "We? Are you joining our little justice league, Sarah Connors?"

"Ye bet yer finely dimpled ass, I am. Hurry now. I'll not have these bastards gettin' away while we lick our wounds. As Sloan said, that serves no one."

"Limerick is the fourth most populous city on the island of Ireland," Sloan says as the five of us take form. "It lies on the River Shannon, at the head of the Shannon estuary, where the river widens and flows into the Atlantic Ocean."

I study the lay of the land as we step to the edge of a copse of trees. In the distance, the ruins of a castle with a five-story tower dominate a rocky crag.

Huh, another Irish fortress. Imagine that.

"Let me guess. This castle has seen tales of history our Canadian buildings could never dream of. It's bursting with character and smells like a rotten root cellar."

Sloan sends me an ocular middle finger, but there's no heat in the look. "The city dates back from 812 CE, and yes, it has seen the violence of Viking raids, English wars, religious uprisings, and now Wiccan fugitives."

"Nailed it." I raise my palm to smack Dillan in a triumphant high-five, then catch Emmet's censure. "Sorry, Sarah. I tend to deal with difficult situations with humor and smartass comments. My bad."

Sarah nods. "Shona was not only my Magis, she was my aunt and my friend. Norah, Delia, Ginny, and Gwen were all friends. I owe it to all of them to bring these witches to justice and honor the goddess."

"We will. I promise."

My phone buzzes in my pocket, and I check the text. "Yeah, Patty says he wants to join the fun. He's ready when you are, hotness."

Sloan winks. "Oh, I like that one more than surly. All right, I'll pop over to the lair and get him."

Dillan raises a finger. "Can I tag along and make a quick pitstop at Granda's to pick up my cloak? I think it'll come in handy for infiltrating the ruins."

"Good idea." Sloan leans in and kisses my cheek. "Be right

back. Don't die while I'm gone. Emmet and Bruin, yer in charge. Bear, are ye on yer guard?"

The flutter in my chest is my signal to let him out. I release my hold on our bond, and he materializes beside me. "On duty and ready to shred."

Sarah squeals beside me, and Emmet catches her as her eyes roll back and she crumples to the ground.

I make a face. "Oops."

Dillan chuckles. "You handle that. We'll be right back."

When they *poof* out, I drop to my knee and brush Sarah's hair out of her face. Her eyes flutter as consciousness takes hold and I squeeze her hand. "Sorry. I should've warned you. I'm bonded to a spirit bear. He looks big and ferocious—"

"And he is," Emmet interjects.

"He is," I agree, "but he's also on our side and is one hundy percent reliable. Would you like to meet him?"

Sarah sits forward and puts her head between her knees. "Give me a moment."

"Sure thing." I straighten and leave her in Emmet's capable care.

"A bit timid, is she?" Bruin says.

"She's a white witch, and she's had a day. Considering what life has thrown at her, I think she's doing well."

"Emmet seems smitten."

I glance back and smile. "Emmet is a caregiver, and right now, Sarah needs TLC. That works for both of them."

"What did we miss?" Dillan says as he, Sloan, and Patty join us.

"In the three minutes you were gone? Nothing. Bruin appeared. Sarah keeled. It's been quiet ever since."

Patty comes over, and I bend down to hug him. He's pulled himself together since I saw him last. No longer the angry leprechaun of Facebook memes and lore, he's once again the loveable imp who taught me the *Jailhouse Rock* pole dance. "How's our queen?"

His smile is wide and infectious. "Och, she's in fine form. She's suckin' diesel but itchin' to have her revenge. Despite being a benevolent beauty by nature, being drained of her lifeforce put her in quite a mood. I wouldn't want to be anyone involved in this mess once she sorts out the kids and gets down to business."

I think about the torched Barghest bodies we found in the Doyle grove. "Agreed. I've seen what happens to people who upset her. It doesn't end well for them."

Emmet helps Sarah to her feet, and I wave them over.

"Sarah, this is my dear friend Patty. He was the one who alerted us to the trouble of the ley lines being siphoned." I consider telling her about the dragon queen but decide she's had enough revelations for one day. "Patty, this is Sarah, one of the white witches of Blarney. I assume Sloan and Dillan filled you in on what happened?"

Patty takes Sarah's hand and kisses her knuckles. "Condolences, wee one. Death leaves a heartache no one can heal; Love leaves a memory no one can steal."

If Sarah's shocked by receiving caring condolences from a leprechaun, she hides it well. "*Go raibh maith agat.*"

After thanking him for his words, she looks at me. "Yer a remarkably interesting woman, indeed."

Patty rests his hand on the top of his hatchet and gets back to the situation at hand. "What do we know?"

"Not much, sadly. We brought you into this the moment we had a target. The Blarney witches tracked the culprits here using a scrying spell, and here we are."

Dillan pulls the hood of his cloak up. "Sloan. *Poof* me into the shadows at the base of the ruins there and let me do some recon. I'll text when I'm ready to return."

"Be careful, D." I peg him with a serious gaze. "No more death."

He winks. "Would I go back on a pinky swear? Hells no. See you in a few."

Sloan nods, grips his shoulder, and *poofs* off. In another beat of my heart, he's back. Emmet and Patty are busy chatting about something while Sarah is sifting through the leaves on the forest floor and picking up stones.

Sloan pulls me around a tree to hug me. "How are ye holdin' up? Ye look tired."

I cling to him and bolster myself with his strength. "When life slows down, I really need a movie night. Flannel jammies, you, my brothers, Da, and Bruin, chicken nachos, the whole deal."

He chuckles. "I love it that *that's* yer perfect night."

I brush at the scrape beside his eye. It's stopped bleeding but hasn't started scabbing yet. "That's my PG perfect family night. Like Dillan says, I'm an onion. Lots of layers here."

"Would ye care to share on yer non-PG perfect night? Maybe it involves some Xs in the rating and someone I know?"

"I do, and it does. See, I said you were smart."

"I try."

"But you're also a dumbass."

He frowns. "What did I do now?"

"You shielded me from the explosion, didn't you?"

He sighs and shrugs. "A lot happened in a few seconds. It's over now."

I won't let him dismiss my concerns. "Don't get killed keeping me safe. Seriously, it will wreck me."

"You make it sound like it's inevitable."

"I hope not. Still, I don't want you hurt. Be more protective of your safety."

"Don't worry about me, Fi. Soon, this chaos and danger will take a back seat. Then we can have movie nights and chicken nachos and use up that box of latex yer Gran bought."

I cover my face. "Oh, gawd. Why did you bring that up? I'm seriously scarred."

He presses his forehead to mine as his body vibrates with laughter. "That was the most awkward moment of my life."

"Mine too."

"It came from a good place though."

I cast a glance at where the other three are still milling around. "Oh, it absolutely did. They're quite a pair, my grandparents."

"They are." As he's speaking, he fishes out his phone and nods. "Dillan's ready. Back in a flash."

I shake off the embarrassment of overprotective grandparents and head back to the others. Thankfully, Emmet hasn't said anything about the condom-tastrophe, so maybe he didn't retain all the particulars from when he was a kangaroo.

One can only hope.

"What are you guys up to?"

"Sarah's making us protection stones," Emmet says. "As a white witch, her attack is a non-lethal spell to immobilize and subdue."

"He calls them my nappy sacks." Sarah pulls a couple of the little jiggly pouches out of her bag and holds them up to show us.

"She doesn't want it to take us out, so she's preparing us counterspell stones."

"Okay, cool. Yeah, we welcome any help you can offer. Thank you."

Sarah sets a handful of stones on a clear patch of dirt and holds her hands over them. When her eyes roll closed, a white glow bursts free from her hands.

Seekers of justice, righteous and true
These stones that I bless will protect you.
Doers of evil will drop and sway
To face the goddess on judgment day.
So mote it be.

. . .

Her words hold power, and I find myself drawn in by the energy she emits when she's casting. White magic feels very different from what I've encountered before. Maybe it's me being new to things, but when she's finished, I feel stronger, more optimistic. "That was cool. Thank you."

Sarah dips her chin and color flushes her cheeks. "I may not wield a sword in battle, but my powers can help, and I want to do my part."

Emmet helps her off the forest floor and shrugs. "I don't have an offensive power either. I'm a buffer."

She giggles, slings her bag over her shoulder, and unzips the top. "I know all about you in the buff."

He waggles his brow. "Not the same thing, but there is that too. The goddess said my powers are as they are meant, but I haven't figured out what that means. She's given me strengths in healing, communication, and backup support, but yeah, I get how you feel about wanting to contribute in a meaningful way to the group."

"Exactly."

The two of them stand smiling at each other for a lot longer than the situation calls for, so I figure it's two's company, four's a crowd.

I step away, and Patty joins me on the retreat. "That's magic in the making, isn't it?"

"Seems so. I've never seen Emmet so consumed."

"Sometimes love is a cool wave lapping against hot sand and sometimes it's a strike of lightning raising the fine hairs tickling yer knackers."

I bark a laugh. "That's poetic, Patty."

He winks. "I thought so."

"What's poetic?" Sloan strides over to join us with Dillan in tow.

"Patty was waxing philosophical while we awaited your return. So, Dillan. What do we know? Where are we headed?"

The dark witches, or at least some of them, have holed up in a hidden fortress beneath Carrigogunnel Castle. Built around 1450 CE, during the Williamite War, the limestone fortress sits on the bank of the Shannon River, near the village of Clarina.

"I'm not sure if they stayed here after they attacked us because they thought they wiped us out or because they don't consider us a threat," Dillan says, "but they don't seem to be going anywhere."

Sloan frowns. "Are there guards on the access points? What's the lay of the land?"

Dillan turns to point. "On the east side is an adjoining house. Along the western side is a range of ruined buildings. The main gate is on the southern side with a smaller entrance to the west. There are guards on the ground and a lookout at the top of the tower."

"How many are we talking?"

Dillan frowns. "I'd guess twenty, but I have no idea how big their hideout is below or how many more they have down there."

"Did you see any sign of the silver casks they used to steal the prana?" I ask. "Anything that tells us that we're in the right place before we storm the Bastille?"

Dillan rakes his fingers through his ebony hair and huffs. "No. Nothing is telling us we're in the wrong place either. Does anyone have a sensitivity to fae prana? Could someone still sense it even if it's contained in those casks?"

That's a big no on that one.

Emmet pockets his stone and hands Dillan and Sloan theirs. "So, we're outmanned by powerful dark witches, have no idea who or what lies below, don't know if the prana is even here, and they know we're coming. Does that sum the sitch up correctly?"

I smack him in the arm. "Well, it sounds terrible when you say it like that. Glass half-empty much?"

He rolls his eyes. "Fi, sista mine, your half-full glass is about to get smashed on the stone floor and ground to smithereens. This is a hard no-go."

I frown. "Then we call Nikon and have him bring Da, Calum, and Aiden. Hell, I'm sure Garnet would come too."

"It still won't be enough."

"Then what do you suggest we do? Let them go? Not try? Since when do we quit?"

"I'm not saying quit. I'm saying we need to come up with a stronger offensive plan. It would be nice to catch them by surprise. Throw something at them they're not expecting."

I shake out my arms, but it does nothing to help the tension in my shoulders. Having a building fall on you isn't enjoyable at the time or in the aftermath of stiffening up. "They're dark witches siphoning the power of the Fae Realm. What aren't they expecting?"

We all stand there thinking for a moment when Sloan's face breaks into a wide smile. "I have an idea. Hear me out before ye say no. It's a three birds with one stone plan. The dragon queen gets her revenge. The young get an adventure and a snack. And it's *definitely* an offensive the dark witches won't see coming."

Sloan goes on to explain his plan, and I'm not sure I'm hearing him right. "Use the dragons as an offensive force? What if the babies get hurt?"

Dillan snorts. "That's like saying what if the mice hurt the herd of stampeding elephants barreling at them."

Sloan shrugs. "I understand yer protective of them, but it's unlikely the dragonborn will suffer any damage."

Patty doesn't look any more pleased with the idea than I am, but he sighs and shrugs. "I'll speak with Her Grand Benevolence about it. We'll see what she says."

Sarah looks at us like we've gone mad. "Yer serious? Dragons?"

I flash her a goofy grin. "Surprise."

CHAPTER SEVENTEEN

When the sky is dark, and the moon hits its zenith, the earth trembles beneath our feet. The flat ground beyond the forested area at the Carrigogunnel Castle opens, and a spiraling beast emerges into the air before crashing onto the grass beside a massive round hole. The first to emerge is the queen herself, then Dart, then twenty-two other dragonets.

The menacing beauty of them never ceases to amaze me.

Yes, I know most of the young by sight and a few of them by name, but they aren't pets, they aren't domesticated, and they certainly aren't obedient enough to consider them under our influence.

They are dragons—a brood of mythological beasts.

"Now, that's a sight we'll not soon forget." Da slings a heavy arm over my shoulder, his gaze locked on the queen getting her excited troop in order. "I'm damned proud ye made that happen, Fi. Ye'll look back on this in later years and realize it mattered."

"Or that I'm responsible for Europe being devoured by twenty-three fire-breathing, people-crunching, water-hoarding monsters."

"Och, ye don't believe that."

Don't I? I study them and consider that. "No, maybe not, but that doesn't mean I'm not afraid of it."

"Well, no. That's a fear that lies in the back of every parent's mind. Will my children do harm or do right by people? Will they take the values and lessons I've taught them and embrace them as their own? I worried worse still because I knew ye didn't have yer mam's softer side to mold ye."

I lean into his shoulder, and he presses his lips to my temple. "I think we fared pretty well."

I watch the queen fuss over her young, and despite the sad echo in my heart where Mam used to be, I'm content. "As much as I wish I had Mam as long as Aiden and Brenny did, or longer, maybe if I had, I wouldn't be the me I am."

"And yer a treasure by any measure."

"Right? I can slapshot into the corner of a net and take a punch like an MMA fighter, and yeah, I'm not girlie, and I don't give a flying fig about makeup, but maybe that was part of getting me here. And I love 'here,' Da. I know you worried, and you never wanted me tied to a life I didn't choose, but I did choose it, and it suits me."

"I won't argue that."

I hug him around his ribs and kiss his jaw. "You did good, Da. We all think so."

"It's easy when yer kids are perfect."

He meets my gaze and manages to keep from bursting out laughing for two whole seconds. "Perhaps perfect is a stretch. I have, however, loved every minute of it."

"Okay, everyone." Patty hops up on a stump and waves us in. "I think we're ready."

Da and I break apart, but he clamps the back of my shoulder as we walk and join the others.

Patty waits until we're all in position and continues. "The

queen will lead the young in from below while we take out the guards and stop anyone from fleein' into the night. I expect more than one will have the ability to portal, but the main objective is to reclaim the casks of prana."

I nod. "That's Mother Nature's primary concern. We'll track down the roaches that slip through the cracks later."

Patty lifts his chin. "Anythin' else you want to add, Fi?"

"Nope. That's about it. Thanks for coming. Be safe. And if for some reason a cask is damaged or leaking, the prana water glows pink with magic. Steer clear of it, and we'll regroup once we secure the site."

I look at Da and Sloan. "Anything else?"

Everyone shakes their heads, and Patty jumps down.

"May the luck of the Irish be with us all," Aiden says.

"May the Force be with you," Dillan adds.

"May the odds be ever in your favor," Calum chimes in.

"May the bird of paradise fly up your nose," Emmet tacks on.

I love my brothers. "May we get this done without becoming dragon kibble or witch fodder."

Da nods. "That one fer sure."

The lookout station at the top of the five-story tower is the first to go. Nikon and Sloan flash up there with two of Sarah's nappy sacks and are back before I have a chance to worry.

Then, we divide into two teams.

Sloan takes me, Patty, Emmet, and Calum to the small entrance on the west side of the castle. Nikon takes Dillan, Aiden, Da, Sarah, and Dora to the ruined buildings and will come in from the east.

Since we'll enter at different times from different points, there's no need to coordinate signals.

Emmet is disappointed about that. Since his highly acclaimed *Cotton Eye Joe* success, he's been dreaming up new ideas and keeping them heavily under wraps.

I'm scared even to imagine.

Sloan and Calum are our stealth team, and between Sloan's skill portaling and Calum's deadly accuracy with his arrows, we've eliminated four guards and are ready to head inside within ten minutes.

"Okay, buddy." I release Bruin. "Go tell the queen it's time." My bear circles us once and heads out. I call my armor forward, and we're good to go.

"Does anyone feel like maybe this is going a little too smoothly?" Emmet asks.

I throw him a look and groan. "Did you need to say that out loud? Geez. Don't jinx us."

"Like me saying that would—" Emmet gets knocked back on his ass as a blue blur pushes in beside me.

"You were saying?"

Emmet blinks up from the ground and frowns. "Manners matter, little dude."

I ignore Emmet's annoyance and pat Dart's head. "What are you doing here, buddy?"

Sloan frowns. "Yer supposed to be with yer mam."

Dart rubs his head against my shoulder and the purr he lets out is so cute it melts me.

"She is his mam," Patty says.

I sigh. "Right. I am, aren't I?"

He nods again, stomps his feet, and flaps his little wings. One day, likely not that far into the future, those wings are going to be massive and capable of carrying him farther than a hop over his siblings. One day soon he'll streak across the night sky.

Not yet. For now, they're two cute appendages with little dewclaws that stand only a foot or two off his back.

"Okay, you can come with me, but you have to be careful, and you have to listen. I don't want you hurt."

He shakes his head, draws in a deep breath, and blows a thin stream of fire into the air.

"Well, that doesn't stand out in the darkness, does it?" Sloan snaps and glares at me. "Can we try not to give away our position while there are still hostile witches around?"

"It's fine. We got the sentries. No one saw—"

A fireball hits the tree inches above our heads and explodes into a shower of magic energy.

Oh, shit. "Okay, so maybe someone saw it."

An incoming barrage scatters our group like pigeons in the park.

"Where are they?" I shout, crouched behind a rock.

"I need a higher vantage point," Calum says. "Sloan. *Poof* me up the tower."

Sloan crouch-runs a few steps and dive-rolls as the ground at his feet explodes. He grabs Calum's ankle, and they disappear.

Patty curses and joins me behind my rock. "How good is yer brother with that bow?"

"He's a sure shot and has an Eternalfull Quiver."

Patty nods. "Can't ask fer more than that, can we?"

I roll to my knees to peer over the rock, and my hair singes as another bolt of magic fire nearly takes my head off. "She's still there."

"Apparently."

"Emmet! You good?"

"Skittles and ponies."

"Glad to hear it." Dart grunts and my smile fades. He's in the open and exposed. "Buddy, get down. There are bad people—"

A bolt of magic hits Dart in the side, and he lets out a pitiful bellow. My hold on my dark side bursts beyond my grip.

My eyes sting as they burn through the glamor to keep them

normal. With violent fury in my heart, I search the darkness. Suddenly the black void is black no longer.

The ruined site flips into night-vision, and I see them. Three women, evil and hidden in the ruins around me. I see their malignant auras flaring against the backdrop of night.

It's like a heat signature. Only instead of them being orange-red from giving off thermal energy, they're a toxic olive green with clawing swipes of purple. I stare up to the tower and see the aura of Calum standing at the open window up top. His aura is tropical blue. I look down at Patty beside me. His is a swirly green. Emmet's is the same as Calum's.

"Fiona, get down." Sloan *poofs* in beside me, but before he can *poof* me out, I swipe away his touch.

"I see them. It's the eyes. I can see their evil." Sloan looks freaked. I can't help that. "Heal Dart. I got this."

Leaving Sloan behind, I call *Insect Plague* and throw my hand out at the two women crouched behind a mossy wall. Connecting with the beetles and bugs deep in the soil and the flying ants and horse flies, bees, and midges in the area, I call them to do my bidding.

"You shouldn't have struck my baby dragon," I say, my voice not my own. "That will be your last mistake."

As screams ring out, I kneel and connect with the stone beneath the last woman's feet. It's the work of a moment to open the ground up and have her swallowed. I let her fall into the caverns below to become a dragon snack.

When that's taken care of, I scan the area and ensure no one is hiding in the shadows. With my fingers pinched beneath my tongue, I let out a shrill whistle. "Okay, people, topside is clear. Let's move into the tunnels and see how the dragons are doing."

After wandering the endless tunnels of Gobekli Tepe, descending to the lower levels beneath Carrigogunnel Castle is a matter of a moment. Our group reunites with the others at the entrance Dillan detected with his gift. Earlier, we introduced everyone to the dragons so they'd know the difference between friend and foe. I'm still worried that if they're in a feeding frenzy, they might chomp one of us by mistake.

"I can't promise it won't happen, Fi." Patty jogs to keep up. "Only that I don't *think* it'll happen. The kids are maturing rapidly. They're smart."

I run a hand over Dart's scaly shoulder and pat him. "Too smart for their good sometimes. I don't want you to step into the line of fire again, dude. Thank goodness Sloan was able to heal you."

Dart gives me a sappy gaze, then rubs his cheek against Sloan and purrs.

"Looks like you soothed the green monster of jealousy at the same time you healed his owies."

Sloan chuckles and runs his palm over the bony framework of Dart's wing. "I'm glad we were able to build a new foundation. Make love not war, right Dart?"

Dart snorts and a puff of smoke escapes his nostrils.

"Besides," he says, "I understand the pull of yer magnetism. I explained to him that none of us can expect to be the only one in yer heart. Yer heart is far too big for that."

I smile and rub a hand over Bruin's furry rump. "True story. My heart is big enough to accommodate everyone—"

"Och, gross, is that all blood?" Sarah scrunches up her face, staring at a wide path of dark soil ahead.

I follow her pointed finger and yikes, gross is right. "My guess is yes. It might be best not to look too closely at things. The kids are messy eaters."

Bruin was right when he said Sarah seems a little timid. Aside from her determination to help us catch the witches and bring them to justice, she doesn't have much of a stomach for the fighting aspect of bringing bad guys down.

Not a lot of white witches on the execution trail.

"The good news is there don't seem to be any half-digested women lying around."

Emmet snorts and squeezes Sarah's wrist. "That's our silver lining girl. Careful, Fi. If you keep shining on us like that, we'll be stuck with our heads in the clouds."

I chuckle and resume playing the part of the raid party cheer-leader. "If you want to hang back for a little Sarah, no one would blame you."

She shakes her head. "No. I'm good. I want to help secure the prana so I can tell my coven the loss of our sisters wasn't for nothin'."

"It absolutely wasn't for nothin'," Sloan says. "We'll recover the prana and save lives. We'll return it to The Source, and the goddess will be pleased. Many of the women captured for their crimes instead of being killed are alive because of yer wee nappy sacks."

Emmet nods. "They'll face the judgment of the goddess and perhaps, in some small way, that will give purpose to the tragedy of their loss."

We come to the end of a torchlit corridor, and I stop at a closed door. My shield awakens and starts to burn. Stretching out my senses, I probe our surroundings for trouble on the horizon. When nothing definite comes back to me, I call in backup. "Bruin, you're on recon, big guy. I'm getting a full-on warning not to proceed."

"Yer shield?" Sloan asks.

"Yeah, it's lit up like a Griswold Christmas."

He frowns and raises a palm. *"Detect Magic."* After a long moment, his frown increases. "I've got nothin'. Yeah, Bear, ye better see what ye can find. Fi's shield has never let us down before."

"On it." Bruin dematerializes, and I step back from the door until he gets back. "Anything?"

"Ye could say that."

"What? What's behind the door?"

"A bomb. It seems armed and ready to blow up anyone stupid enough to barge in."

"I'll take a look," Nikon says. "Hang tight."

Before I have time to argue, he's gone.

CHAPTER EIGHTEEN

"Yep. It's a bomb all right," Nikon says when he rematerializes with us two minutes later. "Does anyone have any experience with such things?"

"Always cut the red wire," Calum says. "Or is it the blue wire?"

"Do f-bombs count?" Emmet asks. "If so, Dillan's definitely your man."

"Fuck off," Dillan snaps and rolls his eyes.

"Dude, you just proved my point."

Sarah steps forward. "Would ye like me to take a look at it? I might sense what spells they used to arm it."

Nikon looks at Da for the answer.

"No." Da purses his lips. "I think it's best if we simply portal to the other side and leave it alone. We can send someone down to disarm it later, but for now, let sleeping bombs sleep."

Sloan nods and holds out his hand. Nikon does the same.

Before we go, Nikon raises a hand, and a flashing red neon sign that says "Bomb. Do not open," appears in front of the door.

"Good thinking." Emmet smiles. "Wish I'd thought of that one."

Once we're all safely on the other side of the door, we continue down to the main cavern.

The space down here is less hole-in-the-ground, and more secret hideaway with the comforts of civilized living: tables and chairs, cots with blankets and pillows, they even have a little kitchenette counter with appliances hooked up to a witch disc.

My mouth falls open. "A prana-powered generator? Really? Does that seem sacrilegious to anyone else?"

Nikon seems equally offended by the setup. "So they steal the ultimate fae power and use it to make tea? What's the end game here? Are they magical preppers or something?"

"That's a good question." I stare at the massive hole in the wall where the dragons came through and can only imagine how terrifying that was for the witches.

Here they are, thinking they're snug in their hideout with bombs on the tunnels to take care of intruders and a cup of chamomile in their hands when a dragon family invades and chomps them up.

Sorry, not sorry. Sucks to be you.

Da and Aiden right an overturned table and gather some paperwork and maps off the dirt and blood-soaked floor. "We don't know why they stole the prana water or what they intended to do with it," Da says. "Once we have the motive, the answers might fall into place."

I scan the space, but it's obvious there aren't nine casks of prana power lying around. "The witch disc proves we're in the right place, so where are the casks?"

"I guess we spread out and do things the old-fashioned way. We investigate."

"But be careful of witch traps and bombs," I add.

Everyone spreads out and starts looking around. Aiden and I end up going through some of the notes he picked up off the floor. "It's all encoded," Aiden says. "Anyone know how to read witch cipher?"

He and I flip through the pages, looking, but come up empty-handed. "Hey, how's the housing issue going? Dillan mentioned your landlord is selling. Have you and Kinu found anything promising?"

Aiden shakes his head. "Being a cop gives me a unique knowledge of the areas in the city. Anything we've found to rent in our budget is either too small, not in the school district Kinu wants for the kids, or I know of some unsavory element in the area that I want nowhere near my family."

"That sucks. How long have you got?"

"He gave us sixty days' notice, so the countdown is on."

I squeeze his arm. "Everything works out the way it's meant to, right?"

"Right."

"So, as soon as we get this prana problem worked out, I'll help with the search. I'm sure the perfect answer will present itself."

"I hope so. If not, the basement at home is going to get very crowded."

"Meh, we can handle it. S'all good."

Aiden snorts. "You say that now."

We search a while longer before I get frustrated. "Does anyone have anything that tells us what they were doing down here? Anyone?"

"I might be able to help you there, Fiona." The dragon queen slithers through the hole in the wall and arches up like a cobra about to strike.

"Holy fuck," Aidan whispers behind me.

Yep. The queen dragon is piss-your-pants scary at the best of times. A casual chat in her lair—scary. Commenting on your latest Elvis dance moves—scary. And yep, leading her young on a witch-chomping mission of revenge—very, very, scary.

"Young Chua found something in the tunnel that accesses the waterway. I think you'll find it of interest. Come."

The queen arches in a turn and slips back into the tunnel like the fifty-foot deadly serpent she is.

"Does anyone else need a moment to make their trembling twigs work?" Dillan shakes out his legs.

Yeah, I'm pretty unsteady too, and I'm used to her. "I didn't know her eyes glowed like that."

Patty casts me a surprised look. "How'd ye think she sees when she's tunnelin' in the earth?

"Night vision?"

"Well, the ocular glow is her night vision."

"Good point."

Sloan pulls out a moonstone, rubs his thumb over the surface, and the smooth, white gemstone glows brightly enough to lead our way. He steps into the queen's tunnel, and we file in behind him.

"Which one is Chua?" I ask.

Patty frowns at me. "She's a little green drake. You know, the one who likes to lick yer ankles."

"Oh, right." I have no clue which one he means, but what kind of a mother of dragons can't remember her twenty-three dragon babies by their names and species types?

Fake it 'til you make it.

I pat Dart's back as he shuffles along beside me. I get at least one point for knowing a dragon's name.

This is Dartamont. Yay me!

The tunnel we're exploring is long and flat, and by my estimation of the queen's comment about it accessing the River Shannon, takes us under the grounds of the property toward the river.

The tunnel itself is dark although there are torches mounted on the walls at regular intervals. Sarah lights them as we go, so even without Sloan's magical moonstone, we'll be able to find our way back to the main cavern.

The flames burst to light behind the power of her magic and

cast a warm glow to mark our way. They also smell heavily of sulfur and lime. I'm not sure the light to stink ratio makes it worth being able to see, but I keep my opinion on that to myself.

"*Soooo*," Emmet says, "is it horribly dark, damp, and creepy down here, or is it just me?"

I shake my head. "Not just you. If ghosts haunted the catacombs of old castles, this would be prime spook territory."

Emmet scowls at me. "Aren't you a breath of fresh air today? First, the half-eaten witches comment, and now you're conjuring up images of dark hauntings."

"You were the one who said it was horribly creepy."

"Kids, stop it," Da says.

Emmet makes a face at me. "Fix your eyes. You're freaking me out."

I shrug, but he's not wrong. My comments aren't usually so macabre, and my eyes are totes creepy.

I step to the side of the tunnel for a second, recite Sloan's spell to restore the glamor of normalcy, and rejoin the flow of footsteps.

"Da? Are we there yet?" Dillan says.

It's a question we've heard a million times from him, and the Cumhaills in the crowd giggle. Dillan was our impatient child growing up. He was also the one with violent motion sickness, so it was understandable he wanted out of the car before the puking started. Truth was, we all wanted out of the vehicle before that.

"Yer in luck, Dillan. We are." Da steps into a chamber at the end of the tunnel, and we follow him inside. "I believe the queen is right. I think we now know what the witches are up to."

Since I stopped to fix my Marilyn Manson eyes, I'm at the back of the bus. When I finally stand shoulder to shoulder with the others, I'm not happy about what we're looking at.

Not one bit.

"This is bad, right?"

Dora dips her chin. "Yes, girlfriend. This is very bad."

In front of us, a huge section of the stone and dirt of the riverbank is gone. The current of water flows by, held back by an invisible forcefield. Two silver casks of prana are hooked up to the field and seem to be pumping prana through tubes connected through a witch disc. The maze of the Hecate's Wheel on the witch disc glows as it emits a steady buzzing hum.

The little green drake dragon that comes over to greet Patty and me is all prance and smiles. She's about the size of a Malamute, so a little smaller than Dart and without the horns and wings. "Did you find this all by yourself, sweet girl?" I scrub her cheek. "Great job."

Dart moves to get in between us and I hold up my finger. "Don't be like that. You're the oldest of the litter. You have to show the others how to behave and get along like my oldest brother did for us."

I wave Aiden over to join us.

He and I might be the farthest apart in age, but with the red hair and blue eyes, we look the most alike. "Aiden, this is Dart. He needs to learn how to be a good oldest brother."

Aiden arches a brow like I might be going soft in the head, but he humors me. "Fiona's right. Being the oldest is a very important job…"

As he takes Dart under his wing, I join Da, Sloan, and the others staring at the wall of swirling river water held back by the invisible field.

"Not to gain another point on Emmet's macabre musings scale, but are we all in agreement that if something disturbs the spell holding back the river that this tunnel will flood and we'll all drown?"

"That's my take on it," Calum says.

"Me too." Dillan nods.

Da frowns at the pink swirls. "Okay, first thing. Madam Queen, I think it would be safer if ye take yer young either topside or back to yer lair now. If this goes poorly, I don't want any harm to come to the little ones."

The queen bows her head, the broad, scarlet scales shimmering in the light of torchlight and fae energy. "Agreed. They've had enough fun for one night. I don't want them overstimulated."

She emits a squelching noise and heads back into the tunnel followed by Chua and, after a moment of hesitation, Dart.

I wave as they go, urging Dart to continue with his family. "Don't worry. I'll visit you before I go home. I'll see you soon, buddy."

When they're gone, Da turns to Nikon. "I'd appreciate it if ye took my kids and Patty topside as well. Sloan, Dora, Sarah, and I have the combined knowledge and power to take care of things here. If they don't object to stayin', we'll have all the hands we need."

I snort. "Nice try, oul man. You don't get to vote me off the island when this is yet another grand adventure I dragged you all into."

Da frowns. "I have the tactical skills here, Dora has both druid and wizarding skills as well as knowledge from the ages, Sarah is a witch and will understand the workings of what's been done better than the rest, and Sloan is not only smart but can portal us out in a flash if things go badly. What skillset makes it necessary for ye to stay down here?"

I make a face at him. "Geez, Da, talk about undermining my self-esteem. What about Fianna shield early warning, or quick wit, or charm and winning smile? If those don't fly, how about… there's no freaking way in hell I'm leaving."

Da scowls. "Yer determination used to be cute. Now it's a constant pain in my arse."

"You're welcome."

"It's sweet ye think that was a compliment." With a huff, he nods at Nikon. "If ye wouldn't mind takin' the others to safety."

Dillan holds up his hand. "Aiden and I want to check out the main cavern again before we go. We'll gather the papers from the table, and I'll do another sweep with my hood up."

Da growls and glares up at the rock ceiling. "Sweet mercies, will *any* of my kids do what they're told and step out of harm's way?"

I chuckle because as annoyed with us as Da sometimes gets, there's never any doubt that he loves us like crazy. "Calum and Emmet are going, aren't you boys?"

Calum nods. "Yeah. We'll check on the prisoners."

"Can we grab a few more of your nappy sacks, Sarah?"

Sarah hands over her bag. "Help yerselves."

Emmet accepts the little bundles of oblivion and hesitates. "Are you okay with staying? Da's accustomed to all of us jumping into the cray-cray of life, but you get to take a pass if you're not comfortable with it."

"I'm fine. Off ye go. We'll wrap things up here and be breathin' fresh air before ye know it."

I give the girl credit. She talks a good game. Too bad Da taught us how to read lies and evasions. Busted.

Sweet Emmet lets her have her moment though. "Yeah, you will." He lifts his gaze and smiles. "Good luck."

When it's only the five of us, Da exhales. "It's like herdin' jumpy cats most days, I tell ye."

"Har-har. I can hear you."

Da flicks his hand at me and points at the contraption we're facing. "What do we see here?"

Dora leans in, studying the force field and the disc mounted against it. "I'm sure we've all come to the same conclusion. The witch disc is pumping raw prana into the flow of the river water."

"Why?" Sloan says. "Exposure to raw, source power will poison people."

Dora frowns. "It can also award ordinary people gifts and transform them into fae creatures and empowered folks."

I stare at the magical energy disbursement and scowl. "You think after seeing what it did to their friends they're tainting the water to create more empowered folks?"

"Actually," Sarah holds up her finger. "That makes sense with two possibilities. There's a sect of dark witches that believes hiding magic in the shadows is beneath us and the empowered should reap the benefits of the planet. If fae magic is outed, they wouldn't have to restrain themselves."

Da frowns. "They wouldn't be the first to try to expose what goes on behind the faery glass of the hidden folk."

"You said two possible explanations," I prompt. "What's the second?"

"That they know very well what will happen to people who drink and swim in the magic-tainted water and they're looking to capitalize on it in some way. Maybe it's not that different from what the Barghest did a few months ago when they tried to siphon the fae they kidnapped."

I roll my eyes. "Why can't everyone just play nice?"

"I'm with you, girlfriend," Dora says.

Sloan sighs. "It's a moot point at the moment why they tainted the water. The question is how do we reverse the polarity of the discs and have it siphon again instead of pumping the magic out into the river?"

Sarah shrugs. "That shouldn't be too difficult. I mean, the discs themselves were created to draw magical energy. It stands to reason once we figure out how they work, we should be able to do just that."

"Pitter-patter let's get atter." I gesture at the glowing faces of Hecate's Wheel on the disc. "While you guys work on that, maybe a couple of us can reform the wall of this river and block it from tidal-waving in on us."

Da nods. "Who's doing what?"

Dora straightens. "Sarah and I can figure out the discs. Sloan, can you study the casks and figure out how to seal their magic flow so we can disconnect them?"

"I can try."

Da smiles at me. "I guess that leaves you and me on landscaping, *mo chroi.*"

"Perfect. I'm getting good at *Wall of Stone.*"

It's close to three in the morning when Sloan *poofs* the five of us out of the tunnel, and we join the others topside. I texted them at regular intervals so no one was panicked, but yeah no, that didn't work. No signal. Eventually, Nikon started popping down for updates and to verify we're all safe and accounted for. Even knowing that, they're relieved when we're done and have gotten out safely.

"Did Patty go back with the queen?" I ask.

Nikon nods. "I popped him to the lair once you said you were finishing up and all was well. I don't think he's used to these crazy druid hours. The poor guy was beat."

I yawn and stretch out my tired and bruised muscles. "Same. Shower, massage, healing, and bed. Love you all, night-night."

Nikon chuckles. "We waited here for that?"

I yawn again and smile. "Who are you kidding? You waited to make sure we didn't get dead. We didn't. Success. S'all good."

"What about them?" Calum points at eight witches lying slumped in a pile unconscious on the ground.

I groan. "Damn. I forgot about them. Mother Nature? Goddess? Would you like to gather some more offenders and get an update on the night's events?"

I wait, searching the starry night sky above, hope dimming with each passing moment.

"Well, crap."

Sloan chuckles. "Did ye think the keeper of the earth's nature is sittin' by watchin' and waitin' for us to call her?"

Sort of. "All right, do we know of a magical prison or holding cell where we can drop them off until we finish this?"

"Aren't we finished?" Emmet asks.

"Nope. We found two casks. If the witches are trying to pollute waterways, we have another seven casks to recover before this is over. And we still don't know who's behind it."

Emmet frowns. "Well, Dillan and I gotta work, so it's back to the grind for us. We used up all our days off, so it's Calum and Nikon up next."

I sigh. "Sorry, guys. You deserved to have your downtime, but you spent your entire block off chasing crazies across Ireland with your sister."

Emmet snorts. "Chasing crazies across Ireland is way more fun than Xbox and the pub. I could've done without the dip in the waters of a primary ley line, but according to the powers that be, all is as it's meant."

"And you turned into a kangaroo," Dillan adds.

Emmet grins. "Well, that part was cool."

Calum looks at me and presses his hands together. "You got pictures, right?"

"Of course."

"Okay, children," Da says, his voice heavy with the late hour. "Back to the prisoners and the casks. What's the plan?"

I pull out my phone and text Garnet.

Does Ireland have a Guild of the Empowered Ones?

Not exactly, but I have people. What do you need?

To imprison eight witches who are part of a conspiracy to taint water with fae prana and expose us all. It's a goddess-sanctioned mission.

The **goddess...as in the Divine Lady?**

Yeah, long story.

You're unbelievable.

So I'm told.

Where are you?

Carrigogunnel Castle. Village of Clarina.

Give me five.

"Okay, prisoners taken care of. Nikon, man o' mine, buddy, pal, can you take Dora, Da, Aiden, Dillan, and Emmet home? We'll drop Calum off at Gran's, Sarah back home, secure the casks, and regroup in the morning."

"I can do that," Nikon says.

"We owe you huge, Greek." I make a heart with my fingers and press it to my chest. "Mad affection for the immortal."

He snorts. "You're never boring, Red. I'll give you that."

I roll my eyes. "Oh, how I wish I were."

"Yer sorted on the prisoner front?" Da asks.

"Sure am. It's not what you know; it's who you know. Garnet's a good one to know."

Da snorts. "If ye consider a man who knows where to hide bodies an asset, ye missed a few key points in the lessons I taught ye along the way."

I chuckle. Da's annoyance with Garnet isn't nearly as hostile or judgmental as it used to be. In fact, I think they might even have found some common ground.

A redhead lass with a penchant for trouble.

"Night, all. Love you huge."

CHAPTER NINETEEN

I wake with newfound energy and excitement for the day. I'm not sure where the burst of optimism came from until I'm out of the shower and catch a glimpse of myself in the mirror. My leg looks much better. I probe the pink flesh of my thigh. It's still a little sore and might scar, but the gray scales of putrification are finally gone.

Could I be free of Morgan le Fey's grimoire?

I take stock of the grimy film of evil residue that I've felt the past week. Yeah, that's way better too.

Yeah, baby! I'm me again.

With my teeth brushed, damp hair combed out, and clothes on, I practically skip out of the bathroom. I smile at Sloan coming out of his walk-in closet. He's got designer jeans on and a collared jersey that stretches nicely over the musculature of his upper body.

Barefoot on the stone floor, I run at him and catch him by surprise. Jumping in the air, I wrap my legs around his waist, and he staggers to catch me and steady us.

His deep chuckle vibrates against me as I claim his mouth and kiss him like I miss him. "Good morning, hotness."

"Good morning to you too, *a ghra*. What's all this?"

"Does a girl need a reason to express her affections?"

"Not at all. Express away."

I'm about to do just that when I sense movement behind us by the door.

"Pardon, sir." Dalton is frozen in place. He's holding a tray with a long, stainless steel cover and is wearing a horrified look—like his shoe just squished into a steaming pile. "Apologies, I didn't mean to interrupt."

Sloan chuckles. "Not your fault, Dalton. Please, set the tray down. No harm done."

I giggle at Sloan using one of my go-to expressions. He's becoming less rigid by the day. I give him a last quick smooch and wriggle against his hold for him to put me down.

He refuses to set me free. Instead, he walks over to the table and checks out the morning breakfast offerings. "This looks perfect."

"And it smells divine." I wriggle again but am still unable to coax him to set me down. I tilt my head back and look at Sloan's butler upside down. "Thank you for taking such good care of us, Dalton. You rock."

"My pleasure." He dips his chin. "Will there be anything else, sir? Miss?"

Sloan waits until I shake my head, then dismisses him. "Please close the door on your way out."

Manx sneaks in before the latch of the huge panel of dark mahogany clicks into place. "Hey, puss. How are things in the halls of Stonecrest Castle?"

"Boring. As usual."

"Hey, don't jinx it. After the past four months, I'll never knock boring."

Sloan gives me one more squeeze and sets me down on one of the four chairs. "So, boring, am I?"

I snort. "Not what I said and you know it."

He removes the lid of the warmer and sets a plate in front of each of us. "I do. So, back to your burst of exuberance earlier. What brought that on?"

"Oh, this smells amazeballs." I lean closer to the plate and breathe in the aroma of raspberry pancakes with bacon. "I love fruit pancakes... oh, and the bacon is chewy, not crisp. My favorite."

The cocky arch of his ebony brow tells me he already knew that.

"Have you been quizzing my brothers?"

He lifts one shoulder and hands me the syrup.

I stare at the bottle, and my mouth drops open. "This is Ontario maple syrup. How do you have that here?"

"It's your favorite. I may have bought a case and brought it with me on one of my return trips to give you a taste of home away from home."

I chuckle and cover my pancakes with the rich, sugary goodness. "So, my first thought here is, that's very thoughtful and sweet. You're adorable. My second thought is...really? Were you that sure we'd be sitting here one day that you bought a case of my favorite syrup?"

His cocky grin morphs into a full-blown smile. "I was, and here we are."

"And if we didn't get here you'd still have a case of the best syrup *evah*."

"Win-win. Now, less talking, more eating."

I dig into my breakfast, and it's as good as I imagine. We eat in relative silence for a while until my tummy is happy and my mind starts to wander. "Did you happen to give me one of your healing touches last night while I was asleep?"

"Why do you ask?"

When he's not looking, I slip a strip of bacon under the table to the lynx lying with his chin on my thigh. "Because last night I felt like a beaten rug. A building fell on me, and I was tired from fighting, and the leftover residual gloom of darkness was still dragging me down."

"I thought as much. You should've told me."

I shrug. "But this morning, I'm rested, strong, and feel better than I have since before Fionn took me back to Camelot. Your bed is amazingly comfy, but I have a sneaking suspicion that my rejuvenation is about more than six hours on a Posturepedic."

He wipes his mouth with his linen napkin and smiles. "Ye know how much I like to watch ye sleep."

"Yes, it's odd and a little creepy."

"No, it's not. Yer bein' intentionally difficult."

I chuckle. "Guilty as charged. Okay, go on."

"Well, yer very expressive in yer sleep. If yer happy, ye smile and let out the odd giggle. When yer sad or scared, ye cry, and when yer hurtin' ye grimace and moan. Last night, ye were hurtin'. I took liberties and eased ye until ye sank into a restful sleep."

I finish chewing my last bite and take a swallow of my juice. "Well, thank you. You're amazing, and I feel great."

"I'm glad. That was the idea."

"Careful, though. If you keep this up, I may never leave."

He waggles his brow. "Did ye hear that, Manx? Our evil plan is workin—"

An alarm goes off somewhere in the distance.

At the wail of a klaxon, I jump to my feet. "What's that?"

"An intruder," Sloan says.

I'm right behind him as he swings open the bedroom door and races out. Manx is hot on his heels, and I release Bruin to join the crew. "Where's it coming from?" I wince at the volume of the alarm.

Out in the hallway, it's so loud that it seems to come from everywhere at once.

"The clinic." Sloan *poofs* out. Either he didn't stop to think of bringing me, or he intentionally ditched me, I'm not sure.

That's an argument for a later date.

I bank right around the corner from Sloan's wing and head down the stone, spiral staircase. Sloan's bedroom is on the third floor of the castle in the east wing. The clinic is on the ground level of the west wing. It faces the courtyard and fountain out front next to the parking lot where clinic visitors park.

On the second floor, I bolt across the gallery walkway that runs along the front of the house. I glance out the windows as I go to see if there are any cars parked there.

None I haven't seen before.

Once I get into the west staircase, I descend the final floor and call Birga forward. *Tough as Bark.*

With the whisper of a thought, my body armor activates. After a building fell on me yesterday, I won't forget again.

Manx and I arrive in the clinic to find a huge hole in the south wall and the fight spilling out onto the grass beyond.

"What the frickety-frack is that?"

"A marauder giant," Manx says. "A big one."

That's the understatement of the century. It also explains how the south wall of Wallace's clinic is now a pile of rubble. The intruder stands an easy nine or ten feet tall, with knee-high fur boots and hide armor. Despite being humanoid, with red war paint on his face and sneering rows of spiky teeth he's nothing like any man I've ever seen.

And he seems quite set on taking Wallace with him.

Sloan and Janet are both fighting to slow him down. He's got Wallace tucked under one arm and is swinging a spiked club at them to keep them back.

There are still so many things I don't know about Irish lore and creatures who live on both sides of the faery glass.

Better to err on the side of caution. "Do we kill marauder giants?"

"If ye try, ye best be willin' to die for it. Their skin is as tough as yers with that enchanted armor, I expect."

Damn. "Bruin, see if you can scare him. Don't engage though. Not when he has Wallace. One wrong twist and he could crush him."

Bruin materializes beside me and races into their midst. His roar merges with the growled grunts of the giant. My bear bellows, and the giant bellows right back.

Bruin's reaction is almost comical.

He's not used to people standing their ground with him.

That will piss him off.

I may not be able to kill a marauder giant, but Birga is sharp and powerful. She can at least slow him down. Rushing in beside Bruin, I take a ready stance and swing. "Put him down, you hairy brute!"

With a growl, he steps back and shakes his head. "You not my goddess. I don't obey green druid goddess."

I blink and look at Sloan. "Is that me?"

"Sounds like it."

I'm not sure whether I should be flattered or offended with his take on me. Not that it matters. In the end, he stopped waving the club, and he's not stomping away anymore.

"Put him down."

"No. Goddess needs him."

"Needs him for what?"

Janet Mackenzie shifts her position to get a better look at her husband. The giant matches her movement to block her line of sight. "Healer magic. Poisoned children."

Oh, that's not what I expected him to say, but it beats the 'hungry for healer meat' I was worried about. "Okay, it's understandable you made a rash choice. Children are sick. You're trying to get them help."

"Goddess needs him."

"Let him go," Sloan snaps.

The giant rushes forward and raises his club.

"Stop!" I shout, raising Birga and taking aim. "Don't even think about it. Lower your club and let Wallace go."

"You not my goddess." He shakes his head again and grunts, showing me his spiky teeth.

"Obvi, but that doesn't mean you can't do it. Set him down and we'll talk about what your goddess needs."

"Needs him."

"Put. Him. Down."

He leans forward and roars at me. Hot, fetid breath washes my face, and I try not to inhale. Gross. He does, however, set Wallace on his feet.

I'm not sure what Wallace is being hailed for but if children are being poisoned and a goddess has sent for help, I'm willing to find out. "Wallace? Are you willing to go with him to see about the poisoned children?"

"Don't be stupid," Janet snaps. "He's not going anywhere with that monster. I don't care if he knocks our home to rubble. He has no right to demand Wallace's gift."

Wallace straightens behind his wife and frowns. "True enough, but if there is trouble and I can help, I must try. Sloan, grab my bag from the clinic, son."

Janet turns on her husband and glares. "Ye'd go with a behemoth of the mound? What if yer imprisoned or cursed or ground up for his dinner?"

"That won't happen. I assume ye'll all be with me."

"You assume correctly," I say.

Wallace sweeps a hand toward me and Bruin and smiles. "I couldn't ask fer a stronger force of protection. Besides, it seems the man is compelled to answer to Fiona."

Yay me. "Yeah, I'm not sure what that's about."

"The ways of the Tuatha De are not ours to judge or try to figure out. As servants of the fae and guardians of their gifts, we must ever endeavor to honor our stations within their realm."

I like the sound of that, in theory, and hope it works out

like that. Pulling out my phone, I send a quick text to Calum at Gran's to tell him Sloan and I have an errand with his parents before we continue with the plans to recover the prana casks.

Once that message is sent, I tuck my phone away. "Locked and loaded."

Sloan *poofs* back after a moment. He brings me shoes, socks, and a jacket, and Wallace his medical bag. We walk over a few hills and into the woods that border the Mackenzie property to the south. The marauder giant's steps are quick-paced, and with his long stride and my average height, I'm jogging to keep up. When we get to an arched arbor in the wood, I hesitate before crossing the threshold.

"Anything?" Sloan asks.

I search my instincts and other than a worrying pressure on my bladder and wishing I peed before I left the house, nothing comes back at me. "No. S'all good."

When I step through the opening of the archway, it's like passing through a pressurized bubble. I open my jaw and pop my ears, trying to recall where I've felt this sensation before.

It doesn't take long.

It's the same feeling I get when I visit Garnet Grant's home compound. When we pass under his brick archway in front of his house in Toronto, it magically transports us to a sunny compound on the plains of the Savannah in Africa.

This is like that.

Only, we're not in Africa.

"Where are we?" I ask.

"The River Boyne," the giant snaps.

Sloan's gaze searches the lush, green riverbank and he nods. "And not far from the Hill of Tara if I'm not mistaken. Fi, do ye remember yer history from when Fionn fed ye the Salmon of Knowledge?"

"Some. Thankfully, Calum and Kevin helped me write most of it down. Why?"

"Because this is the land of yer ancestry. Ye told me Fionn's mother was the granddaughter of the High King and his wife, a deity of the Tuatha De Danann."

"Yep. I was chuffed I have the blood of the Tuatha De Danann running in my veins."

"Right. But not the blood of just any member of the sect. Yer a descendant of the pantheon of gods and goddesses of the fair ones."

I scratch my forehead, still not a hundy percent sure what he's getting at. "Your point?"

"I don't think the giant set Da down and stopped to answer yer questions because he wanted to. Did ye see how muddled and frustrated he got when ye told him what to do?"

"That's not uncommon. I frustrate men to a fluster more often than not."

He arches a brow and smiles. "No argument there, but I don't think it was what ye said so much as who said it that confused him."

Hubba-wha? "Speaking about muddled and frustrated, what are you saying, Mackenzie?"

"I'm sayin' I think he senses yer royal goddess blood and he *had* to obey."

"Seriously? Fionn's grandmother being a goddess goes *waaaay* back. Do you think it's even detectible? Isn't there like a magic half-life that saps it out of descendants generation after generation?"

"Ye make is sound like yer radioactive. No, it doesn't work like that. It's magic."

Oh, yeah. "Okay, let's try out your theory." Running to catch up with our hostile tour guide, I lift my feet high to clear the long grass. "Mr. Giant, will you do something for me?"

"Not my goddess."

"Yeah, you've mentioned that. Still, I want to try something. Ready?"

"No."

"Put your right hand in." I stab my right hand into the air between us.

He frowns, rounding on me with violent fury. I'm a hair's breadth from whimpering and cursing Sloan for getting me eaten by a giant with terrible gingivitis when I put more feeling into it.

"Put your right hand in!"

He shoves his right hand at me and glares.

"Put your right hand out."

He does.

"Put your right hand in, and shake it all about."

I smile as he follows my lead. "Thanks, dude. That was a good bonding exercise. I appreciate your time."

He roars as he stomps off, and I stop to wait for Sloan to catch up. "Are my eyes deceivin' me or did ye just compel a marauder giant to do the Hokey-Pokey?"

I giggle. "I thought it was a quick and effective way to test whether or not he has free will over my suggestions. I'm quite sure if he could've said no, he would have."

"Agreed."

"The question now is, how can we use that to our advantage if things go south on us?"

"Which they inevitably will," Sloan mumbles.

"Such a pessimist...but a pessimist with a damned fine ass." I smack the ass in question and jog to catch up with Wallace and Janet.

He's right of course. It's only a matter of time before the next bomb blows up in our faces.

But I'm not going to admit that to him.

The five of us stop on the bank of the River Boyne, and our giant escort plunks down, pulls off his tall fur boots, and wriggles his feet in the mid-morning breeze.

Ew, gawd. The stench of his feet is worse than his breath.

It's a small mercy when he lies back and lets his feet dangle into the water's current. It's been warm for the last week in October, but I can't imagine the current swirling around his feet is anything but freezing.

Then again, if Manx is right about his skin being as tough as armor, maybe he doesn't feel the cold.

"So, what are we waiting for?" I ask.

"The goddess, I expect," Wallace says. "If he fetched us on her behalf, I assume she'll want to speak to us before we're set on our task."

Janet huffs. "Or it's an ambush, and he's waitin' fer his assassin brothers to come along and cook us fer lunch."

I blink at Janet and now understand where Sloan's bright and sunshiny disposition comes from. Deciding to change the subject, I look at the Mackenzie men. "So what goddess do you think we're dealing with here? Brighid? Anu? Eostre?"

Sloan waves those suggestions away. "According to Irish mythology, Boann is the Irish goddess of the River Boyne—thus the name although it's been modernized over time. Boann is also a member of yer ancestry in some fashion as she was the daughter of Delbaeth and a member of the Tuatha De Danann."

"A cousin. *Noice.* What's her story? How'd she get to be the goddess of the River Boyne?"

Sloan frowns. "According to legend, the sacred well of *Sidhe Nechtan* contained the source of knowledge. All were forbidden to approach the well, except for the god Nechtan, who was Boann's husband, and his servants."

"Rude. Let me guess. She wanted to get a closer look."

He nods. "Boann is said to have ignored the warnings and strode straight up to the sacred well."

"Thus violating the sanctity of her hubby's secret spot."

"Exactly. It's said that when she did, the waters of the defiled well swelled and transformed into a raging river that pursued her across the Irish countryside as she raced away and fled for her life."

"But she managed to outrun the currents?"

"Some legends say she did. Others say she drowned. In either case, the watercourse became the River Boyne, and Boann became the presiding deity."

I gaze out on the blue waters of the river and think about that. "So, the goddess of a river is upset because people are being poisoned?"

Sloan stiffens beside me. "When you say it like that…do you think it's connected to the witches polluting the River Shannon with prana energy?"

"My instincts say yes. I bet that somewhere around here, there are a couple of casks of stolen source power being pumped into the river. The question now is, where?"

CHAPTER TWENTY

Sloan and I look around but find nothing. Next, we consider speaking to the giant. I'm not sure if he's asleep or simply ignoring us, but that gets us nowhere. "Hey, hotness. There's a druid spell to detect magic, right? What's it called?"

Sloan smirks. *"Detect Magic."*

"Oh, good name. Do you have any proficiency at it?"

"Some, but I think since this river is seventy miles long, we'd have more luck finding the point of power pollution with a divining spell instead."

"Not it!" I hold up my hands and take a step back. "I don't need poison ivy on my girl parts, thank you very much."

"Why would you get poison ivy on..." Wallace stops speaking mid-sentence, his brow drawn tight. "What are you two plotting?"

Sloan fills his parents in on our past few days working on behalf of Mother Nature and what we suspect. I interject his commentary with color and points of interest when needed.

It's sad. When he speaks to his parental unit, Sloan gets all stiff and formal. I can't imagine feeling like I can't be myself around Da. My father has always been my safe refuge from the storms of life. I know it's the same for my brothers as well. Isn't that how it's supposed to be?

When Sloan finishes his recap, Wallace and Janet give the winding ribbon of sparkling blue water an assessing glance.

"Why is this the first we're hearing of this?" Janet snaps.

"When we got in this morning, it was close to four. We slept, finished our breakfast, then the alarms sounded. I didn't keep it a secret. We simply hadn't seen ye yet. We mentioned it to Da yesterday before we headed out."

Wallace sighs and shields his gaze against the glare. "Yer right, son. Yer odds of finding the source of pollution using a divining spell are much better than by using *Detect Magic*."

"At least until ye get within range," Janet adds. "And yer makin' assumptions that one problem relates to the other problem based on what a marauder giant says. Ye know they are, at best, chaotic neutral. He's more likely isolated us so he and his friends can come to eat our faces."

Wow. Okay, Janet is a barrel of rainbows and sunshine.

"No one is eating our faces, Mam," Sloan says.

"I'm glad yer certain."

"I'll portal us out before that ever happens."

"Unless they have a dampener and yer unable to portal."

"My shield isn't activating," I say, hoping to quell Janet's additions to the conversation. "I sense when danger is closing in, and right now I've got nothing."

Janet rakes me over with a disparaging look and apparently finds me wanting. "And ye think yer qualified to have an opinion in this discussion, why? Ye've been a druid how long now? What formal trainin' have ye completed?"

"Mam, don't," Sloan snaps, his gaze growing hard. "Not here. Not now. I mean it."

Her brow arches. "Och, and since when do ye take a tone with me? Yer not the adult here. I get to have my say."

Sloan's hands ball into fists at his sides, and he straightens to his full six-foot-two. "I *am* an adult, and ye've had yer say. I simply disagreed and chose to make my own decision."

My gaze ping-pongs from Sloan to his mother and back again. "Sorry. I'm new to this convo. I take it you have a problem with Sloan and me. Or is it just me in general?"

"A problem?" Janet props her hands on her hips and scowls. "Ye might say we have a problem. Our boy is an elite, full-blooded druid male with prestige and education and he's set his sights on an urban half-blood who couldn't sense the difference between a charm and a compulsion."

"Don't be rude," Sloan snaps. "Yer intentionally being snide, and Fiona doesn't deserve it."

"And we do? We deserve the way ye've treated us the past months?"

"Now yer bein' dramatic. I've not treated ye with any disrespect, and ye bloody well know it. I've sat through yer rants and listened to ye go on about things, and I've never once been disrespectful."

"She has ye hopping halfway around the world like a love-sick puppy at the drop of a hat. She puts ye in danger at every turn. And she's twisted ye up in her seductions so ye can't even see yer ruinin' yer life."

My mouth falls open. "And here I thought we were getting along well. Obvi, we're not on the same page."

"We're not even in the same library, ye reckless, wee—"

"Enough!" Sloan steps in front of his mother, his finger pointed in the air. "Don't ye dare finish that sentence."

Janet's eyes grow wide, then she glares at me. "Do ye see? He would never have spoken to me like this before ye got yer hooks into him."

"Don't blame Fiona for me finally growing a pair of knackers. No, wait, go ahead and give her the credit. That, at least, is her doin'."

Noice. Throw the girlfriend under the bus.

"Spendin' time with Lugh and Lara all these years gave me a glimpse of life beyond the propriety of druid life. But nothin' taught me what family meant like stayin' with the Cumhaills in Toronto. Yes, they're a rough and rowdy bunch, but they love each other to a depth of commitment I admire. They cod one another and fight and celebrate their triumphs and their failures. When have you ever celebrated who I am or anything I've ever done?"

Janet scowls and turns to Wallace. "There now, ye see. I told ye she's fillin' his head with poison against us."

"I would never." I blink against the sting of evil eyes and pray I can hold back the freak show. "You are his parents. He loves you, and you love him. This isn't about me versus you two. We all want Sloan to excel and be happy, don't we?"

"We do." Wallace's tone is much like his son's when he's calming the waters. "But as much as we've tried to rear our son to a certain level of standard, we've never seen him as animated and self-involved as he's been these past months."

Animated? "Thinking for himself isn't self-involved. It's independent. Don't you want him to thrive on his own?"

"Ye see, this is what Janet is talkin' about. Ye fill his head with ideas we don't support. It's wrong to lay that as blame, but perhaps ye'll agree inadvertently, yer still the cause."

"Both of ye need to stop," Sloan says, his cheeks flushed. "Yer makin' a scene and insultin' Fiona for no reason. I'm twenty-seven years old and a man in my own right. We don't agree on all things but why can't that be all right?"

"Because yer throwin' yer plans to the wind," Janet says.

"No. I'm not. *My* plans have never been discussed. I simply went along with yer plans because I didn't have my path figured out."

"And now ye do, do ye?"

He shakes his head and sighs. "Can't we do this another time in a more appropriate place? Fiona and I were up all night trackin' and fightin' dark witches. Can we please focus on why we're here?"

"Good idea, hotness." I grip his wrist and smile at the glowing female rising out of the river. "Now would be a really good time to get back to the whole poisoned children part of our morning."

Sloan stops glaring at his parents to study me. "Why did ye say it like that?"

I tilt my head toward the water. "We have company."

"My Goddess." The giant pulls his hairy toes out of the water and jumps to his feet. He points at Sloan's father. "Druid healer."

"Blessed be, Knuruk." She offers the giant a warm smile. "Merry meet, druids. I am Boann, goddess of the River Boyne. I appreciate ye takin' the time from yer day to heed my call."

I stifle the urge to mention we had little choice since her behemoth messenger crashed through the wall of the castle and kidnapped Wallace.

"It's our pleasure to be of service." Wallace recomposes himself after the public discord. That's one thing about Sloan and his family. At the drop of a hat, they can cut off their emotions and put on a professional air. "Yer messenger mentioned poisoned children? How can I be of assistance?"

The goddess waves toward the water and a wooden boat appears. It's like one of those Viking ships that have those swoopy front and back ends that swirl up into the air with what looks like fiddleheads. "Come. I shall show ye."

Sloan looks at me, and I know what he's asking without him saying a word. "S'all good."

He smiles at the goddess Boann. "It would be our pleasure, milady. After you."

I've always loved boats.

The boat the goddess of the River Boyne manifests isn't huge, like the ones that would have thirty oars coming out each side, but a smaller version of the same model.

A compact edition raiding ship, if you will.

Thankfully, Knuruk's task is complete, and the goddess dismisses her messenger. I know boats are buoyant, but I feel better not having a marauder giant on board as we whisk along the river.

And we are whisking.

With no sails up to carry us forward, the ship is still skimming through the waters at quite a clip. I wonder how far into the seventy miles the trouble will be?

"When we were kids, my parents used to take us on the ferry across Toronto Harbour to Centre Island on the weekends in the summer. Since I was the smallest, Mam held me up so I could see over the rail."

I lean over the side rail as the wind picks up my hair and stare at the surface of the passing water. "I remember telling her to hold me tight so I wouldn't fall in. Sometimes, in my dreams, I still feel her arms wrapped around me and feel so safe. I loved the boat ride as much as the day we spent at the kid's amusement park there."

Sloan leans in beside me, hooking under my arm so that he can link our fingers. "That's a beautiful memory, *a ghra*. Which is better, I wonder, to be cherished deeply for a short time and lose it, or to be raised with moderate affection for a lifetime and endure it?"

I consider our two situations. "I pick cherished."

"Yeah, I think I do too." Sloan voice is tight. "I'm sorry about what they said about you."

I pull a loose chunk of hair out of my mouth and lean on my elbows. "You don't have to apologize. They're your parents. They want better for you. I get it."

Sloan rolls his eyes. "Their idea of better has nothing to do with any measure of worth I value. I don't care what yer bloodline is or yer bank account or whether or not ye went to a fancy university. Anyone who spends ten minutes with ye can sense yer value. Yer one of the smartest, kindest, bravest, most authentic people I've ever met and yer heart holds a capacity for love and acceptance I've never seen rivaled."

I shrug. "Still, you're their only child. They've invested their hopes of legacy on grooming an uber-druid wonder son."

"And that's my destiny? What about what I want?"

"I asked my father the same question the morning after you manhandled me and made my Fianna mark appear. What about what I want?"

He chuckles. "I didn't make yer mark appear, and ye know it, but what *is* it ye want? Or what did ye want?"

"It seems like a million years ago. It was the morning after Emmet's graduation, and I was mad that everyone had their thing they loved except me. They all chose the police academy. I chose to work part-time at the pub and help run the household. Yes, I could've gone to college or university, but my family always stood out as my priority."

"There's nothin' wrong with that."

"I know. Da always says you should never regret what happened in the past because it's what propels you forward. I like where I am and who I am, even if it doesn't hold up under your parents' scrutiny."

"Och, please, don't let them make ye feel bad about yerself. So many things have changed on ye since yer mark appeared. It's a testament to yer personality that ye've handled it as well as ye have. I love who ye've become and am proud to stand at yer side."

My eyes sting, but it's not the evil freak show trying to break free this time. It's worse. I swipe my cheek and draw a deep breath, refusing to cry in front of strangers.

"Damn. I'm not usually a waterworks girl."

"Aw, Fi." He shifts to drape his arm across my shoulders as we stare out at the water. "Take it from the one who knows best in this situation. Don't shed a tear for them. It's not worth it. Honestly, they'll never see what's right in front of them, and they'll never understand the damage they do by being who they are."

I swallow against a thick throat and fight to tamp down my emotions. "I guess it caught me off-guard. I thought they liked me—your dad anyway. It kinda came out of left field, you know?"

"We like ye, Red." Manx stretches up on his hind legs and rubs his furry cheek against my arm. "In fact, we love ye. It doesn't matter what they think because their ideals are skewed with old-world nonsense. Yer a treasure. Them not seein' it is their short-coming, not yers."

I hug Manx tight to my side and bend over to rub my face against his velvety fur. "Thanks, puss."

He lets out a rumbling purr, and I close my eyes. "Don't let them drive ye off. We need ye around to keep us on our toes. Life only started gettin' fun once ye invaded ours."

I chuckle and press a hand on the flutter in my chest. Bruin is sending me his strength, and it fills my heart. "Thanks, guys. I don't need reassurance often, but it's nice to know it's here when I do."

Sloan presses a kiss to my temple. "No woman is an island... even the fiery, Fiona Kacee mac Cumhaill."

"Mac Cumhaill?" the goddess says behind us. "Are ye Fionn's kin then?"

We straighten from leaning over the rail, and I expect to find Boann standing right behind us. When she spoke, her voice was clear and close. When we turn, we search the lower deck and find her up on the steering platform forty feet away.

"Yes. Fionn mac Cumhaill is my ancestor and my mentor and friend."

Boann smiles. "That makes us kin. It also explains the magical power signature I sense coming from ye."

"Yep, somewhere way back, our family tree shared the same roots."

"Well then, merry meet, cousin. I'm glad to know ye and thank ye for coming to help my waters."

The boat slows, and although we've only been on the river for ten minutes, we've traveled a great deal farther than that should've allowed for.

Magic is cool.

"Come, let me show ye the source of my concern."

As she waves a gentle hand, her ship eases to the bank of the river and steadies. Wallace helps Janet off. Manx leaps onto the grass on his own. Sloan helps me off and turns to hold out his hand to the goddess. "May I help ye, milady?"

She smiles and holds her fingers out. "So gallant."

"He's a keeper all right." I wink as he escorts her onto the grass beside us.

When she's settled, she strides over to me, takes my hand, and sets it at the crook of her elbow. "Come, cousin. Let me show ye what has me concerned."

———

The moment we arrive at the scene of chaos, Wallace and Sloan are consumed by the state of five people gathered by a village pump. Well, people is a blanket term that may or may not apply. From what the one still able to communicate tells us, the village water system went down early this morning, and they volunteered to fetch water from the artesian well.

It didn't go well for them.

Since it hadn't been used in a while, one member of the group tested the water. When it tasted off, he passed it to a few others for their opinions. Voila, five altered humans in the process of transforming into fae beasts.

I scan the area. It's set back from the river, but there doesn't seem to be a pump-house or anything. "Where is the access point of this pump? Where is it drawing from?"

None of them seem to know, or they're too freaked out by gills and scales appearing on their bodies to be much help.

Wallace has his stern healer face on, which I know from my experience being on his doctoring table, isn't the look you want. "I need my team," he says to Sloan. "Portal to the clinic and bring them back. Then I need ye to track down Ciara and have her join us."

"Ciara? What the hell do you need her for?" The cutting edge to my words is audible—and inappropriate. "Sorry. That came out harsher than I meant."

Janet frowns. "Ciara Doyle is a talented druidess with cultivated skill in dealing with poisons."

Not surprising. The girl is toxic.

I manage to keep that outburst to myself.

Sloan looks from me to his parents and seems torn.

"Don't worry about me. Go. People are suffering."

He looks over at Manx, and the lynx's head turns in response. I see the dip in the cat's chin before Sloan's animal companion trots over to stand next to me.

I scrub Manx's cheek and smile. "You're sweet, Mackenzie. Now stop worrying about me and go."

He winks and flashes off.

Left to my own devices, I head over to the trees with a dutiful gray wildcat trotting along beside me. "If I'm right, there will be a couple of casks set up somewhere close by."

Let me out to help look. Bruin flutters around in my chest, and I release my hold. My bear manifests in the trees next to me and scrunches up his face. "Do ye think the casks will be easy to find?"

"No, I think we need to *Detect Magic*, but I don't know that spell, so I moved on to divining rod." I pull out my phone and scroll back through Sloan's texts to the instructions and spell he gave me last month for making a divining rod. "Okay, we need a forked branch from an oak or ash tree or a yew shrub."

I'm getting better at recognizing different types of trees and leaves, but Janet is right. I'm decades behind in my training. The first problem is there are so many variations of trees to learn, and when you add to that issue how species change by location, I'm playing a nature guessing game.

Manx is a big help.

After a five minute trot rummaging through the fallen leaves and between the trees, he returns from behind a grouping of evergreens with a forked branch in his mouth.

I take it and pat his muscled shoulder. "Thanks, this is perfect."

Stepping further into the trees, I hold the stick out in front of me, modify Sloan's spell to fit the situation, and focus my intention:

Branch of yew, I cast this charm,
Find the poison doing harm.
Where casks hide, you shall see,
and feel the pull to guide me.
Protection spells hinder you none,
We find the casks, and this is done.

With my connection to nature deeply rooted in my desire to cleanse the River Boyne's water, I push power into my spell. When Emmet and I did this spell to find the ley lines in the rivers and waterways, I was juiced with naiad magic and put too much power into it.

It was a wild and dangerous ride for poor Emmet.

Hilarious…but wild and dangerous.

Today, though, the power behind the spell is mine alone and is much more controlled. When the divining rod shimmies to life, I slide my phone into the pocket of my pants, and away we go. "Game on, boys."

CHAPTER TWENTY-ONE

O ur trundle through the woods is quite peaceful and soothing. If it weren't for us searching for raw fae magic that could turn us all into swamp creatures, it would be fun. Even still, I admit, it's a little fun. Who would've thought my destiny would be to thwart the plots of dark witches trying to expose the fae realm?

My life is so cool.

When my divining rod pokes against the rough face of a stone wall, I frown and turn away from the rock. Holding the rod out once again, I wait to see if it finds a way around.

The divining rod pulls back the same way and pokes the stone again.

"Bruin, can you spirit your way above this rock and see what's on the other side? I'm not sure if my stick wants to go into the rock or through it."

"On it." Bruin disappears and is back a moment later. "There isn't another side to this. The landscape slopes and the forest continues on a steep uphill climb."

"Do ye think there could be a cave behind the rock?" Manx

asks. "Maybe yer witches transformed the cave opening to conceal their workings."

"Anything is possible, I suppose. Okay, let's see." After thanking the divining rod for a job well done, I set it on the ground and have Manx sit on it, in case we need it later, and it decides to continue without us.

After seeing Emmet dragged through the forest, I know how determined divining rods can be.

Pressing my hands against the cool, damp rockface, I connect with the energy of the minerals involved.

"Stone to Sand." Magic tingles at the back of my neck as the solid wall before me starts to dissolve.

My shield flares.

It catches me by surprise. It's too late.

The stone wall between the witches and me is gone—

Tough as Bark. I'm calling my armor forward as a blast of magic hits me and knocks me flying into the air. The blow is stunted but not blocked completely. My momentum comes to a hard stop when I hit the trunk of a tree and drop to the ground in a heavy flop.

Ow. That hurt.

I press my palms into the soil and push myself onto my hands and knees. Bruin's growl thunders through the forest, and I don't even care that my bear will get all the action on this one.

There will be no dialing back my Killer Clawbearer now.

Regaining my footing, I try to make myself useful.

Birga responds to my call without hesitation, and I stumble toward the mouth of the cave.

Manx is snarling and swiping at a witch he has pinned against the cave wall. He's covered in leather battle armor I've never seen before, and it's wicked cool. He lets out a hideous *mrowl* as an orb of energy knocks him flying.

My eyes sting as my fury burns away the glamor on my eyes. "You okay, puss?"

What comes back at me is a string of Irish cursing that would make Patty proud. That's good.

Manx is pissed, but okay.

Birga and I engage with the one woman left standing, but we don't even get past our first jab when Bruin slices her from shoulder down to her opposite hip. His massive claws pierce through her and cut her almost in two.

I'm covered in the splattered spray of a dead witch and scowl at Bruin. "Really? Was that necessary?"

He snarls at me, his teeth bared in fury. "Aye, it was. When they hurt you, they die a horrible death. It is the way."

I snort. "Did you just quote the Mandalorian?"

"Maybe." He shakes his head and the fur on his massive neck and shoulders sways and shakes off blood like a dog coming out of the lake. "I think it's catchy. It is the way. It has a nice cadence to it. I think I should have a tag line."

I roll my eyes, thankful every moment of the day for my bond with him. "Okay, let's see what this cave is about and how we did. Manx, you good to join us, my man?"

Sloan's lynx tromps back into the cave still spouting obscenities. Beware the quiet ones. I try to hide my grin and wonder if Sloan knows half as many curses as his cat does.

That's an interesting convo for another day.

Taking inventory of the cave, the three of us explore deeper into its depths. Bruin is right. The slope of the ground drops, and soon we're in an underground grotto.

"Hello, my precious." I point at the two casks and the glowing discs pumping raw fae prana into the river.

Even after watching Dora, Sloan, and Sarah disarm the same setup at the River Shannon, I'm doubtful I can do it alone. "I think I could reverse the function of the discs back to siphon and dismantle them, but I don't have a clue about the witch magic Sarah disarmed. We'll need to phone a friend."

"What's this?" Sloan joins us. "Fiona Cumhaill is both logical and cautious in the clutch of a situation? I never thought I'd see the day."

I stick out my tongue and regret it. I'm still covered in witch bitch, and apparently, some is on my lips. "I'm a work in progress."

Sloan eyes me up and down and frowns. "Yer a bloody mess is what ye are. Are ye all right?"

"Fine. This was Bruin being overprotective and killing my opponent in the most explosive way possible."

Sloan nods at Bruin, and the two share a private look. "Well done, Bear. And I see my Manx got into the mix."

"He sure did. And holy schmoly, puss, you look badass in your leathers."

Manx is licking his wide, tufted paws and grooming his face. His leathers are no longer visible, and I wonder how that works. Can he call them like I call my armor? "Nice of ye to notice."

I chuckle. Sloan says that all the time too. Cute.

Pulling out my phone, I text Sarah. A moment later her response *pings* back. "Sarah's ready to be picked up. Can you grab her to help?"

"Back in a flash."

It's nearly two in the afternoon by the time Sloan and I finish with Sarah in the grotto. We take her home, then stash the two River Boyne casks with the two River Shannon casks in the safe room in Sloan's wing in his castle. It's not ideal, but we can't put them back without Mother Nature or all three pieces of the key together, so we're holding them here until we're ready to return them to the Cistern in one trip.

After Sloan gets his parents and the medical team and the mutant people back to the clinic, we are officially finished with our morning from hell.

"There ye are," Ciara says.

Or so I thought.

"Let the morning of hell continue," I whisper.

Sloan chuckles beside me and turns as we reach the hall that leads to his room. "Ciara. What can we do for ye?"

"Yer da's been askin' about ye. He wants ye to help out in the clinic for a few hours."

Sloan drops his head back and sighs. "I can't. I'm dead on my feet already, and we're four hours late pickin' up Calum to track down the dark witches."

"Which one is Calum?"

"The gay one," I answer. I wave my hand through the air in my best Obi-Wan impression. "He is not the druid you are looking for."

Sloan chuckles. "Yes, he's gay and very much off the market. He's only here to help us track down the other kegs."

"It's true then. Yer workin' for the Divine Lady?"

He nods. "It's true."

Ciara eyes me up and down. I'm still plasma-covered and sporting ode to witch innards, so pretty much disgusting. She shakes her head. "I admit I don't see what all the fuss is about, but I'll not second guess Our Lady. Yer doin' somethin' right, Cumhaill. I'll give ye that."

"Um…thanks?" Ciara and I will probably never be friends, but it's nice not to be at war with her either.

"Oh, and just so ye know." She meets my gaze. "Janet asked me to turn on my wiles and seduce him away from ye. Watch yer back. She's not keen on havin' ye around her thoroughbred son."

I search her expression and wonder what her angle is for telling me. "I take it you declined?"

"Officially, I never commented either way, but between us, I don't need to scheme for sloppy seconds."

"Of course not." When she frowns, I wave away her skepticism. "No. Seriously. You're gorgeous and educated. I don't think for a second you need to set your sights on picking anything but the top fruit on the tree."

She nods. "Besides, it's moot. One look at him, and it's obvious he's a lost cause."

"Hello, ladies...him's standing right here."

I chuckle and take his hand. "Actually, you're not here—*we're* not here. You didn't see us. You didn't find us."

Ciara nods. "I can do that. Off ye go. I have to go play poison Florence Nightingale to five very distraught fae-infected humans."

"Does Wallace think he can help them?" I ask.

Ciara raises a shoulder looking bored. "Help them during their transitions? Yes. Help them return to who they were and the lives they had before this morning? No."

"That's sad."

Ciara nods. "It is at that. Now go before someone else sees ye and yer stuck."

"Thanks for the save." I lace Sloan's fingers in mine. "Manx, you too. We're getting outta Dodge, buddy."

The lynx lifts his chin and trots in between us. "And off to our next adventure."

———

By the time we get to Gran's, shower, and eat, it's nearly three in the afternoon. A message *bings* in on my phone and I check to see what it's about. It's the death benefits guy again. As much as I don't want to acknowledge Brendan's death, Myra's right. Da's not the only one who's not getting over the loss well.

This guy's only doing his job, and I'm acting rude. I open the text and type my response. *Out of town for a few days. I'll be in touch as soon as I'm back in Toronto. My apologies.*

When that sends, I realize there's a missed call from Garnet. I leave Sloan, Gran, Granda, and Calum in the living room and slip into the kitchen to call him back. "Hey there. Sorry I missed your call. What's up?"

"Not a problem. I figure you were probably battling dark witches or taming a dragon or something."

"Yes on the dark witches. No on the dragons. I don't need to tame the dragons. They're my friends."

"Right. I forgot." The line muffles as if he's cupped his hand over the mouthpiece of his phone, then he returns. "Sorry about that."

"Not a problem. So, what do you need?"

"What do *I* need? No, no, Lady Druid, it's what *you* need that's in question."

"All right, I'll bite. What do I need?" Saying that out loud brings so many answers to the fore. A vacay from cray-cray, an afternoon with Liam, a visit to my grove, and quite a few things involving Sloan's healing hands, King Henry, and a lot of almond oil...

I pull back from my mental meandering and focus.

Garnet has piqued my curiosity, and now I'm looking forward to his news. "Would the location of the dark witches' targets and the purpose of it all be on that list?"

"That would be awesome. Is this a bait and switch or is that what you've got? And how did you get it?"

"My colleagues you met last night may have taken it upon themselves to interrogate your witches today—unsolicited by me, I assure you—and ended up with some answers you might be interested in hearing."

"Hells yeah. What did they find out?"

"According to Jimmy, the witches confessed to making away with nine casks of primal fae energy before they were discovered. They stashed two at the River Shannon, which you know, two at the River Boyne, and four at the mouth of the Three Sisters."

"What is the Three Sisters?"

"It's a river basin that splits off into the Rivers Barrow, Nore, and Suir." Sloan joins me. "Sorry, ye've been gone a while. It's always prudent to check when ye've gone missin' again."

I hit speaker on my phone and hold it out for Sloan to hear as well. "You're on speaker now, Garnet. Carry on. You were saying the witches have four casks at the mouth of the Three Sisters?"

"So I was informed, yes."

"That's a lot of ground to cover for a search," Sloan says.

"Then you'll be happy when I say you won't need to cover it."

"What? Why?" I make a face at Sloan, and he arches an ebony brow at me.

"Jimmy is in charge of what you might call a privately funded force. When they heard the witches' stories, they went out and located your silver kegs of prana poison. All you need to do is show up and collect them."

"Seriously?" I blink, my heart picking up speed. "You mean we might have really, actually, finally caught a break?"

"What's the catch?" Sloan looks skeptical.

"They mentioned they might have a favor to ask."

Sloan's skepticism blooms into a fully darkened scowl. "What kind of favor? Are ye barterin' with Fi's safety, Grant? How well do ye know these mercenaries?"

The long growl that rumbles out of my phone speaker makes me thankful that Garnet is an ocean away. "Careful, Mackenzie. I allow Fiona to play it loose with me because of her connection with Myra and because she likely couldn't behave with any sort of formal propriety if her life depended on it. That doesn't mean the same liberties extend to you."

I smack Sloan's shoulder and point at the phone.

"Apologies, Governor." Sloan scowls right back at me. "The world is forever takin' more than Fiona can give. I get a little protective because I care about her."

Well, now he's trying to butter me up.

It works. I roll my eyes, and my annoyance fades.

"Fine. I understand posturing to protect your female." There's a long pause on the other end of the phone while his voice muffles and he speaks to someone on his end. "Needless to say, I won't let anyone take advantage of you, Lady Druid. Jimmy assures me this favor will be quick and painless."

"Well, they've hosted our hostages and found four more casks. It's the least I can do in return to talk to them about this favor they need. *Quid pro quo*, amirite?"

"Right you are," Garnet says. "That's good business. It never hurts to make powerful friends and acquaintances in the empowered world."

I nod. "True enough. Thanks for the assist, Garnet. I want this one done so I can come home to my city."

"You sound tired, Lady Druid."

"I am."

"Myra wants you to know she misses you and wants you to come home soon. She has lots she wants to tell you."

I chuckle. "You know most of that will be gushing about you being a big studly lion, right?"

"I assumed as much. Still, it's nice she has a girlfriend she trusts."

Yeah, it is. "Tell her I miss her right back, and once we wrap this up, I'll come straight home."

He chuckles. "She's squealing and bouncing on the bed beside me."

Before my mind goes to Garnet and Myra lounging in bed, I change the subject. "When does Jimmy expect me?"

"Knowing Jimmy, an hour ago. The clock is ticking. The end game is a Samhain ritual, and that would be tonight."

Awesomesauce. "Okay, tell Jimmy I'll gather my hazmat team and be there ASAP."

"Will do."

"And Garnet…thanks, I owe you one."

"You owe me more than one."

"I heart you hard, lion man. Seriously. If you weren't so

damned far away, I would climb your muscled bod and lay one right smack on your lips."

"Yeah, you would, girlfriend," Myra yells in the background. "And I'd let you do it, too."

"All right, you two," he says, amusement thick in his voice. "Let's try to keep this professional."

I snort. "Okay, so where am I going?"

"I'll text you the info. Jimmy will explain the rest to you in person. I'll let him know to expect you."

"He knows not to touch the casks, right?"

"He's aware. The witches described in great detail the workings of their plans. He has no interest in growing gills or a tail."

"Good enough. Laters."

When the call ends, I step into Sloan's personal space, and he hugs me tight to his chest. "When will this day be over? I can't feel my body anymore. Am I standing up? Am I speaking English? Do I have a stunt double who could take the next scene?"

His chest bounces against my cheek. "Tell me where to meet this Jimmy bloke, and I'll collect the casks with Sarah. You head into the spare room and take a nap."

So tempting.

"No. I should go. Garnet's likely told him I'm coming, and he has that favor to ask. I don't need Irish mercenaries on my hate list. It's long enough already."

He squeezes me tight and kisses my forehead before stepping back. "Fine. Fill yer brother in, text Sarah, and give me five minutes. I'll be right back."

"Where are you going?"

"To buy a case of Red Bull."

"Good call. Sugar-free for me, please."

CHAPTER TWENTY-TWO

Sloan, Calum, and I pick up Sarah outside the Blarney Mill before three-thirty and fill her in on the next four casks. "What kind of favor are they askin' for?"

"We don't know."

"But they jumped the queue on findin' the casks so that they can blackmail us to get them back? I don't like the sounds of that."

True story. "It's not my favorite play either, but it's the hand we've been dealt. I want those casks, and if the favor isn't unreasonable, I think we should play their game and make sure everyone wins."

"Do we know anything about these men?"

Calum shakes his head. "I ran the name Jimmy Duncan through the system and got a few hits. No one who matched the man we met last night though. Either he keeps his dealings under the wire, or his name isn't really Jimmy Duncan."

"That's not comforting." Sarah scowls and turns her collar up against the autumn wind buffeting against us. "Very well, I still have a few nappy sacks in my bag, and I tossed in a few other gems in case trouble rears. Emmet suggested that any time I'm out with ye, I prepare for the unexpected."

I shrug. "I can't argue that. So, are we ready?"

When everyone nods, Sloan holds out his hand. We all stack ours, and he places his other hand on the top of the pile. "I've never been to this location, so I'll get us as close as I can."

"That's all you can do, hotness. Your best is always good enough for us."

Sloan *poofs* us to Waterford, a seaport city in southeast Ireland. When I look around, it doesn't take me long to figure out why he's been here.

"So, Waterford. Tell me about its architectural history. I assume this ancient stone wall bears some significance."

Sloan hails a taxi. Once we're tucked inside, and our driver has our destination's address, Sloan sinks back into his seat beside me. "Waterford is Ireland's oldest city and was founded by Vikings in 914 CE. The stone wall ye noticed is part of the original city's core fortifications."

I smile as my historian geek gets his groove on. He loves dates and history. I think about Janet saying that she's never seen him so animated since he's been with me. It's a shame she doesn't take the time to see how he lights up when he's passionate about something.

"And of course, Waterford Crystal began here in 1783. The factory is near the historic district and offers tours. We should come one day. It's a fascinating process."

I smile, take his hand, and rest my head against his shoulder. "Sounds like a great idea. For today, I vote we get the casks, find out what this favor's about, then seal ourselves inside King Henry for five or six hours before we face the witches tonight."

"That sounds amazing, but let's make it the spare room at Lugh's and Lara's. My parents are still lookin' to keep me busy and separate us."

"Good point." I close my eyes and yawn. "Calum, we're taking your bed for an afternoon nap when we've finished here."

"It's yours, Fi. You look like you're about to drop."

"It wouldn't be so bad if my body wasn't made out of lead. Damn, my limbs are *soooo* heavy."

Sloan chuckles, and that's the last thing I remember until he pats my leg sometime later. "We're here, Fi. I hate to wake ye, but it's time."

I blink and groan. "I was having the best dream, too. Remind me later to tell you about it."

The side of his mouth lifts in amusement. "Not something yer willin' to share with the class?"

I waggle my brows and smile. "Not even close."

"I'm intrigued. I will definitely remind you later."

I chuckle and accept his hand to get out and stretch.

Last night, when we first met Jimmy Duncan and his crew, I wasn't sure if Garnet's acquaintances were part of the empowered sector or not. Even in the daylight, I can't tell. To me, seeing them standing outside a concrete water purification station, they look like eight human military men wearing black assault gear and carrying automatic weapons.

"Howeyah, Jimmy. What's the craic?" I approach the crew. "I heard you had a busy day."

Jimmy Duncan is a fit and wiry blond with a crew cut and scruff on his jaw. He steps forward and extends his hand. I wait to see if my shield lights up, but when nothing happens, I meet his palm. "Every day there's an opportunity to keep our skills honed is a good day."

I'd argue that, but whatevs.

I'm sure not everyone would kill for a PJ day.

"I'm thrilled you were able to figure out what the witches are up to. I admit, it's been a long week and to not have to track down these casks is a welcome surprise."

"Did Mr. Grant happen to mention a wee favor?"

I nod. "He didn't mention any more than that. He simply said in return for your efforts that you might expect a little *quid pro quo.*"

Jimmy flashes me a wink. "That's the gist of it."

"You know we're the good guys, right?" Calum shifts in behind me. "We're not druids for hire and won't be part of anything illegal or anything that puts innocents or civilians in danger."

Jimmy nods. "Not a problem, sham. This favor won't put anyone out except the witches themselves. Ye see, as well as tellin' us about the casks and what they're up to tonight, they also mentioned a bit of intel the boys and I found of personal interest."

"Yeah? What was that?"

"They said they robbed a leprechaun's den and found his hoard of gold."

I straighten and raise my hand. "Wait. Before you ask me to steal from that particular Man o' Green, you should know he's a very dear friend of mine."

"Aye, the witches mentioned that. They also mentioned the place was lousy with dragons."

"And?" My response comes out more tersely than I intend, but so far this favor is crossing some very personal boundaries.

"The witches stole a few extra items when they stole the dragon claw dagger."

"Oh? That's news to me. Patty never mentioned anything else that might've been missing."

"Can't help ye there. Maybe he's been busy and hasn't taken inventory. The item we're after isn't made of precious gems or gold."

"And that matters why?"

"Because leprechauns can track gems and gold. The item we're looking for is the wee man's shillelagh."

I strum my fingers to play an imaginary instrument and look to Sloan for clarification. "Is that like a ukulele?"

Sloan shakes his head. "No, it's a wooden walking stick or cudgel made from a stout, knotty blackthorn stick. It usually has a large knob at the top that's good for crackin' someone's noggin'."

"So, it's a walking stick you can use as a weapon in a pinch. Why do you want it?"

Jimmy frowns. "Because an authentic leprechaun walking stick is a high-value item. We have a buyer who will pay a pretty penny for it."

"You only found out they stole it a few hours ago and yet you already have a buyer? Does this buyer know you don't have the item or that it's stolen?"

Jimmy shrugs, unperturbed by my assessment. "We're businessmen, Miss Cumhaill. In business, sometimes ye gotta bend the rules a little to keep yer clients happy."

"Blackmailing me to steal an item that was already stolen from a friend of mine seems like more than bending the rules. It seems like an out and out dick thing to do. I'll be honest with you. It doesn't make me happy in the least."

Jimmy shrugs. "Maybe from atop yer high horse that's how the view looks but from where I stand, four casks of pure fae prana is a much more valuable commodity than one wooden stick. Yer gettin' the better end of the deal here."

I can't argue that, and yeah, my priority is to recover the casks of prana and return them to the cistern. "Fine, but Patty isn't happy about being robbed once. He won't be any happier to learn he's been robbed twice, and I won't lie to him."

"Fair enough. Ye can fill him in, but not until after we have the shillelagh in hand. To that end, ye'll all need to hand over yer phones."

Calum snorts. "Yeah, and you can kiss my precious—"

Four of the eight raise their automatic weapons, and each one of them points at one of us.

Like that is it? "Well, you're not going to shoot us, so you might as well put down your guns."

Jimmy flashes me a crooked grin. "That sure of things are ye?"

"It's basic logic. If you kill us, you don't get what you want." I hold up my finger before he can argue.

"Yes, you'll have the casks, but you already know the Goddess wants them back, so she'll not take kindly to you double-crossing her envoys."

He feigns disinterest, and the guns remain poised.

"Fine, if pissing off a goddess doesn't scare you, then you know Garnet Grant will track you down because he vouched for you and he's a close friend of mine."

I give him a chance to let that sink in.

"If Garnet's fury doesn't deter you enough, maybe you should know I'm bonded to a mythical spirit bear that will rip you all to shreds for hurting me. Even after you kill me, he will hunt you for eternity and dice you up to bits."

I release Bruin, and he swirls through the air and materializes in front of the men with guns, snarling and growling into the air in front of their faces.

"And if that doesn't deter you, then I'll add in the queen dragon and my friend Patty, the Man o' Green you want me to rob because I guarantee you they will hunt you down too."

Jimmy eyes me up and down, and I get the sense he's assessing how serious I am.

"I'm not bluffing Mr. Duncan, and you must know it. I find it very difficult to believe you'd ask me any of this unless you already knew my connections and abilities."

After a long moment, Jimmy lifts his hands and gives me a slow clap. "Well done, Miss Cumhaill. Ye may talk like an American, but ye've got the Irish in ye."

I chuff. "I talk like a Canadian, and you bet your precious ass

I've got the Irish in me. Now have your men lower their guns, or this meeting of the minds ends in bloodshed."

He hesitates a moment more, then smiles. "All right, we'll play it yer way, but I'll need yer word that none of the four of ye will tip the leprechaun off to where we're goin' or what we're doin' until it's over. No phonin'. No textin'. No warnin' him where we'll be."

"You have my word. Now, where are we going? I'm tired and would rather be horizontal right now sawing logs. Let's get this over with."

The address Jimmy gives me for where the shillelagh is stashed is back in Dublin. A moment after he gives us our instructions, Sloan *poofs* me, Calum, and Sarah into a shadowed stoop outside a seedy-looking pub.

"The Witch's Brew." I read the glowing fuschia neon. "Do you think the name is cute for the non-magical, or enchanted to draw only those who are empowered inside?"

Sarah holds her hand up and tests the air. "The second one. There's a warding spell creating a barrier. It's subtle, but it's there."

I sigh. "Damn. I was kinda hoping it was the first one."

"Why's that, Fi?" Calum asks.

"Because now we have to go into a bar of witches when we're in the process of dismantling an evil witch plot and have recently killed or imprisoned two dozen of their friends."

Sarah chuckles. "Not all witches are friends, and we certainly don't talk about coven business with other witches. Odds are, no one will give us a second glance."

That goes a long way in easing my nerves. "Okay, let's get in there, scope out where Patty's walking stick might be, then grab it and get gone."

"Easy as pie," Calum says. "Hell, you and Sloan will be spooning and catching up on your shuteye in no time."

My eyes flutter closed at the mention of it. "Fair warning, Mackenzie, the more exhausted I am, the higher the odds that I'm going to snore."

Sloan chuckles. "Ye mean there are nights when ye *don't* sound like yer a buzz saw?"

I smack his six-pack and frown. "Ow, you flexed."

He laughs harder. "I tend to do that when someone's about to hit me. How's yer hand?"

I roll my eyes. "Like you care."

He wraps his big, ropey arms around my shoulder and kisses my cheek. "Yer cranky because ye need sleep. Let's finish this up so we can rest before the Samhain witch ritual tonight."

"Yes, let's," I huff, glaring at the door to the witch pub. "FYI, you're no longer invited to nap time. I want the whole bed to myself."

He chuckles and eases back. "Not a chance. Now, stop stallin' and get inside."

I yawn. "I'm not stalling. My legs aren't responding to my mental command."

Calum gives me a shove from behind and gets me started. "Thanks, bro. I needed that. Okay, so let's keep a low profile and get out of here without drawing attention."

"Got it. Unobtrusive it is," Calum says.

Despite the pub's skeevy exterior, The Witch's Brew is cool and exactly the kind of place I'd hang out in if I lived in Dublin. The main floor boasts a long bar along the back wall with a smoked-mirrored wall behind, lit shelves, and glowing drinks giving off wisps of smoky color.

The clientele is a mixed bag of modern-day witches, some

obvious fae—judging by the pastel rainbow of skin colors, horns, and wings—and other magically empowered mages, wizards, moon called, and the like.

"Fiona and Sloan!" someone shouts off to our right. "What the fuck are ye doin' here?"

As the majority of the conversation stops, all eyes turn to the four of us coming in the door. Awesome.

"Remind me what unobtrusive means again," Calum says. "Because if this is that, I've got it tangled up in my head somehow."

"Har-har." I raise my hand and head over to the table of the heirs of the Nine Families. "Hello, Tad. Was that necessary?"

Tad McNiff, a tall, slick, frat boy-type flashes me a cocky smile. "Necessary? No. Amusing as fuck? Yes."

Sloan gives him the finger and frowns. "From now on, assume that when we frequent a place such as this that we're on druid business and we're tryin' not to be noticed."

The eight heirs in attendance straighten.

"Druid business?" Eric Flanagan repeats.

"Is it somethin' we can get in on?" Jarrod Perry asks.

I look at the eight of them, and part of me is sad that Sloan doesn't feel more connected to them. They are, after all, his peers. In a world where he has no siblings, and his best friends are my grandparents, it would be nice if he could at least count on the heirs as being part of his crew.

Well, if they weren't so dick-ish.

"Found it." Calum steps in so we're shoulder to shoulder and indicates with his thumb behind us. "Over the bar above the top shelf under the signage."

I glance back and groan. "It's ten feet in the air, and there are three bartenders. How the hell are we gonna get it down and get out of here without being stopped?"

Calum frowns. "We need one of Emmet's distractions."

Ciara rolls her eyes. "Don't remind me. After the battle in the clearing at Ross Castle, I had *Cotton Eyed Joe* playin' as an earworm in my head for a week."

Tad grins, and for once, it's genuine instead of there for show. "That was classic. I love that guy."

"So why do ye need the shillelagh off the wall?" Jarrod asks. "And why are ye stealin' it?"

I sigh. "We're not stealing it. We're re-stealing it back. It belongs to my friend Patty."

"The Man o' Green who kept ye prisoner in the dragon's lair?" Tad asks.

I tilt my head back and forth. "I wasn't so much a prisoner as an unwilling bystander while the dragon eggs gestated. Anyway, yes, that Patty."

Sloan catches the server's attention and orders a round.

Once we sit and merge in with the crowd at the table, the curious gazes end, and the other patrons go back to their business. As the pitchers arrive, Sloan fills in the heirs on what we've been up to and what we're dealing with now.

Tad, for once, seems to listen without needing to make some smart-assed remark. Maybe there's hope for him yet. When Sloan's done, he takes a long swallow from his pint and nods. "So, ye need the shillelagh to give to the mercenaries, to get back the casks of stolen fae prana."

"That's about it." I steal a wing from one of the Perry twins. I know their older brother's name is Jarrod, but now that I think about it, I don't know their names. Everyone calls them the Perry twins.

"Well, then." Tad smiles. "We'll create the diversion. The white witch—"

"—her name is Sarah," Sloan snaps.

Tad raises his palms. "Fine, Sarah can remove whatever spell binds it to the wall—because we all know there will be one—and lover boy here can grab it and portal out with his booty."

I roll my eyes. "Can you not say lover boy and booty when

you're referring to Sloan? It triggers images in my mind that shouldn't be there."

Sloan scowls at me. "No. Let's not do that."

Calum chuckles. "Okay, now I'm imagining the two of them. It's pretty hot."

Tad holds up his palms. "Please stop. It's horrifying. Now, does everyone know their part?"

We all go over things one more time and nod.

"Okay, here goes nothing."

CHAPTER TWENTY-THREE

What kind of trouble can eleven young Irish druids, a white witch, and one spirit bear get into at a witch bar? When they put their minds to it—a lot. Honestly, when Tad lays out the nuances of his three-part plan, I know, without a shadow of a doubt, I've been cast in the perfect role for me.

I get to punch Ciara Doyle and start a catfight.

Although we've managed to be civil the last couple of times we've interacted, I owe her one—more than one.

Funny, as much as I despised her at first, now I sort of get her. What I originally took as her being shallow and judgy is her defense mechanism.

Snide is her armor.

Humor is mine.

Look at that, common ground.

Sarah catches my attention from the back hall, and I refocus. She's on her way back from her fake trip to the bathroom to get into position by the bar.

I finish my Guinness and stand. "Guys, stop getting mesmerized by her boobs. She's not all that."

Ciara arches a perfectly plucked brow. "Says the girl that

hasn't progressed from her training bra. Hater's gotta hate. Maybe one day you'll grow a pair."

I laugh, wave my arms in the air, and draw more attention. "Maybe if you spent less time glossing your lips and picked up a book you'd have something to offer men other than a booty call."

"Yer only sour because ye haven't got the goods to catch a man's eye."

"Please. You ain't pretty. You just look that way. What have you got going for you other than your glamor?"

Ciara laughs. "And what? Yer a centerfold pinup? Yer Canadian. It's almost November. Have ye taken out yer thermal underwear and hats with ear flaps?"

No, but I have to. Admitting that wouldn't win me any points in this argument though.

In my peripheral vision, I watch Tad ease closer to the bouncers as they hear our raised voices and turn.

"And what were you thinking when you put on that shirt?" I point at the designer t-shirt she has tied at her hip. "Have you ever heard of an iron?"

"I was thinking your boyfriend should learn not to strip a girl and toss her shirt into a heap. It got wrinkled."

"Bitch."

"Whore."

Ciara charges me, and I punch her in the gut and toss her onto the next table. I call my armor forward and let Bruin loose. My bear plays his part perfectly and snarls and roars.

Witches scream and scatter.

Tad, Jarrod, and Eric cut off the two bouncers as they turn and move to rein in the chaos. Whatever spell they hit the brawny brutes with knocks them on their asses. Sarah lobs nappy sacks at the bartenders, and they drop too. Bruin roars again and sends a table spinning across the floor. Sloan sips his beer at the end of the bar, taking it all in.

Our server girl legit pees her pants.

Ciara rolls me onto my back and gives me her best right cross. "Feckin' hell, Cumhaill."

I laugh as she shakes out her fist. "Armor's up."

"No kidding."

I roll her off me and check to see if anyone is watching us anymore. Nope.

Sarah hops over the downed bartenders and onto the chair Sloan brings to her. The two of them are just getting started when a woman storms out from the back looking like she's ready to raze the world.

I drop to the floor and plant my palms on the floorboards. Reaching deep into the foundation of the soil below, I conjure up an earthquake. The woman grabs the frame of the doorway and scowls. She totes sees it's me causing her building to shimmy-shimmy-shake and she doesn't look happy about it.

She fires off a bolt of energy. Damn, she's fast.

There's no way I have time to counter or defend. I lift my hands to shield when Ciara shouts something, and the bolt veers left and hits the power box on the wall.

The pub goes dark, and another round of screaming ensues. My weird freaky fae eyes flare, and now I see everything in evil aura heat signatures.

It kinda makes me feel bad.

Almost everyone here is a good person minding their own. I suppose not all witches be bitches after all.

I glance over at where Sarah is finishing with the binding spell on the shillelagh and marvel at her aura. It's so pretty and pure it amazes me. Okay, so maybe there are witches who adhere to the harm none tenet and who are genuinely non-violent and nice peeps.

I stand corrected.

Red, time to go. Sloan's got Patty's walkin' stick. Let's get gone.

Done deal. I run through the chaos and grab Sarah's wrist. "It's Fi. Time to go."

"Can you see?"

"Yep. Trust me. We're good."

A few seconds later, we emerge out the front door, and the brilliance of the streetlights blinds me.

Sloan is waiting and *poofs* us straight away and onto a rooftop across the city. He deposits us and is gone again. A second later, Tad flashes in with the Perry twins laughing their asses off. Sloan's back with Ciara and Calum. It goes like that until we're all accounted for.

When we're all there, I flop on my butt and take a breath. "So, we got it?"

Sloan holds up the shillelagh and nods. "Yep. Now the question is, what are ye goin' to do with it?"

I shrug. "Give it to Jimmy and his crew. A deal's a deal."

Calum makes a face as if he's surprised.

"Patty's linked to his treasure. If he wants it back, I have no doubt he can reclaim it. Given the fact that it's between an old, gnarly walking stick and raw, fae prana, I vote we secure the casks and worry about the stick later."

"Fair enough. What does it do?" Calum asks.

"An authentic shillelagh belongin' to a Man o' Green is said to offer the owner untold luck," Tad says. "It's likely why the witch proprietor of that pub had it mounted above her bar. She was hopin' to cash in on the magic of the thing."

"It sucks to be her. My guess is she's in league with the dark witches somehow and knew it was stolen. Sorry, not sorry."

Sloan nods. "Agreed. Now to get it back to Jimmy and his men and unhook the casks from pumpin' into the water in the purification station."

I groan. "Right. There's that still."

"Then the ritual tonight."

I drop my head forward and want to melt right there onto the roof of the building. "Gawd, when will this day be over?"

"Not anytime soon, I'm afraid." Sloan helps me up. "There's still work to be done."

"Yeah, yeah." I cover my mouth as I yawn. "Let's go get those casks."

"Yer dead on yer feet," Ciara says. "After ye make yer trade with the mercenaries, Sloan can take ye home for a nap, and we'll help with the casks. Ye don't have to do everything yerself, Cumhaill."

"No, she doesn't," Sarah says. "Sloan and I have disarmed the casks enough now that we can do it. Ye'll need to get some rest before tonight."

The Perry twins nod. "Yeah, hangin' out with yer family has been the most action we've ever been included in for the Order. We're pleased to help."

My head drops back, and I smile up to the heavens. "Thank you, baby Groot. I'm not even gonna pretend to argue. Let's give Jimmy his stick, then I'm going to bed for a few hours, or I'll never be able to take on the witches tonight."

"We're helpin' tonight too, right?" Tad asks. "Tell us where and when and we're there."

Sloan frowns. "We won't know where and when until we hand over the shillelagh. Then the men we're dealin' with are supposed to give us the final pieces to the puzzle."

Tad nods. "Well then, I'll take everyone home to change, eat, and rest up. Text me the details when ye get them, and we'll meet ye wherever and whenever ye need us."

I look at the heirs and smile. "Thanks, guys. Seriously. We're happy to have your help."

I wake to a gentle pat on my leg and the warm smile of my Gran peering down on me. Well, not only me. Sloan's asleep behind me, his face nuzzled into the back of my hair, his hand draped over my hip. "It's time to wake up, luv. Sloan asked me to wake ye at ten-thirty so ye'd have time to eat and stretch before ye head out."

"Okay, thanks, Gran. I'm awake."

She brushes a gentle hand over my forehead and cups my cheek. "I'm sorry this life demands so much from ye, luv. I truly am. Yer granda and I had no idea things would turn out as they have. Yer destiny has been such a tumultuous storm."

"It's okay. Other than the narrow brushes with death, I wouldn't change a thing."

I think the sound of our voices stirs Sloan from the depths of his sleep because he shifts behind me and grinds his hips against my ass.

Gran's eyebrows raise as my cheeks flare scarlet. I pat his wrist, and he startles awake. "Gran's here to wake us up."

He relaxes and scrubs a hand over his face. "Good. Thanks, Lara. I appreciate it."

Gran's smile is far too knowing, and after her condom intervention, I'm fighting the urge to pull the covers over my head. I figure my best course of action is to slip out from under the quilt and show her I'm fully clothed and decent.

I am, however, careful to drop the covers to keep Sloan covered because he's sporting wake-up wood and would likely die if Gran commented on that.

"Is there tea, Gran?"

"Have ye ever known me to be out?"

I chuckle. "No. Forgive me. I'm still half-asleep."

"Forgiven. I'll go heat ye both up a plate of supper."

"Sounds great. Thank you." I sit on the edge of the bed, and when Gran leaves the room, I giggle and flop back onto the mattress. "Hey, I love the sentiment, but if you could tell Mr. Big Idea to keep the pelvic grinding to a minimum in front of my grandmother, that would be great."

Sloan's dark eyes grow wide. "I didn't."

"Oh, you did. I expect we'll receive another box of condoms soon. Maybe she'll go the Ostara route, and it'll be like an Easter hunt, and we'll find them everywhere tucked into our things and hidden under our pillows."

Sloan shakes his head as if trying to clear the cobwebs. "Sorry about that."

I chuckle and wave that away. "A man can't be held responsible for his body's base instinct while sleeping, especially while he's snuggled up cozy with his girlfriend."

He looks like he might argue that or apologize, but honestly, s'all good.

"All right, change of subject. How did the cask retrieval go after you *poofed* me home?

"Blissfully uneventful. As Sarah said, we've done it enough times now that it's rote."

"And we know the location for their Samhain ritual celebration in a few hours?"

"The Ring of Rath."

"Oh, that sounds foreboding. What is that?"

Sloan swings his long legs out from under the quilt and pulls out his phone. "Its proper name is the Rathgall Hillfort. It's an eighteen-acre hill fort near the town of Shillelagh on the Wicklow/Carlow border. It's considered one of Ireland's most ancient faery rings and dates back to the Bronze Age. It's a sacred site for a sacred night."

"Okay, what does that tell us?"

"Nothin' good that I can think of. All we know is that they're usin' the Sabbat to pierce the veil and call forth a dark fae lord and are offering themselves up for his favor."

"It's like a bad joke. What do you get when you put ancient faery rings, dark witches who stole fae prana, and Samhain together? A Hazmat Sabbat."

"Are ye done?"

"Yep. Sorry. Carry on."

"It says here that the Ring of Rath consists of three roughly concentric stone ramparts with a fourth masonry wall dating from the Medieval period at its center."

"So, if I were a dark witch and I wanted to get dark and dirty with an Unseelie fae dude, this might be the kind of place where we'd hook up?"

"I would say so, yes."

"Okay, so we need to get there and cock-block."

"Now that ye won't fall over."

I nod. "I feel much better. Better enough to go stop an evil orgy and recover the last cask."

"Call yer brothers and see if they're ready. I'll text Nikon and tell him the address of where we'll be so he can Google it. Tonight, we end this."

According to the intel Jimmy Duncan and his men gleaned from the witches we captured, the grand finale of their dark plan is to host a Samhain celebration and offer themselves up to an Unseelie fae prince.

It seems they want to offer the last cask, the location of the Cistern of The Source, and the mutants to prove their value. Then, to further please the fae dark lord, to have sex with him and prove their devotion.

While Sloan *poofs* off to get Sarah and Patty, Calum and I sit on the edge of the roof of a building a few hundred feet from the bottom of the hillock.

Sitting shoulder to shoulder with my older brother, we let our feet dangle down the side of the structure while we wait for the arrival of both our Toronto and Ireland support teams.

"You gotta wonder where life went off the rails for these women." I stare out at the lantern lights being lit in the distance. "I mean, when did they start thinking it's normal to say, hey, on Samhain this year, instead of celebrating our ancestors, why don't we mutilate people and have orgy sex with an Unseelie fae and become his pets?"

"What? That's not blinking at the top of your to-do list?"

"Surprisingly, no. It doesn't even make my top hundy."

"Weird."

"Right?"

"Does Wallace think he can fix the people they transformed already?"

"No. Ciara said they're toast. The Source energy is too powerful for us to reverse. They're now fae beasts for life."

"That sucks."

"Yep."

"You're sure Emmet's going to be all right?"

"I'm not going to argue with Mother Nature."

"No. I guess not. Good point."

I shrug and think about my brother. "I think there's likely more to come of his plunge into power, but I also think that it's drinking the stuff that's the kiss of death. Nikon's father only touched it, and his entire line of descendants became immortal and juiced with power."

"Can you imagine Emmet with unlimited power?"

I laugh. "We should plan for the alpaca-lypse now."

"Right? I can see him wishing alpacas roam the streets."

"They do have lovely, soft fur."

"And have better manners than their llama cousins."

"Llamas should realize spitting is socially unacceptable and clean up their acts."

"Then they can tell the camels, and their family might get more love."

We sit there in easy silence for a while before he bumps shoulders with me. "You're rocking the druid thing, sista. We're all mega proud of you, but we worry too. Remember to take time for yourself. This afternoon you were *way* too tired. Don't let yourself get run down like that."

"Sloan and I joked that when this is over, we should spend a week with King Henry's drapes pulled and hide away in his bed."

"Go on." He waggles his dark brows and flashes a smile. "How's the private time going with the studly Sloan?"

"Really good, but I meant sleeping."

"Sleeping, eh? That's disappointing."

I chuckle. "That's as far as we've gotten. I don't want to make assumptions or mistakes with him. He's too important to me, us, Gran, and Granda. We're taking it slow."

"No one ever took it slower than Kevin and I, and it turned out pretty well. Seriously, we waited eleven years."

I laugh. "You met when you were five."

"It still was a long wait."

"True. You and Kev inspire me. I want that."

Calum takes my hand from where it lies on my thigh and kisses my knuckles. "I have no doubt you'll have it. You deserve every happiness this world offers, baby girl. You inspire us every day."

I hug Calum's arm and take a mental snapshot. The Irish countryside is so much darker here at night than anywhere in Toronto. It's eerie, but it's cool.

"Look at that." Sloan appears behind us. "Yer exactly where I left ye, safe and sound. That's such a refreshin' surprise."

"Hey, surly," I roll to the side and get up and away from the ledge. "I'm not a total danger magnet. There are moments when things go smoothly."

Sloan chuckles. "Be sure to point them out. I don't want to miss one."

"Har-har, you're hilarious." Swallowing, I tilt my head to the side and catch Patty's attention. "Can I talk to you for a second in private?"

"Sure. Why the long face?"

When we're far enough from the others that I can speak to him privately, I fill him in on our day's events: finding out about the shillelagh, stealing it from The Witch's Brew, then giving it to Jimmy in barter for the details about tonight and the four casks at the purification plant.

"I'm sorry, buddy." I rub the ache in my chest when I see the disappointment in his gaze. "I pride myself on loyalty, but I was stuck with this one. I needed those casks, and I figured if I help you get them back, it might make up for it a little."

Patty waves his stubby fingers in the air and shakes his head. "Och, I don't care about that old chunk of wood. My ex-wife gave me that thing. Sure, it gave me great luck when we were together, but the moment we ended things, that shillelagh turned nasty. It's like a harbinger of doom. I'm afraid whoever ends up with it is in fer a rude awakenin'."

"So, you're not mad?"

"With you? Never. Ye did what ye thought was right and that's all I can ask."

"Then why did you look so upset?"

"Because the beauty of havin' a secret lair is the 'secret' part. Through no fault of yers, a dozen of yer friends and family have been through there this week. Before that, the witches came through. Baba Yaga knows where we are. And now a band of mercenaries has the location. It doesn't sit right with me at all. I think the queen and I will have to find ourselves a new place to live."

"I'm so sorry."

He pats my hand and winks. "Don't give it another thought, Fi. It was bound to happen one day. I'd rather move than have more intrusions into our private space."

"I suppose." Still, I feel awful. "If I can help, let me know. Oh… will I still be able to portal there or are you talking super-secret?"

Patty frowns. "Yer family, Fi. We'll make sure yer portal band still works. Ye need to keep tabs on the kids, after all."

I nod, thankful to make the cut. "I do. Thanks for not being mad, Patty. I was worried."

Patty shakes his head. "Don't give it a second thought. Of all the gold, gems, and priceless things I own, yer one of my greatest treasures, Fi. Let the world steal from my hoard. As long as yer well, we're good."

I hug him and take the first deep breath of the day. "Thanks, oul man. I didn't know you were such a romantic."

"Och, it's a curse, I swear. How do ye think I ended up with thirty-six ex-wives?"

"Thirty-six? Wow. How did I not know that?"

"Weel, that's a tale for another night."

CHAPTER TWENTY-FOUR

The Ireland heirs arrive bursting with energy and bouncing on the balls of their feet. Thankfully, Nikon arrives with our Toronto backup team almost immediately after. I'm both surprised and thrilled to have everyone here. "Emmet and Dillan, don't you have to work?"

"We're on afternoons," Dillan says. "The real question is 'don't we have to sleep?'"

Emmet shrugs. "And apparently, the answer is no. So, we're set to go."

I blow them a kiss and get started. "Okay, so, here's what we know and what we suspect. The witches we caught last night—gawd was that only last night?"

"Seems like a week ago," Sloan says.

It does. "Anyway, Garnet's associates, Jimmy and the mercenaries interrogated the witches."

"Hashtag, tortured." Da frowns.

"Not necessarily. They might have some kind of a psychic info puller on their crew. We don't know."

"Och, I'm fairly certain I know."

Cranky pants. "I'd argue, but you're Irish so there's no point.

Also, they aren't the most scrupulous bunch, so you're probably right."

"I usually am."

"Point to you. You usually are." Turning back to the others, I continue. "In some manner of information extraction, the witches confirmed that their end goal was to come here on the eve of Samhain when the veil between realms is thinnest, and contact an Unseelie prince."

"What for?" Aiden asks.

"From the sounds of it, to put themselves up for an orgy offering and win his favor."

Aiden's brow arches. "Have they tried Tinder?"

"I think it's less about the hookup and more about entering into a partnership with a powerful dark fae."

"To what end?" Da asks.

"Undetermined. More power would be my first guess."

"Does the sinister sex partner know about this arrangement?"

"Not that we know of. From what we heard, it's kind of a first impression thing."

Emmet snorts. "Hi, howeyah, we brought you Source energy, fae mutants, and a boner bonus bonanza. Will you be our baleful bae?

"How about my heinous horndog?" Calum adds.

"Or my murderous love-muffin," Dillan says.

"Woeful Wookie?" Tad chimes in.

I raise my hand to slow their roll. "Yeah, that's about it."

"Sweet deal for him," Emmet says.

"Are the last casks down there?" Dora looks a little lost in my brothers' chatter.

"We've managed to track down and secure all but one. Supposedly, it's here as part of the offering."

"You've been busy, girlfriend," Dora says. "No wonder you look so tired."

I nod. "After this is over, consider me on vacation for a month. Seriously, I'm shutting off the world."

"It would be good to confirm that the cask is here and how heavily it's guarded," Dillan says.

"I sent Bruin to scope things out. He should've been back by now." I glance over my shoulder and stare out across the dark expanse. "I hope everything is all right."

Tad chuckles. "You hope Bruin, an ancient bear spirit and the unstoppable killing warrior, is safe against a bunch of posturing dark witches that won't even know he's breezing through their midst?"

"Well, fine. When you say it like that..."

"It's hard not to worry when danger abounds, *mo chroi*. It's natural." Da squeezes my arm. "What do ye think about the cloven courter? Will he engage in a fight against us or step back and stay out of it?"

No one seems to have an opinion about that.

"I vote he takes his leave and bows out."

The wind picks up, and Bruin manifests beside us. "Well, now the gang's all here. Hello all."

Da nods. "What did you find out, Bear?"

"It's a sight to be seen down there, I'll tell ye."

"What do ye mean?"

"It's like a Jamaican hedonist resort surrounded by a carnival freak show. Between the outer rings, there are fifty or more mutant fae abominations, and in the inner rings, all the women are naked and oilin' themselves up in front of a cluster of civilians."

Tad busts up laughing. "How does yer spirit bear know about Jamaican hedonist resorts, Cumhaill? Where have ye been takin' him, and why wasn't I invited?"

I flick my hand through the air to wave that image out of my head and sigh. "Your internet privileges will be scrutinized a lot more closely, Bear. Seriously, I'm putting on the parenting filters."

"Back to the problem at hand," Da says. "Why are there civilians here?"

Bruin shakes his head and his long fur flutters around his face. "By the look of things, they're volunteers to transform for the guest of honor."

Emmet grunts. "They're volunteering to drink the killer Kool-Aid? That's whacked."

"People are so stupid," Dillan snaps.

"Now, now." Da sends them both a quelling look. "Dial back the condemnation. We don't know the situation. Maybe they were misled or compelled in some way. It's not our place to judge. The point is, now we also have to secure them, clear their memories, and deposit them back into their lives."

"Sloan and I can clear them after things are taken care of," Ciara says.

"So, back to the oily rubdowns," Calum says. "I'm not looking forward to seeing Moira's girl parts in battle."

Bear chuckles. "There are others for you to face off against. I admit I got distracted enough to forget to come straight back."

I roll my eyes. "And here I was getting worried."

His deep, bass laughter says he's not sorry.

"Naked isn't good," Sarah says.

"How so?" Dillan asks. "Works for me."

He raises his hands when we all turn and scowl. "I mean, if they're all naked, they aren't carrying weapons, they can't run off and blend, and they might even be distracted about facing off with an army of studly dudes. Geez, such dirty minds."

I chuckle. "All right, you talked your way out of that one like a boss."

"Thank you."

I gesture at Sarah to continue. "What did you mean by naked not being good?"

"Well, if they were in robes, we could at least try to infiltrate and get closer. With all the women naked, there's no chance."

Emmet chuckles. "Weeeel, that's not quite true. You girls could take one for the team."

I give my brother a droll stare. "We're not getting naked. They know the women in their group, dumbass. Then they'd capture us and as Dillan said, we'd have no weapons and wouldn't be able to run off and blend."

"You'd have Birga," Emmet corrects.

"The girls aren't gettin' naked, Emmet," Da says. "We'll have to encircle the stones and come in from all sides in a coordinated assault."

"Agreed," Sloan says. "And sooner rather than later. Bruin, was the cask there? Either Nikon, Tad, or I should commit to getting to it and flashing it out."

"You do that," I say. "You know where to stash them and can get back here for the fight. Then we'll transport all of them back to where they belong, and we're finished."

"Not entirely," Sarah says. "I want justice for my coven. We won't be done until that's taken care of."

I nod. "Agreed. Sarah gets justice for her lost coven sisters. *Then* we're done."

"Agreed," the others say.

Emmet looks at the heirs and chuckles. "You were jelly because we get all the action, weren't you?"

"Um...yeah," Tad deadpans. "Share the battles, bro. Some of us have trained our entire lives and been sitting on our thumbs."

Da arches a brow. "Well, with a moat full of mutants to deal with as well as the witches, the more, the merrier."

Emmet nods. "Da brought us up right. We know how to share. We'll probably need a distraction, don't you think?"

"No. We should be good."

Sloan fights back a smile. "No, Niall, I think Emmet's right. If

I'm portaling in to go for the cask, an Emmet distraction is likely a solid idea."

Da rolls his eyes and shrugs. "Fine, Emmet. Delight us with yer strategic wit."

Emmet fist-pumps the air. "Oh, I will. And thanks, Irish. You win big points for making this happen. In fact, I'm taking you off boyfriend probation."

Sloan smiles. "Much appreciated."

I peg Emmet with a look. "Do we get a hint on the distraction or is it a surprise?"

Emmet grins wide. "Oh, it's a surprise."

Tad, Nikon, and Sloan take us down to the rings in three groups. The plan is set. Draw the witches away from the cask so Sloan can get in and get out. While he's busy doing that, the rest of us will assess the fae creatures and capture the witches—sedating them when possible.

That last part is Sarah's addition.

It makes me wonder what she meant when she said it won't be over until she gets her justice. What does a witch's revenge look like when it's demanded by a passive white witch who believes in harm none?

The way the rings are set, there's a small rise in the land-scape as we move closer to the center. A wide circle of stacked stones divides each ring. They stand six feet tall in some places and up to twelve feet thick. From the rooftop where we observed, we couldn't grasp the sense of how truly involved the stonework is.

It's quite impressive.

It also plays to our benefit because when we materialize on the outside edge of the rings, no one can see us.

"So far so good—"

I jinx us, and Moira Morrigan lights the bonfire with her arms extended toward the night sky.

Prince Keldane, our Unseelie male,
Visit us from behind the veil.
With offerings of both flesh and power,
Our intentions lain this sacred hour.
A joining of both body and aim,
To dominate and lay your claim.

I blink at Dillan. "I guess that covers things."

Dillan chuckles. "If I were in charge of the spell writing, I would've finished with more of a hook...

So, slip on through the faery glass,
To get you some dark witch ass."

"I like it. Catchy and super classy."

Dillan nods. "I'm a poet."

Something shifts in the night and a call of darkness tugs at me. My eyes sting as the glamor burns away and my freaky night vision activates.

Dammit. I'm not immune to the taint of Morgana's darkness after all. Still, being able to see the witches highlighted against the darkness is a boon. I choose to take the silver lining for what it's worth.

Sloan frowns. "When yer brother activates his signal, I'm goin' straight for the cask. Call yer armor and watch yer back until I'm done and can watch it for ye, yeah?"

I call forward my body armor, and my skin hardens to shield me from physical damage. "Don't spill any of that pink liquid on you. I try not to judge, but I don't think I can love you if you're a fae mutant who tries to eat my face."

"Understood. I wouldn't think less of ye for it either."

Calum crouch-runs over to us and flashes hand signals. I interpret and whisper in Sloan's ear. "Everyone's in position. We're holding until the signal."

Sloan nods and takes a guarded peek over the rise of stones. Turning back, he points at his eyes and into the circle, giving me a thumbs up.

He sees the cask. Good. That's good.

The wind picks up, and I grip my hair as it smacks against my face. The sky above lights up as if we're in a drive-in theater and the projector is using the night as a backdrop screen. The sepia scene above is of a wooden farmhouse caught in the tumultuous winds of a twister. "Auntie Em?" The house spins and spins until it comes down with a thud, and all that's left of the witch it crushes is her shoes.

I chuckle at my brother's sense of humor and grab my hair as wild wind sweeps over the stone circles bringing the impact of the images to life. Nice touch.

Moira drops her arms at the end of repeating her incantation for the third time. Like every witch in the circle, she looks up at the sky as the iconic scene plays out.

The movie breaks into a chorus of Munchkins singing *Ding Dong The Witch is Dead*, and Moira searches her surroundings.

Too bad. So sad.

By then, Sloan has *poofed* in and *poofed* out.

Da, Emmet, Dora, Sarah, and I are the ones taking on the witches on the inner ring from our side. Nikon, Dillan, Aiden, and Patty are coming in from the opposite side. Bruin gets to Killer Clawbearer his way through the crowd as he likes, and Tad, Ciara, and the others from the heir's group are on mutant guard dog duty.

"We've been robbed," Moira shrieks.

I chuckle as I Bo Duke it over the stone wall. "Technically, you're the thieves. We're the repo officers."

Moira throws her hand out, and a bolt of purple magic shoots at me. I barely manage to drop to the grass in time to evade. Still, the crackle of the power surge it gives off singes my shirt.

Damn. She's juiced up. I roll to the balls of my feet and look at my charred outfit. "I have to talk to the Order about having a clothing allowance."

Nikon chuckles. "With what you make as a Guild Governor, you should be able to buy a new shirt."

I raise my arm over my head and block the blow of a boulder hurled at me. My body armor makes it feel more like a pebble. "Wait. What? I get paid to be on the Guild of Empowered Ones?"

"Of course you do." Nikon drops to the grass and sweeps the legs out from under the witch he faces. "What? Oh, my gods. You were honestly going to hold the seat because it was the right thing to do, weren't you?"

"Maybe."

The moment Nikon's witch is down, Sarah moves in and slams her in the belly with a knock-out water balloon.

Nikon chuckles. "It's a lot harder to wrangle naked and oiled up women than you'd think. I'm out of practice."

I spin and crack Moira with the blunt end of Birga's staff. She grunts and buckles at the waist. "Have a lot of experience with slicked-up nudes, do you?"

He laughs and grabs a discarded wand off the ground. Waving it with a little flick and pointing it, he sends off a series of blue bolts like laser rapid-fire.

Pew, pew, pew.

That's the second time I've seen him do witch magic. I really have to ask him about his abilities.

"Life in Ancient Greece is hard to describe."

I spin Birga in my hand and am about to swipe left and take Moira out when Sarah rushes in and pelts her hard in the head with one of her nappy sacks.

The bitch doesn't drop.

I spin Birga in my hand and crack her on the side of the face with the wooden staff. She goes down for the count. Although she's unconscious, Sarah pegs her with another witchy water balloon.

"Does that make you feel better?" I chuckle as I search for my next opponent.

"Not really," Sarah says. "I wanted it to, but it doesn't."

"Sorry. Yeah, I get that. My brother was murdered a couple of months ago, and I'll never get over the injustice of it. I want everyone involved to die a fiery death."

"You're speaking my language, female," a guy says behind me.

A slender man with opal-white skin and a malevolent grin stares at me. He's bare-chested, his jacket covered in long, black raven feathers, his head covered with a thicket of silver and grey twigs, his eyebrows a gray moss.

When our gazes meet, my dinner curdles in my stomach. My evil eyes register him, and the malevolence is off the chart.

He steps right up to me, and I'm too caught up in his gaze to step back.

"Shit, how tall are you?"

"Six-foot-seven or above. Over seven now. I haven't had my twigs pruned in a while."

I shake my head as the burning heat of my shield scalds my nerve-endings, and I snap out of whatever hold he has on me. "Sorry I ruined your orgy, Prince Keldane."

He glances around at all the dead and unconscious women. "Me too. I usually like to have my needs met before I kill them, but breathing is not a deal-breaker. I can still work with this."

"Um…no, you can't. For one, that's gross. For another, these women have to stand before the Divine Goddess to face their crimes."

"Then who will sate my thirst to consume, little one? Will it be you?"

"As tempting as that sounds," *not*, "I'll have to pass. The goddess expects me, and I'm sure you have to head back.

Samhain's almost over. I bet you can still make a fae party or two back home if you hurry."

I sense Sloan's presence as soon as he *poofs* in behind me. Holding my hand open, I signal for him to keep his distance for the moment.

A second later, Tad's there with the heirs, Da arrives with Clan Cumhaill, and Nikon arrives with Dora, Sarah, and Patty.

Keldane eyes the opposing force and smiles. "As much fun as it would be to prove you all foolish to challenge me, you're right. The power of the hour is waning, and I have yet to find a plaything to sate my needs for the year."

Oh, like a New Year's resolution.

"Take her." Sarah points at Moira on the grass. "She's the one who called you and made promises of flesh and fealty. It's her you want."

Okay, mystery solved. Sarah might not serve up vengeance personally, but she has no problem ensuring it's served.

A witch's revenge served cold.

"Very well." Keldane tosses Moira and a couple of the others over his shoulder and heads back to the altar.

Morally, I object, but they were the ones who wanted to play this game.

Wow, to see their faces when they wake up later.

Before Keldane passes through the veil, he turns and meets my gaze. "I'll see you again, little one."

I shiver as he returns to his side of the realm and the dark energy conjured by his portal evaporates. "Not if I see you first."

Everyone looking at me has the same worried glare on their faces. "I can't help it. It's this stupid Fianna mark. Stop looking at me like I have any control over it."

Funny. After a week of tracking witch madness and battles and dealing with magic-infused mutants, I'm not sure what to do with myself after the final battle.

Sloan and Dora wipe the civilians' memories and get them sorted with a member of the Order who will handle getting them all back to where they belong.

The heirs go back to Tad's for a few celebratory bevvies.

Nikon transports the rest of us to Sloan's panic room to get the casks and return them to the Cistern.

Emmet is uncomfortable about going into the lake area, so Sloan asks him to stay out in the antechamber with Sarah and me while they take in the recovered casks and carefully return them to the lake.

"A job well done." Da sets his empty cask down twenty minutes later.

Dora and Dillan take the last two inside, and Sloan, Aiden, and Nikon bring out their empties.

Nikon props the silver cask with the others. "At the very least, they had a decent containment vessel."

"Yeah, goddess forbid they contaminate themselves," Sloan adds. "They wanted to make sure they saved all the torture for the innocent and unwitting."

I rub the ache in my chest. He hasn't said much about what Moira and the witches did to him, but I know it's still upsetting for him.

Dillan and Dora exit the cistern chamber and Dora seals the stone wall. She removes the key, separates the three components, and hands the other two pieces to Sloan and Patty. "May the key never be reassembled."

"To that end," the goddess steps through the stone wall. "If you don't mind, Sloan, I'll take the base of the chalice into my possession."

Sloan is already on his knee and holds up his piece of the key. "Of course, milady."

"Rise, all of you. I deeply appreciate your devotion, but you needn't supplicate yourselves before me. You have each earned the right to stand at my side."

The look of bewilderment on Da's face says he disagrees. She looks at our group and smiles. "There is a great deal of love and camaraderie in this group...but there is suffering too. The losses of late have taken their toll. The hardships of standing against evil weigh you down."

She steps over to Sarah and places her palm against Sarah's forehead. The golden glow encompassing Mother Nature expands to encompass Sarah as well. Sarah's eyes close, but her tears still leak and drip down her cheeks.

"Yes, child. I shall see those involved held responsible."

When she lowers her hand, she moves to Sloan. Part of me doesn't want her to do her mojo thing on him, but I know the pain she senses from him. I feel it too. "These witches have caused quite a bit of turmoil in the lives of good people."

Sloan tenses as the golden glow surrounds him, but his resistance doesn't last long. With a heavy exhale, his entire body eases. "Thank you, milady."

Then she comes to me.

Her palm is warm against my forehead. The instant we're connected, I feel her healing power awakening my cells. The last of the grimy film of darkness peels away, and a cool sensation of relief washes through my body. "There you are, child. Everything is as it's meant to be."

"Thank you." My words come out more like a breathy sigh than an exclamation. I didn't realize how much the taint of Morgana's book weighed on me. "That felt so good."

"I'm glad." She brushes my cheek with a gentle caress of her finger. "You deserve to be eased."

With loose limbs, I step over to Sloan and Sarah as the goddess spends a moment with every member of our party. She tends to each of my brothers, Da, Nikon, Dora, and Patty, then faces us all.

"You made me proud today, children. Standing for justice and fighting for those who can't fight for themselves is a tiring and often thankless calling. Always know I am cheering you on."

"You honor us, goddess," Dora says.

"You honor me in return. Now go. Resume your lives and let this chapter of your adventures be over." She turns and holds out a hand to Sarah. "Come with me, child. Together we'll address those who wronged you and your sisters."

Sarah looks back at us, and I shrug.

How do you say no to Mother Nature?

You don't.

When they disappear into the stone wall, Nikon sighs, still looking a little shaken. "Shall I escort everyone to Gran's and Granda's to say goodbye before we head home?"

I nod. "You take Dora and the fam jam. Sloan and I will take Patty back to the dragon lair to say goodbye to the Dragon Queen and the kids before we join you."

CHAPTER TWENTY-FIVE

"I'm going to miss you, dude." To hug my baby dragon's head, I have to use both arms to get around his neck. He's growing so fast. "I'll be back to visit soon. In the meantime, be good for your queen mama and Patty, okay?"

Patty pats my blue boy's scaly spine and winks. "Och, he will be, won't you Dartamont?"

Dart dips his chin, his pleading gaze pretty much doing me in. "Don't be sad, buddy. I promise. I'll try to find a way to bring you to Toronto for a visit in the spring. The weather is yucky in the winter, and you won't fit in my house. I'll figure out something once things warm up again."

Patty smiles. "The way time passes in the human realm, lad, it won't feel like any time at all. Besides, we'll be busy with the move."

"So, it's set then? Where do you think you'll go?"

Patty shrugs. "Undecided at this point."

"Why are you moving?" Sloan asks.

I fill him in on the convo Patty and I shared on the rooftop earlier tonight.

"What kind of Man o' Green would I be if I left my hoard out where people knew how to access it?"

"A poor one." I smile. "See what I did there? Poor, as in bad and poor as in people could take your gold."

"Och, I got it before the explanation." Patty chuckles and waves me away. "Off with ye now. Get home and get rested up before the next calamity crashes through yer doorway."

I hug Dart, and Scarlet and Chua come over to get a squeeze goodbye, then I wave to the rest and say goodbye to the queen. "I'm glad you feel better, Highness."

The Wyrm Dragon Queen cants her head to the side and smiles—at least, I think it's a smile. It's hard to tell with dragons. "Be safe, Fiona Cumhaill, and thank you. I owe you a life debt, and I shall never forget it."

I dip my chin and reach out for Sloan to take my hand.

It's almost dawn by the time we finish at Granda's and head home. Nikon takes my family home, and Sloan and I make a quick stop at his place before we follow.

"You sure about this, surly?" I ask as I roll his large suitcase to the center of his bedroom.

"I'm sure." He finishes packing a duffle and slings it over his shoulder. "Are ye ready, Manx?"

Manx is sitting beside the suitcase as if to ensure that we can't leave without him. "Do ye have bacon in Toronto?"

"Definitely. We have the traditional kind as well as Canadian back bacon, which is also delish. Do you have anything you want to bring?"

"Just my bowl and my blanket."

I lean into the depths of King Henry and grab his blanket. When I straighten, I find Sloan's spellbook on the bedside table. "We can't forget you or Beauty will be heartbroken."

I slide the bowl and the book into my red suitcase and fold the blanket over my arm. Setting my suitcase next to Sloan's, I watch him take one last tour through his room.

"This is your home, hotness. You don't have to leave it behind. Your parents can only hurt us if we let them." The look Sloan pierces me with is so haunted, I want to cry for him. "They love you the most and the best they can."

He nods. "That used to be enough. Now, after seein' yer family, I want more. I think I deserve more."

"No question. You definitely do."

He purses his lips and sets a handwritten note on the table in his room. "How about it, Manx, my boy? Are ye ready for an adventure?"

Manx flicks his tufted ears. "Beyond ready. I'm proud of ye, sham."

I grip the handle of my suitcase with one hand and Sloan's arm with the other. Sloan grabs his suitcase and Manx. When he's sure we're all secure and connected, he flashes us to my bedroom in Toronto.

Home sweet—*Hubba-wha?*

As exhausted as I am, it takes a moment for my mind to catch up with why my bed and carpet, and dresser are heaped with small boxes. Condoms?

I groan. "Very funny, assholes," I shout to the house in general. "You're lucky I'm tired."

"Night, kids," Calum calls from next door.

"There was no stopping them, Fi. Sorry," Kevin shouts.

"Not your fault, Kev. I still love you."

"Thanks."

"Just you."

"Oh, you know you love us," Emmet says.

I roll my eyes and shake my head. "How could I not?"

Sloan grabs an empty laundry basket and clears a path across the floor. With a straight arm along the surface of my comforter, he scoops what has to be forty boxes of condoms off my bed. "Ye can make their life miserable tomorrow, Fi. Right now, ye need sleep."

"True story." I stagger over to the first window and draw the blinds. "It's not a castle, Manx, but when we wake up—"

"In a week," Sloan interjects.

"Good call. When we wake up in a week, we'll take you on a tour of the Don Valley wildlands next door. Until then, you have the run of the house and the grove in the back yard."

Manx meets me at the last window, stands on his back legs, and searches the Toronto skyline. "I'll be fine. You two rest. We'll unpack and settle tomorrow."

"You don't have to tell me twice." I pat my chest and release Bruin. "Night, boys. Love you."

Too tired to shower or change or even untie my boots, I flop onto my bed and close my eyes. The moment my head hits my pillow, I'm sinking into the oblivion of sleep.

"Let me help ye off with yer boots." Sloan's voice is quiet and in my current state of near unconsciousness, very far in the distance. "That's it. Let the world slip away, *a ghra*. Yer home now. We all are."

I wake to the smell of sweet seduction and an empty bed. My alarm clock says it's six-thirty, but with the late-night witch battling and the continent-hopping, I'm not sure if that's a.m. or p.m. I roll over and stare closely at the time—p.m. for the win. I permit myself to be a lazy daisy. Truth is, I feel a little like a pulped orange abandoned on the kitchen counter.

Scrolling through my contacts, I pull up Myra and hit send. She picks up on the second ring.

"Fi! Are you home? Tell me you're safe. No, tell me you're home."

I smile. "I'm home and safe."

"Thank the goddess. You sound tired."

"Beat to a pulp was what I was just thinking."

"My poor girlie. Don't worry about work then. Take a few days and get your wind back. I wouldn't mind a friendly visit though if you feel up to it. I have so much to tell you."

"I can't wait. It's top on my list. I'm just waking up, so today is shot, but yeah, as soon as I come up for air, I'm there."

"How about I come there? You've asked me more than once about visiting your grove. If that invite is still open—"

"Of course. We'd love to have you."

"Good. It's settled. Let me know when you're rested, and we'll catch up."

"Sounds perfect. Thanks. I've been a dismal employee lately."

She laughs. "Oh, honey. It's hard for a superhero to hold down a job. I've run the store solo for over fifty years, and it's my joy. Any time you have to help out is welcome whenever it comes. Don't worry about that."

"Best boss, *evah*."

"Love you too. Now, roll over and kiss that Irishman of yours from me for bringing you home."

"I'll have to find him first. I think he's downstairs cooking me dinner."

"Oh...I love that boy. Remember, a kiss from me. Oh, and I'm a French kisser."

I laugh. "Now you went and made it weird."

Myra's melodious laughter at the other end feeds my empty stores. "Take care of yourself. See you soon."

"Looking forward to it." I hang up and send a quick text to Liam. "Home. Just waking up. All is well. Have a good night at the bar. Let's catch up tomorrow."

I slide into my slippers and beeline it into the bathroom to pee, brush my teeth, and pull myself together. As I'm washing my face, I look at my eyes and my heart sinks.

I honestly thought that when Mother Nature cleansed me of the darkness, my eyes would've gone back to normal. Since our palm to forehead moment, the burn of evil eyes is gone.

I'm pretty sure she fixed me.

Maybe Sloan's right and they're more about triggering a dormant fae trait.

"Thank you, Goddess," I whisper to the mirror.

It's horrible to look in the mirror and not recognize yourself, but maybe this is the new me...

Nope. Can't do it.

I glamor my eyes and give myself one last smile before jogging down the stairs to check in with the fam jam.

"Good evening, Lady Cumhaill. How fare thee this fine November day?"

I giggle at Sloan using my fancy morning address and take my place at the kitchen table with him, Calum, and Kevin. "Did I smell baking?'

"You did," Calum says. "Sloan made us ham, scalloped potatoes, and honey-glazed biscuits. Too bad you slept so long. You missed out."

I frown, but Sloan shakes his head. "I had to fight yer brothers off to save ye some, but yer worth the bruises." He slides an oven mitt on and grabs a plate off the top rack. "Since I was the first up and about, I took liberties in the kitchen."

Kevin gathers Calum's plate and takes it to the sink to rinse off. "We told him the first up rule is only for Sundays, but hey, he insisted."

I break open a biscuit and grab the butter knife. "Who are we to argue, amirite?"

"That about covers it," Calum says. "Hey, guess what?"

"What?"

"I was chatting with Mark at the mailbox an hour ago, and he said they're putting the house up for sale."

I almost choke on my bun. "No way. For reals? I didn't know they were considering moving."

Kevin glances back over his shoulder and makes a face. "Apparently, the neighborhood is in decline."

I grab the teapot from the center of the table and pour myself a mug full. "What does that mean?"

Calum chuckles. "It was his passive-aggressive way of pointing his middle finger at us. He said between the fight in the back lane with the hobgoblins a few months ago, the tussle on the front lawn with the doppelganger a few weeks ago, and losing Skippy to a coyote right in front of our house, they've decided this isn't the place they want to raise a baby."

"A baby? Is Janine preggers?"

"Not yet, but they're planning. With the way houses are priced right now, they can sell here and get a huge place with property in the burbs."

My mind starts whirling. "Wouldn't it be awesome if Aiden and Kinu could buy it? Then we could take down the fence, expand the grove, and have them right next door."

Calum's dark brows rise. "Awesome, yes, but they'd never be able to afford it. They're asking one-point-six."

I sigh. "Good point. Even with the death benefits payout from the TDP, there wouldn't be enough."

"No, there wouldn't. You need to wrap that up while things are calm. Charlie Mantle has been calling."

My third biscuit seems to clog my throat. Or maybe my throat is clogging around my biscuit. "Yeah, I know. It feels wrong to boil Brendan's worth down to money in the bank." I blink against the sting of tears burning in my eyes.

"Agreed, but if something happens to any of us, there's a process that has to be followed. That money can do really good things for our family. It can put Jackson and Meggie through university, pay off a landscaping bill, or maybe buy a new furnace."

"I get that. Yeah, our furnace is wheezing its last breath. Okay, I'll pull up my big girl panties and take care of it."

Sloan squeezes my hand. "How much money would ye be short?"

"For what? A furnace? Oh, there's plenty for that."

"No, I meant if ye could buy out the neighbor's house and expand to include Aiden and his family?"

I frown, not liking his tone. "Too much to borrow. I haven't spoken with Mr. Mantle, but since Brendan got killed while undercover, I know the payout will be big. Still, it won't be one and a half million dollars big."

"But having the house next door would solve more than a few issues. Yer family could spread out more, and ye wouldn't have to worry so much about pryin' eyes watchin' yer backyard when enemies attack and try to kidnap ye."

I squeeze his hand and smile. "I'm not taking your money, Mackenzie. You save up and buy yourself a castle of your own. Manx and you deserve to rock the bachelor pad life. We'll find another answer for Aiden and Kinu."

Sloan shrugs. "If ye change yer mind, I'm happy to help."

Calum frowns. "How much money have you got, Irish?"

Sloan shrugs again. "More than I need."

I pat his hand and start in on my ham and potatoes. "That's awesome and generous, but Cumhaills pave their roads forward."

Manx trots in the kitchen door with Emmet, and the two of them look suspiciously happy and wind-blown.

"Where have the two of you been?" I ask.

Manx goes to where his bowl is on the floor and laps up water. Emmet drops into his chair and smiles. "I showed Manx the grove and introduced him to the gang. Everyone asked about you, Fi. You should visit them."

"It's my first stop after dinner. How do you feel?"

"I haven't sprouted a tail lately if that's what you're asking. So far so good."

I look him over, and yeah, he looks healthy and normal and not at all like he's transforming into a fae creature. "Have you heard anything from Sarah? Do we know what she and the goddess did after they left us in Turkey?"

"Yeah, she emailed me." He pulls out his phone, calls up his email, and smiles. "She's happy to report that the two of them gathered the witches from the Ring of Rath, and the goddess stripped Jimmy and his crew and all those involved of their powers. Mother Nature visited the coven of the Blarney white witches, and that went a long way in restoring her sisters' faith that they did the right thing in helping us. She also says that she's been named the new Magis of the coven and looks forward to rebuilding."

"Och, that's good news," Sloan says. "She's a lovely lass. She deserves the honor."

Emmet nods. "Yeah, it's a good thing. It'll give her something to focus on beyond the guilt of feeling like it was her fault."

"It wasn't her fault." I finish my plate.

"No. It wasn't." Emmet closes the email and smiles.

"So, when do you see her next?" I smile at the lovestruck grin on his face.

Emmet shrugs. "Nikon said he'll take me after my next block when he picks up Suede."

"Ohmygawd, Suede!" I stare at Sloan and cup my hand over my mouth. "How horrible are we? We forgot about her and left her behind in Ireland. We have to call her and apologize. Oh, I feel terrible."

Sloan chuckles. "We're not horrible...well, I'm not, anyway. I kept in contact with her and chatted with her before we came home. You may have forgotten about her, but I didn't, and I didn't let on."

I shake my head. "Okay, so *I'm* a horrible person, and you covered my butt."

Sloan chuckles. "It was my pleasure to cover your butt. Now come, there's something the boys and I want ye to see."

———

Sloan, Emmet, Calum, Kevin, and I slide into our shoes and jackets and trot across what little backyard we have left. The moment we step into the grove, I feel the strength of the ambient magic feeding my soul. Sloan slips his palm against mine as we wander deeper into the trees. I reach out and catch Flopsy in the air and cuddle her against my chest. With a wave, I greet Pip and Nilm, and Mopsy, and my deer.

"And hello up there." I smile at all the little lights twinkling in the branches above. "What are you?"

"Winnots." Sloan smiles. "Remember when we set up the lights in the grove and I told you that my grove is lit by tiny faery bugs called winnots? I also said that I would see if any of them fancied the idea of relocating to the new world."

I blink against the onset of tears blurring my vision. "All of you came to live with us here in our grove? I'm so honored to have you."

"I told you she'd cry." Calum pats Manx's head.

I blink against the warm moisture leaking out of my eyes. "Thank you. This is so thoughtful."

He chuckles and pulls me into a hug. "Today is the first of November, *a ghra*. For druids, it's our New Year's Day. It's a day of celebration, and it's customary to give a heartfelt gift to make someone happy. It is my honor and pleasure to make ye smile."

I gaze into those warm, dark eyes and sink a little deeper.

He gets me. He sees me. He accepts me.

"Then my November first gift to you is a heartfelt gift that will make you happy. It is my honor and pleasure to make you smile. You said all I need to do is say the word, right?"

Sloan's eyes widen as he stands a little straighter. "And?"

"The word, hotness. I'm saying the word."

Thank you for reading – *A Witch's Revenge*

While the story is fresh in your mind, click **HERE** and tell other readers what you thought.

A star rating and/or even one sentence can mean so much to readers deciding whether or not to try out a book or new author.

And if you loved it, continue with the Chronicles of an Urban Druid and claim your copy of book five:

A Broken Vow

IRISH TRANSLATIONS

a ghra - my love, a romantic endearment

Dia dhuit - a greeting for hello

Maith go leor – all right, good enough

Go raibh maith agat - thank you

The story continues with A Broken Vow, coming soon Amazon and Kindle Unlimited.

Pre-order now to have it delivered to your Kindle on midnight January 31st, 2021.

AUTHOR NOTES - AUBURN TEMPEST
DECEMBER 18, 2020

Thank you so much for reading _**A Witch's Revenge**_—I truly appreciate you spending your time with our characters.

Fiona is growing into her druid-y boots, backed by an amazingly supportive family both in Toronto and in Ireland. I heart Clan Cumhaill hard. They feel real to me and are quickly becoming part of my family. The supporting cast of Sloan, Nikon, Patty, Dart, and even the heirs of the Ancient Order of Druids are coming into their own, too.

I'm excited to see where they take us.

Thank you all for loving the series and joining us on the adventure. The fans are amazing, and I read every review to make sure I'm writing what you love to read.

I will continue to focus on family, fun, and of course, fantasy.

Book 5 of the series – _**A Broken Vow**_ – is up next. It's written and ready to be polished to perfection by Michael's LMBPN super team. What a joy it's been to work with them.

I hope you've enjoyed getting to know more about Toronto and maybe even a bit about Irish and Celtic mythology. Expect more mayhem and creatures of legend in the books to come.

All the best in these trying times. When you need to leave reality behind for a while, I hope you escape into the pages of the Chronicles of the Urban Druid series and find sanctuary.

Wishing you all lives filled with laughter and love.

Auburn Tempest

P.S. If you enjoy my writing and read sexy steamy romance, my pen name for the books I write Paranormal and Fantasy Romance is JL Madore. You can find me on Amazon.

AUTHOR NOTES - MICHAEL ANDERLE
DECEMBER 22, 2020

Thank you for not only reading this story but also joining me back here for a bit of commentary.

Sometimes I'm funny, sometimes I'm poignant, often I'm confusing.

I have one of the best jobs ever and it only took me something like forty-seven years to start it. As an author and publisher, I get to create or talk about stories all day every day, rain or shine.

Further, I get to collaborate with some of the sweetest and nicest authors on the planet. I absolutely include "Auburn" (Jenny) on my list of amazing and fun authors to talk to. Having spoken to her about the family in the books, I know that she is taking her own siblings and their craziness and placing it into the stories.

I asked if she shared that with her family and she admitted she had. And that once admitted, she followed up quickly with "there aren't any royalties included with making up characters based on you."

I laughed. I totally see one of Fi's brothers trying that out on her. Which makes sense, in a roundabout way.

It's almost like "Which came first, the characters or the siblings?"

Well, obviously the siblings. But, for me it was the characters who came first, so in my own version of reality, are the siblings actually the less real of the two?

Ouch, I made my head hurt.

If you enjoy the stories, tell a friend or two. We would LOVE to keep the stories going on for a few more books if we can!

Happy Holidays!

Michael

ABOUT AUBURN TEMPEST

Auburn Tempest is a multi-genre novelist giving life to Urban Fantasy, Paranormal, and Sci-Fi adventures. Under the pen name, JL Madore, she writes in the same genres but in full romance, sexy-steamy novels. Whether Romance or not, she loves to twist Alpha heroes and kick-ass heroines into chaotic, hilarious, fast-paced, magical situations and make them really work for their happy endings.

Auburn Tempest lives in the Greater Toronto Area, Canada with her dear, wonderful hubby of 30 years and a menagerie of family, friends, and animals.

BOOKS BY AUBURN TEMPEST

Book 2 – <u>Jesse and the Magi Vault</u>

Book 3 – <u>The Makings of a Magi</u>

CONNECT WITH THE AUTHORS

Connect with Auburn

Amazon, Facebook, Newsletter

Web page – www.jlmadore.com

Email – AuburnTempestWrites@gmail.com

Connect with Michael Anderle and sign up for his email list here:

Website: http://lmbpn.com

Email List: http://lmbpn.com/email/

Social Media:

https://www.facebook.com/LMBPNPublishing

https://twitter.com/MichaelAnderle

https://www.instagram.com/lmbpn_publishing/

https://www.bookbub.com/authors/michael-anderle

Made in the USA
Monee, IL
06 March 2022

92326409R10174